A Daughter of the Island

Sharon E. Bowman

Sea Lily Publishing— Chebeague Island, ME
ISBN: 979-8-218-16245-0
Library of Congress Control Number: pending
Title: *A Daughter of the Island*
Author: Sharon E. Bowman
Digital distribution | 2023
Paperback | 2023

Dedication

For Cait and Mark—the first to request the retelling of this story

Elegy Before Death
Edna St. Vincent Millay

There will be rose and rhododendron
When you are dead and underground;
Still will be heard from white syringas
Heavy with bees, a sunny sound;

Still will the tamaracks be raining
After the rain has ceased, and still
Will there be robins in the stubble.
Brown sheep upon the warm green hill.

Spring will not ail nor autumn falter;
Nothing will know that you are gone,
Saving alone some sullen plough-land
None but yourself sets foot upon;

Saving the may-weed and the pig-weed
Nothing will know that you are dead, —
These, and perhaps a useless wagon
Standing beside some tumbled shed.

Oh, there will pass with your great passing
Little of beauty not your own, —
Only the light from common water,
Only the grace from simple stone!

"Bates Island in Casco Bay, one of the outside group lying in about the same parallel as Jewell's, was frozen so it could be reached from the mainland for the first time in 70 years. As 83 year old resident of Great Chebeague recalls a time 70 years ago, when Aunt Nancy, the sole resident of Bates Island, died there. A party from Harpswell came up to carry the remains back for burial. When within half a mile from the island they encountered a solid ice over which they walked and dragged a dory to the shore. From Bates to Chebeague it was frozen to a sufficient strength to permit the trip being made on foot. Donald Barton, a professor of Newton, Massachusetts now owns Bates and its one home, a beautiful summer cottage."

Source: Newspaper clipping found in notebook compiled by Sister Mary Regina dated 1918

Part One
Bates Island 1848-1856

Sarah

Chapter One
Bates Island: 1848

The sloop *Hannah Bates* nosed forward running before a stiff afternoon breeze out of the southwest. Her decks carried: two wooden crates, one barrel of flour, one barrel of cornmeal, one crate of live chickens, one jersey cow, one barrel of seed potatoes, a bushel basket of winter apples, twenty bales of winter hay and one smaller wooden chest made up of squash, corn, pea, and bean seed.

Alexander Johnson held the tiller arm steady, skillfully adjusting for the following sea. It was no burden to carry his single passenger and her provisions from his home on Hope Island to Bates, now just a mile in sight. The overcast sky suggested afternoon rain and both were anxious to make the shore and unload the cargo.

His fellow traveler, Jane, knew without a question, that Alexander thought she was making a mistake in moving back to her childhood home. She also imagined that his fondness for his granddaughters, and his feelings of guilt about their father and Jane, had caused the extended silence between them since their departure. He loved his son, she knew, but could not reconcile his inconsistent behavior in light of the responsibility he did not seem to grasp. Alexander, now fifty-eight years, turning grey, yet still possessing the rugged fisherman body of his youth, had his own responsibilities. No matter how many hours he'd spent talking to Jim, there was no changing his mind. Jane may be the mother of his children, but he had consented to marry another woman and that was the end of it. The shame this decision had brought to the entire family did not seem of any consequence to James. He left it to his father to clean up the mess, and up until last winter, no one knew exactly how this would be accomplished. Not until Aunt Nancy's death, leaving the Bates home vacant, had a solution presented itself. Even at that, Jane was the one to make the announcement that she and her three daughters, Mary, Sarah and Rose would move to the island, leaving family, and more importantly, James, to his new wife.

Jane sat at the bow, balanced on the lip of the low gunnel, judging the strength of the incoming tide ripping through the channel between Cliff and Bates. The heavy sloop moved slowly along giving her time to take the island in; to breathe in the faint scent of bayberry and salt. Approaching from the west, they would sail into the first cove below the cottage, keeping inside the bar point, extending out toward Cliff Island. Following the shoreline, she caught sight of the barn's slanted roof against the afternoon's low hanging clouds, wondering if she'd have to re-shingle before next winter. She had no doubts that the cottage needed work as well. A good scrubbing inside and a bit of hole patching would suffice. She'd liked the warmth of Alex's two story farm house. Thinking of the open chamber of her small cape, and the frost clinging to the ceiling beams in January, gave her a momentary shiver, yet brought a smile, recalling how she and her sister hated getting up in the early morning. Aunt Nancy must have slept by the fireplace all winter. They would too if it came to it.

She hadn't visited her aunt since last May and now felt a twinge of guilt that she'd left her to fare for herself, even though she'd insisted. Perhaps stubborn just ran in the family. Or maybe, it was just the way things worked for some. You couldn't know how one moment a decision could lead to either happiness or sorrow, or some mixture of both. A plan is made, you live with the outcome. And so it was for her aunt, she thought. So it was for her. Did returning home mean she'd somehow failed? Was crawling back to the only thing she understood plainly the act of a coward? The sloop could just as easily come about, head into the wind and sail for the city, yet the water slipping beneath the hull, moving homeward, was what she knew. Her girls might have a better chance, but it was too big a step to take. Here she knew boundaries. On these two miles of solid ledge, topped by well-tilled fields, the winter wind and rough sea would pound the shores, but it would hold. The spring would bring the sweet greens of another year and here she could provide. Hard work and sure-footing the island's shores had to be enough for now.

Alexander guided the sloop onto the beach head and together they took to the task of unloading. The cow would be seen to first, which they accomplished by walking her down sturdy planks from the sloop's midship to the beach.

"Thank God she's a little one," Alexander said, breaking the mutual silence of their sail. He did not take Jane's silence as anger toward him, he knew she was taking her time trying to think of a way to smooth over, perhaps bury, all of the scenes of discontent from last winter.

As they worked, he watched her effortlessly hoist the crates and carry them to the house. He marveled at such a strong woman and thought once again that he had little doubt she would make a go of it living on the island alone. He had seen her strength, not just in the physical sense, but in her character as well. After each child, he knew his son had promised marriage, each time holding her off by taking a spot on a fishing schooner, some trips leaving for a year at a time. That she loved him made this decision to leave her family even more difficult for those who thought James to be in the wrong. Time would tell was all that he could come up with and satisfied himself that he really could do nothing to change her mind. His next sail to Bates would be with the girls who would be Jane's only consolation and help.

Watching her from the beach, the last of the cargo unloaded and stored, readying to leave, Alexander thought he would forever hold this picture of Jane as she stood now on the doorstep. Dressed in her usual overalls, hip boots and cotton flannel shirt, all six feet of her made her seem so much like a strong man, save for her long auburn hair falling loose from her cap. Admiration did not begin to express how he felt about her. In her face, the resilience and determination he saw to simply survive the loneliness would be enough to break most men he knew. Even as he sought to provide solace, there was no way through the wall she now hid behind. It would be that image; the wall moving as she moved, and the shoulder to the swollen door, now opening to the shadows of the late April afternoon within, that would stay with him as he sailed for home.

Jane found the house much the same as her Aunt Nancy had left it. The open chamber still held the chill of winter, its one window at the roof peak, swollen tight from rain and winter snows. She'd have to pry it open to let in the sunlight and fresh air. The same cots slumped beneath the eaves, reminding her of her childhood and nights she'd listened to the wind howling through the timbers. She hoped the girls remembered to carry their own feather beds from Alex's house, or they would have to make do. Sweeping away cob webs and layers of dust, she thought it likely her aunt had not bothered much with the room, finding nothing more than an old chest neatly packed with patchwork quilts and yellowing linens. She would find time later to haul them out to the yard for a thorough washing, but today she'd concentrate on the main room; cleaning the fireplace and seeing to stocking the cupboards before the girls arrived.

Patterns of a new life began to take shape as she worked through her chores. The cow stood untroubled, munching tall grass, turning her head by way of greeting, as Jane pulled the kitchen door open and walked to the barn in search of the milk pail. Every step forward in her day presented another next thing that she'd need to tend to, causing her to hesitate before venturing into the barn. Rusted hinges complained as she swung open the tall, planked doors and braced them against the outer wall. Following the family tradition, her father, Edsel, had built a saltbox style barn; shingled over pine boards, favoring just one window at the lower side of the building with a small cubby door in the cow's stall. Allowing her eyes to adjust, Jane reluctantly surveyed the interior. Everything appeared to have been shoved in, as if the last person to close the door took great pains to confound the next person to walk in. What one required on a saltwater farm lay strewn across the main floor: picks, shovels, hand plow, hay rakes, baskets, wagon wheels, seine anchors, rope, chains, clam hods and hoes, gangings and hooks, mismatched oars, and lobster buoys. Molding hay dangled from the loft and the wagon's body hovered overhead like the skeletal remains of some ancient creature. She wondered how long it had been since someone had thought to take stock in the homestead, since anyone had patched a roof, or mucked out the stall. It had all been left to her poor old aunt, who never once complained or asked for help, and Jane had been too busy with her own life to do anything more than a simple visit now and again. The comparison to her own future set dimly into her thoughts, discouraging the keep positive attitude she had been trying to maintain.

Stepping further in, she spied the dory settled against one wall as if she'd just floated in and decided it would be as safe a harbor as any. Jane knew, without a closer look, that she'd reached the end of her rope; a wood boat stored inside for so many years, dozens since last overboard, meant re-caulking, scraping old paint and possibly re-fastening. Casting one last look over the impossible clutter, she set out across the field, placing as much distance as she could between herself and the countless disasters she now called home.

Reaching the east end point, Jane looked across the cove to Bates' sister island, Ministerial, thinking of walking over the bar on the low tide to visit the family graves. Then she guessed she should wait for the girls and plan for a day later in the week when they were more settled. She hoped the girls would love the island as much as she had as a child, but knew they'd miss the excitement of Hope and other children. Mary was only a few days away from her eighth birthday and Jane imagined she would miss it most of all. She counted on Rosy being still young enough to adapt to a new life, and Sarah, two years younger than Mary, was the least of her worries. Of all her girls, Jane never knew Sarah to shy away from a challenge. She reminded Jane of herself, tall and thin, her russet hair in blunt contrast to her sharp features. Her girls all bore similarities to both the Bates and Johnson's; Mary, favoring Jim's side, her blond hair and blue-eyed combination a testament to a Scottish heritage. Dissimilar in looks and character, Jane understood she could always count on daily skirmishes between them. If Mary complained about the chores, or compared their work, it was Sarah's way to smile and make light of the chiding. Where Mary worried, Sarah jumped in, finding her way out of tangles. In many ways, she concluded, they probably made life more interesting, if not unnerving some days.

Standing in the sunlight, more contented, she sighed and turned toward home. Thoughts of the girls arrival had put some cheer back in her day and a bit more hope for their prospects here. Retracing her path through the field, she envisioned the farm restored to her early glory days. She imagined the whole island from the stone wall to the east end, tilled and thriving. She didn't doubt but she too could accomplish what her father had with hard work. If he could row his wife and two daughters in a dory from the main shore, build a house and barn, and clear cut the entire island for planting, then she could make a start where he'd left off. Jane trusted the island's sturdy backbone and rich soil to keep them safe and nourished. What the island could not provide, the sea's arms holding close to her shores would provide the rest.

That afternoon, Jane hauled the old dory out of the barn and set to work. Shaking her head, she surveyed the damage, making a mental list of materials she would need. Rummaging around in the barn she managed to set the tool bench in order, rooting out the tool her father had used to scrape the old paint. Judging the rust would remove itself, she began at the bow and worked her way to the stern, finding more and more damage to the hull, concluding she would need to refasten the planks. She hadn't thought about the dory's age when she decided to leave Hope and realized this miscalculation would cost her. In spite of the setback, she worked on stripping paint, noting areas that would leak and those that might hold. She'd been so engaged in the project that she'd not realized how late it was getting to be until she heard the girls call from the beach.

Although she'd arranged that old Alex would sail the girls over, it appeared from her perch on the hill's crest that it was not grandfather, but father. Whatever he had in mind, there was no time to haggle. Jane wanted to sort out their new home before dark which meant a fair amount of lugging from beach to house. They had not spoken since he announced his marriage to Sarah Pennell. She supposed there had to be a word for what was about to transpire, but could only think of unbearable; and even that did not satisfy her.

Jim and Mary had transferred all the luggage to the shore as Jane met the girls at the bottom of the path. Fussing with the dory anchor and beach line for an unnecessary long time, Jim finally walked up the beach.

"I expected Alex," Jane said. "Didn't think you'd show yourself here."

Jim stood for a moment, awkwardly holding a wooden crate, searching for the best approach. "Said I'd best do the right thing. Pretty much picked me up, set me in the dory, and shoved her off."

"He most generally says what he thinks."

"That's the truth," he said, lifting another crate and starting for the path. "Guess we'd best carry this on up to the house then."

Jane went on ahead without more to say. Whatever Alex had planned for this reunion she could only guess. He was a man who believed that others should act honorably, still powerless to fathom his son's behavior. A less gentle man might have forced his son to marry, given the circumstances, but it was not in his nature to speak crossly to any living soul. Jane recognized this as knowledge that had always played to Jim's advantage.

Once at the doorstep, Jane stopped and placed her parcels to one side. Looking toward Jim, she waited, watching as he pulled off his cap and ran rough hands through his hair. He held a firm fisherman's stance, his legs braced for rough going, mostly uncertain on solid ground.

"Thank you for bringing the girls. We won't be needin' any more help."

Unable to face her, Jim looked out across the yard and spied the dory outside the barn door. "Look, I know you're sayin' that now, but there's no use me not lendin' a hand. I can't just walk away and not put my oar in when need be. I'm pretty handy with boats."

"It's a nice offer, Jim," she said. "I'll keep it in mind, should I need it."

"That's good then. Be glad to come over and get her ready."

Jane knew she should accept, but there seemed a greater need in her to keep him away. His easy way, so like his father's, had managed to keep them together, but broken promises slipped from his lips as easily as taking a breath. Trusting him again would just not do. If she were to make it here, it would have to be on her own terms.

Chapter Two
The Tide Pool

Providence! Her sister, Caroline, would call it. Jane just put it down to good luck and let it go at that. Although, on the first of May, she had recalled her father's story. It began four years before her birth when her sister was just two. In his annual retelling, summer never came to the islands, or mainland, and nothing grew except a few potatoes they'd planted in the seaweed. He'd swear that frost and snow switched days, that the ground froze solid, and he'd had to haul enough hay from his brother's farm in North Yarmouth just to keep the cow. Fish and potatoes kept them fed. Jane didn't doubt his story, as old Alex too spoke of it each spring before planting. Every summer they'd lose sleep until the green sprouts took hold and the corn tasseled.

Standing now in the field, Jane did count her blessings. Enjoying the gentle September wind rustling the corn stocks, she paused and listened to the Oldsquaws calling from the outer ledges. She took in the deep blue water and the sun's glimmering at the shoreline where bright pink rugosa fringed the edges, lifting their perfume across the island. She hadn't realized how much she'd missed her own home until now. There was a certain perfection in the balance of all that she could see and feel. Although, it did not make sense to think of it as balanced when she thought of the how the tree shapes defied symmetry, grew haphazardly around each other, or formed imperfect patterns against the sky. She thought it must be taken in at a distance to see a design, to stand as witness to perfection. Maybe that was the only way to view life, to every once in a while take a step back.

That morning, Jane had promised a picnic at the back shore after tending to chores. When Mary approached with a basket on one arm and Rosy by the hand, she guessed it was time.

"Ready then?" she asked, as Rosy reached up to take her hand, setting herself between them. "I don't suppose you have an idea where Sarah might be?"

Mary grinned and nodded in the direction of the shore. "Guess we both know she's gone on ahead of us."

At the cliff's edge, Rosy raised a pudgy hand and pointed back in the direction of the house. "Look, Mama. There she is." Edging her way along the stone wall, they caught sight of Sarah's tightrope walker act. Completely in her own world, they watched as her bare feet clung to jagged rocks, and her arms swayed and tipped for balance. Not one to give up once she'd started on an idea, she walked to the very end. Looking up to her audience, she put her hands on her hips and took a bow.

"For heaven's sake Sarah, do you have to make such a spectacle?" Mary yelled.

Sarah laughed, jumped down from the wall, and skipped over to join them. "You know, I was thinkin', if I was to string a line from the willow out to the barn, I might be able to walk it."

"Where did you ever get such an idea?" Jane asked.

"Just thought it up. Would be kinda fun."

Mary looked to her mother. For a brief moment she thought she might actually be considering the crazy idea, then she saw the slight smile and knew what her sisters had yet to learn. Their mother wanted to encourage them and sometimes it meant trying on new ideas. Still, Mary had her doubts about Sarah and her risk taking, thinking she'd better keep a close watch on her sister's shenanigans.

The tide was slipping out of the small cove beneath the cliff walk when they arrived, leaving plenty of room for the picnic. Mary spread an old table cloth she'd found in the loft chest over a flat ledge and Rosy plunked herself down, signaling she was ready. Watching Rosy devour food prepared for the family, amazed everyone. Fish or fowl, it mattered little to her. Old Alex thought she'd inherited her appetite from his wife's side of the family, based mainly on the fact that most of the women were inclined to carrying more weight than needed to get by on. Jane's family tended toward thin and tall, whereas Jim was stocky, so she guessed Alex might be right.

After lunch, Mary walked Rosy to the tide pool to wash her face and hands free of chicken grease and sand. This was Rosy's favorite spot. A deep basin held white and rose quartz stones polished in the heavy seas. At the high tide, the pool disappeared, swallowed by the ocean, and reappeared as the tide receded. Here she would plunge her hands into the pool and pull out the glossy stones. Her favorite picks would go into the picnic basket to be carried home. Sometimes Sarah would join her, but it was Mary who helped with the difficult sorting decisions. It appeared that Rosy's preferred the pink stones and would not allow a single white one in the mix. It did not take long for Sarah to make the comparison, calling her sister Rosy Quartz, teasing in good natured fun. She'd keep at the game stringing rhyming verses together until Jane would put quits to it, admittedly turning her face to hide her smile.

They stayed on until the clouds turned the afternoon cool. Walking the path to home with her girls, Jane understood that it was a day to take stock. It was a day to be remembered before the winter fire, one to hold up against others, a chance to keep a memory somewhere safe. It was a day when a profile or a gesture might keep, marked by words forgotten by nightfall. It was a day when all experience might just be held in a basket of pink stones sitting on the doorstep with one white quartz stone on top.

Chapter Three
Sarah

Even though it was April and still cool, the cloudless morning sky mantled the still water and islands, making a promise to the day. Snow patches clumped in the field ruts and clung to the bayberry bushes along the edges of island as they walked to the shore. Running low on wood, they had talked for days about getting a chance, when the wind dropped out after a solid week of blowing hard across the island. Mary walked ahead of the others, balancing the oars on her shoulder, her boots slipping on the path. They hauled the dory on rollers down the beach and across the flats, setting her in shallow. Stepping in, Mary set the thole pins and steadied the oars while Sarah climbed over the side and sat in the stern, leaving Rosy to the bow seat and Jane to give them a final shove to deeper water.

Stave was the closest island as the crow flies and they planned to gather the driftwood tossed up by the winter seas and tides. They had taken all they could find off Bates and what they could carry across the bar from Ministerial. Today, it would take an hour's row.

Jane followed her daily routine from barn to house chores. It was getting on time to scrub the floors and she thought today, with the girls out from under foot, might be the day. Although having the girls to haul the clean sand from the front beach and lend a hand would be helpful, she also knew that she could get it done sometimes more quickly without them running in and out. Once she had made up her mind to tackle the floors before they got back from the wood run, it was settled. The day was bright enough to make the chore doable. It was also cool enough to ensure a reasonable comfort to a task often leaving her sweaty and done in.

It was her mother's way, and her Aunt Nancy's, to wheelbarrow the sand in bucketfuls from the beach to the back door. Having removed all the furniture outside, she spread the sand by handfuls onto the pine boards one area at a time, starting at the back of the room and working toward the door. Scrubbing with a stiff, short handled broom, Jane hummed a tune from her childhood as the grit dug into the wood floor, removing winter's dirt and dust. It was satisfying work and Jane felt a bit righteous, while at the same time, ashamed for thinking that way. "Such an old fool to be down on my hands and knees, playin' like a saint, probably should be prayin' instead of scrubbin'." It amused her to be clever in making fun of herself and she wished that the girls had been there to overhear. "Speakin 'of the girls, they should have been home hours ago," she announced to the empty room. Pulling herself upright she walked to the door, grabbing her shawl off the hook.

The afternoon sky had turned grey and a stiff wind had picked up from the southwest. Jane had confidence in Mary's ability handling the dory, but still she left the doorstep and strode down the path to the shore. Standing alone at the water's edge she studied the bay's response to wind and tide, then walked further to the west end, looking out toward Stave. The island's spruce ridged back lay etched against the gathering afternoon clouds, asleep and indifferent to her search. It was a kind of silence Jane accepted. Knowing that the row from Stave to Ministerial could still be managed, and the toll it would take on Mary, left her wishing again for the money to build another dory. With another dory she could name an action. She could run it down the beach, and pull on the oars, and call out their names. She could turn any thoughts of trouble from her mind with the simple freedom of the strength in her arms. It should be simple, yet the only choice now was to turn and walk back up the path to the house. Determined to drive out the dark thoughts she sought comfort in action. She would put the house back together and they'd be back before dark. She would start dinner, have it ready for girls, light the lanterns and keep watching the shore path.

****

Beaching at the half tide would allow the girls almost a full day to walk the shores and stack their piles above the high water mark. The dory would sit high and dry for hours and not worry their gathering efforts.

Mary hoisted a canvas sail bag from the bow seat Jane had stocked with a tin of biscuits, salt cod and three jars of tea. Sarah set the anchor firmly into the mud giving the tines an extra push with her boot heel. "That should hold her, Mars. We'd better get a move on though. I hate to think about rowing a load back in a chop."

"Maybe the wind will come up and we can sail the lot back. Fingers crossed. I can see Rosy's real worried about it," Mary laughed, setting off across the flats. "Come on, let's get a start then."

A little after noon, the girls rested on the beach drinking cold tea listening to Rosy complain. "We should carry that pile down to the dory and come back tomorrow for the rest. At least that's what I think. It's gettin' cold too, and that tea's not helpin' any."

"You'll be a lot colder if we don't fill that dory, so stop carryin' on so. Let's have one last look on the east end beach and then we can call it a day here," Mary offered. "Rosy, you can walk with me and get yourself all warmed up. How's that sound?"

"Sounds like I ain't got a choice," Rosy groused. "What's Sarah gonna' do then?"

"Don't worry yourself about me. I'll check the dory and catch up."

Mary nodded her approval. "Come on then, Rosy girl. Let's have one more look see. You'll be right as rain soon enough," she added, watching as Sarah walked off toward the dory.

Reaching the east beach, Mary looked back, judging the distance to the wood pile and how much more they could carry in one load. She did not want to make a return trip, but knew the danger of overloading. Standing now at the eastern tip, out of the cove's shelter, she felt the wind quicken. Coming from the southwest meant, if they hurried, they could load the dory, hoist sail and catch a free ride home. She found Rosy sitting on a boulder tossing small stones into a tide pool at her feet. "Busy, I see. Come on then, let's head for home."

"We coulda' done that an hour ago."

"I know. Come on. Get yourself up and movin'."

"Don't have to ask me twice," Rosy answered.

"We've still got to load the dory, so don't get too excited."

Rounding the crest of the second beach, Rosy stubbed her toe falling head first, scraping her wrists and chin. "Now look," Rosy wailed. "This is what you get when you hurry me. First it's stay, then it's go."

"You'll be alright, Rose. Really, just a little scrape. Come on, Sarah will be waiting."

"I'm coming. Don't get all bossy. Besides Sarah isn't even there. So there."

"If she's gone off explorin' on those cliffs after she was told not to, I'm...."

"You'll what, miss high and mighty," Rosy interrupted, then stopped beside Mary, following the direction of her gaze down the beach. The groundswell had washed the dory into the cove, hitting her broadside, tossing her sideways onto shore. Both girls knew at once that the dory would take priority over Sarah's whereabouts. Stifling her anger at Sarah's carelessness, Mary raced into the frigid water, reached in for the anchor line and hauled her bow out to face the incoming waves. Satisfied that she'd hold, she moved quickly to shore where Rosy sat watching her performance.

"You'll catch your death like that," she said. "We'd better get Sarah."

Mary stood, shivering, staring at her sister and what appeared to be her total lack of sympathy. "Do you think you could trouble yourself to have a climb up that beach there and yell to her! She's probably on the other side. I'll get a start on the wood."

"Oh, all right, but she better be there. I can't see why she has to be such a bother all the time," Rosy announced, walking off. Grumbling, she trudged to the island's crest, tripping in tangles of wild roses and bayberries, eventually pausing at an outcropping of bare ledge. Scanning the length of the island in both directions, she sighted a dory close in to shore off the eastern point, and watched as the fisherman hauled at his oars against the wind and tide. Out beyond Stave, white water capped the swells, heaving to the shore, which meant that Mary would stay with the dory, fueling her annoyance at Sarah's disappearance and game playing. Finally, she made up her mind to walk to the back side, since Mary had told Sarah not to go on the cliffs, that was probably where she was. Even though it seemed pointless, she paused, calling out; but Sarah's name seemed to catch in the wind, swirling, unattended and leaf-like, to the ground.

She approached the cliff's edge slowly, watching her step along the broad expanse of shale ledge running the length of the back shore, abruptly plunging to form a tiny cove below. It was possible, she thought, that Sarah might have climbed down to the cove, thinking of working her way back to the dory, but the ledge face dropped straight down to the water and the idea seemed unlikely to her, yet, childlike, she walked to the edge. Moving closer still, she felt pieces of shale loosen from the ledge top and plummet to the water below, drawing her attention to the seaweed twisting with the current, intermingling with patches of white and dark shapes lifting in the tide. She stood transfixed, forcing her mind to work out what her eyes were telling her, trying to believe that the thing in the seaweed could not be Sarah, that she would not be just floating down there in the water. She tried to move closer, to position herself in such a way that she might be able to see more clearly. Struggling to focus, her mind began dismantling the moments of her day, replacing them with disordered fragments and images; Sarah waving at the dory's bow, Mary dripping wet on the shore, a bloody knee, a face, a face tangled in seaweed, the wind taking Sarah's name, lifting her up in the wind…

Jane heard the shouts just as nightfall shut down the April day. She could make out Mary's voice barking an order and heard the anchor splash. Even as she hurried to the water's edge, she planned a scolding about the late hour, yet as she reached the dory and held fast the bow, Rosy lurched forward and clasped her arms about her neck. She felt the clinging wet clothes, saw Mary's hands frozen on the oars, then the horror of Sarah's body awash on the dory's deck.

****

Jane pulled herself up from the rocker and stood before the morning fire, trying to remember if she had stirred the embers and fed driftwood to the flames. She heard Rosy stirring above her in the loft, then turned toward the window's morning light. She had been half dreaming, caught in the same story, reaching the same end. Mary, she now recalled, had taken the dory and was probably half way to Chebeague. She wanted to fetch clean clothes from her room, but she could not think how it would be to open the door and see Sarah there in the stillness. She could not know what to expect. Had Mary done what needed tending to? It would not do to think her still in wet clothes, or her hair matted against her head. Reaching for the

17

chair back she stood still, steadying herself, immobile and staring at the door.

"Mother, come sit down. Mary's been to the hens and left us some eggs. I'll fetch the spider, shall I?"

"Yes, that would be fine, Rosy. We can do it together, shall we?" She smiled, knowing Rosy's eagerness to please her an attempt to find a common moment in the strange day about to unfold.

By late afternoon Barnwell and Mary sailed into the cove towing Barn's dory astern, having taken advantage of the wind to shorten the journey. Jane met them at the shore, holding the bow steady as Mary stepped ashore, noticing the lumber stacked neatly across the seats. It would be like Barn to think of the coffin and the fact that she, no doubt, had nothing for such a task. He didn't speak until they'd secured the dories and carried the pine planks to the bank's edge.

"I'm so sorry, Jane. How in God's name did this happen? Mary couldn't speak of it to us without tears. I heard enough to understand, I guess. Has anyone been to Hope?"

"Mary's just gone for you, Barn. It's not likely we need to hurry 'bout tellin' her father."

Barn stood looking out toward Hope, then nodded. "Guess you know best."

"Best as I can think of right now. Come up to the house and we'll eat somethin' before we get started."

"You go on ahead with Mary and Rosy. I'll take these on up." Jane started toward the path, then turned back to him.

"I'm no good at this sort of thing, Barn. Mary and Rosy can't say what happened so's it makes sense to me. As near as I can say, Mary and Rosy was 'round the beach on the east end. They left Sarah to tend the dory with the tide, and when they got back, the dory was rollin' onto shore. Guess she was nowhere to be seen. Should have known to go with them because she was bound and determined to go off to that other side. Seems someone gave her an idea that there was some gold pieces found there and she'd a mind to have a look. Told her it was foolishness. 'Spose she slipped on that loose shale."

Barn shoved his hands in his pockets, then kicked a stone across the beach. "God damn this island! You and the girls should come right back with me tomorrow. I've got half a mind to just put you three in my dory and sail you right out of here. It's just too damn hard here. Now this." She followed his gaze out across the island's crest, its barren fields holding a grip at the shale edges of the bank, then turned back to the house. A thin smoke stream slipped lazily from the chimney, a slight remark against the darkening afternoon sky.

Chapter Four
Frank

Three shale stones marked the family graves, gray and indistinct, on the eastern tip of Ministerial Island. Jane's father, Edsel, her mother, Mary, and now Sarah, lay at peaceful rest in the morning sun. Jane had crossed the sand bar early, her only chance to visit today. In an hour's time she would have to retrace her steps. Three months to the day and still the horror of Sarah's death sank like a stone in her heart. She knew it must still be beating, yet she did not care. To lose a child before you was the worst that could happen to any woman or man, yet James had not sent word. He'd missed the burial. Now, his silence at the death of his child, made the fact unbearable. If time would heal all wounds, as she had heard from many in her time, Jane thought it was just probably too soon to tell.

As she rounded the shore to the bar a shout lifted her from her sorrow. The *Hannah Bates*, now weighing anchor, swinging her bow to the wind's directive, gave her hope that James had at last found the courage to come and pay his last respects to his daughter. Jane could make out three, yet not until she saw old Alexander, did she realize that a woman and a boy also stood on deck. Although not unusual for family to visit, today's gave her an unsettled feeling, perhaps because she had just been to the graves.

She was greeted by old Alex, his daughter and James's sister, Elizabeth, and her son Albert. Named for his father, Albert was called Frank by everyone to make home life less confusing. Frank Coffin stood by the dory hanging on to the painter with one hand and helping his mother onto the beach with the other. He was tall for a boy of ten and possessed his mother's quick smile and easy manner. The Johnson's were all blonde as a rule, and Frank, taking after his father's side, took considerable joshing about his olive skin and thick black hair; meeting each joke with a smile and often a sly return in kind.

Taking the painter from Frank, old Alex tied on the anchor, set it on the bow stem, and gave the dory one swift shove, watching as the anchor dropped into deeper water. Running the other end up the beach, he walked toward the path, reached down and wrapped it around a stone. As a customary method for ensuring the dory would neither go adrift, or aground, it was good enough for a short visit.

Having traversed the stretch of bar between the two islands, Jane looked up and waved to her family, then hurried across to greet them properly.

"If you're all not a sight for sore eyes!" Jane shouted, as she drew nearer.

"I suppose we must be," Elizabeth answered. "We weren't entirely sure how'd you'd been keepin' since... the accident."

Jane's lack of response came as no surprise to them, as she had refused to talk about Sarah's death, or how she felt about it. Elizabeth, kind to a fault, had offered to stay with Jane and the girls in April, but soon realized that Jane was too stubborn to take the offer, she supposed fearing too much sympathy and hand holding. They all knew Jane's inability to take, or ask, for help was legendary, which made the reason for today's visit all the more difficult. Breaking the silence, Frank walked over to Jane standing at the water's edge.

"You know, Aunt Jane, these two have been treatin 'me somethin ' awful. I haven't had but bread and water for a solid month. I don't reckon we could go up to the cottage and have a mug-up or somethin'."

"That's a good idea, seein' as how your gramps probably already has the kettle on," Elizabeth responded, relieved to see that Frank seemed to be handling well the prospect of the discussion they both knew might be challenging.

They walked single file up the path reaching the doorstep in time to greet Mary just stepping outside, bucket in hand, on her way to the well.

"Aunt Liz! And Albert! This is a nice surprise."

"What 'bout your poor old gramp, girly. You didn't forget 'bout me, did you?"

Mary's face reddened, but she caught herself soon enough to cover, giving the old man a big hug. "Now, that's more like it. Where's Rosy hidin'?"

"Rosy's over to Caroline's for a visit. You know how she loves to follow Uncle Barn 'round," Mary quickly answered, hoping to avoid the real need to explain her absence.

"Mary, any doughnuts left from yesterday? According to Frank, he's been losin 'weight due to very bad treatment." Jane looked a slow smile in his direction.

"It's all true. And I'll swear to it too, Mary. A fella can't get a decent meal over to that farm if he goes to hell."

"Albert James! That's no way to talk. Brought you up better than that and you know it. Alexander, would you please speak to your grandson right this instant."

"He didn't mean no harm, Liz. Still and all, mind your manners in company boy, or you'll be answerin 'to me one of these days."

Albert knew his gramps and a hollow threat when he heard one, but apologized all the same. He thought about how a man should talk; how they did talk at the shore mending nets or traps. His grandfather knew it too. They all knew that the long established bond felt among the men at the shore did not pass across the doorstep. The rough talk went unnoticed when he was with the menfolk and Frank had begun to realize how it signaled a change in his status. At ten he felt he needed to be twenty, to be someone who could hold his own if he had to.

Elizabeth took stock in the exchange, understanding what it meant to her son, knowing that he was making a sacrifice for the family, that he was letting her know in his own way that he was up to it. She felt a moment of pride mixed with sadness. Her oldest son was about to leave her for a while, perhaps forever, and even as she wanted to hold the memory of it for a moment to herself, she spoke the reason for their visit. "We've had some trouble, Jane. God knows I shouldn't be burdenin' you with it, but if you can see your way clear, Albert and I would like you to take Frank in for spell." It was out, sitting among them in the dark morning kitchen like a stranger at the table. She had planned to ease into their request, but once started, she finished the rest. "There's diphtheria with the Estes family, and just before we left, we heard with Ellie Thompson's girl, Flora."

Jane circled both hands around her mug, as if warming them might warm her thoughts, might stem the unbearable sadness in this news. She knew Elizabeth well, knew of her grace and kindness toward others. Frank would be kept out of harm's way and Liz would be nursing the neighbor's children. She loved her for the sacrifice she was making and rose to shake off a weakness she could not hide. "Frank's more than welcome, Liz. There's nothin' else to say 'bout it. He's like my own. He'll have to sleep in the open chamber with the girls. Help on the farm, but I think we'll find time for him to go haul a few traps this summer."

Part Two
1856-1876

John

Chapter Five
John Brown

When the ship settled into her berth in Portland harbor, John Brown thought he'd never seen a prettier sight. Although an overcast April day, with a strong northeast wind causing them to tack most of the afternoon all the way into port, he still felt a thrill holding his secret close. During the long winter sail from England he had made up his mind. The crew had growled from Portsmouth to Portland. Sitting now on the edge of his bunk he looked down, all that he owned packed in the battered sail bag at his feet. No one at home looked forward to his return. It was time to start new. This bay launched a hope within him the likes of which he had not felt in years.

The ship's cabin boy, slipped up beside him on the bunk and planted his fist jokingly into John's shoulder. "What's matter mate, no woman waiting for you ashore?"

"Jonesie, you can only think down one track. You know that, don't you boy?"

"Ah, get on with ya, I'm just joshin'. It'll be fine to plant our feet on dry land though."

John leaned back against the bulkhead and removed his watch cap. He liked the boy sitting beside him, always smiling and willing to take a shift, he'd even thought of asking him to go along, but John could see the boy he used to be too clearly every time Jonesie climbed aloft. Besides, gambling on a boy of thirteen keeping quiet with the crew could not be risked.

In the morning they were given leave. The Tars often found the lure of Boston harbor too enticing, which was why John waited for Portland, besides he'd loved sailing past the islands in this bay. The forests growing right down the islands 'backbones, right to the water's edge, pines and spruce so tall, spoke of a promise to anyone with the will to match the work. In this bay, a man could make a living from the sea. John counted nineteen schooners anchored just below the big hill when they entered port and had seen the sloops and pinks sailing freely beyond out into the bay.

Following the directions he'd been given on the wharf, he set off up India Street. Tossing his sea-bag over his shoulder, he held tight to his plan as he walked the short distance to the Seamen's Home.

Stepping inside, John gave his eyes a chance to adjust in the hall's dark interior. He peeked inside a large room, and with the exception of a few men sitting at tables arranged along one wall, the place seemed deserted. Backtracking to the outer hallway, which ran the length of the bottom floor, John walked slowly, passing door after door until he reached the end. A tall man leaned on the front desk chatting with a man half his height. Not wishing to impose on the conversation, yet considering this to be the place to make inquiry for a room, John waited for the right moment. It came easily, as the more noteworthy of the two stood away from the desk, straightened his black coat and held out his hand to him.

"Reverend Pratt," he said. "How may we be of service to you sir?"

The smaller man pulled his thin lips into a crooked smile at what apparently was a common enough occurrence, finishing with a quick swipe across the counter top with a rag for emphasis. "What can we do you for?"

"I'll be needing a room and hoped you could help with that."

"Just one qualification required here my good man. Are you a sailor tossed from the sea in need of guidance from the Lord and your fellow man?" asked Pratt.

"I guess probably I fit that and then some, Reverend."

"Then seek no more your wanderings, you'll find Mr. Pike here to be a most accommodating fellow. I will say good day to you sir and hope to see you in my flock this Sunday....Mr...?"

"Brown, John Brown. And you surely will Reverend." Having his response, the Reverend satisfied, took his leave, his black tails flapping against his legs as he strode down the hall to the front entrance. Watching the Reverend disappear John thought he seemed more like a ship's master than a preacher, yet he also thought he should keep his impressions to himself, fearing he might offend the little man who would now aid in the first step to his freedom.

"Mr. Pike, might I inquire as to available accommodations?"

"Not so complicated, Mr. Brown, just put some coins in the jar there and find yourself a room," he replied. "And be sure to get yourself up the street to St. Stephen's this Sunday at ten, if you know what I mean. The Reverend's been awful generous to us and some need a square meal more than others, if you know what I mean. Couldn't make it without he brings the guidance of the Lord, if you know what I mean."

John nodded, guessed that more than likely he knew what the man meant. Reaching into his pocket, intending to do his part, he realized too late that British coin might not be acceptable currency. But Mr. Pike returned his nod by way of thanks and turned back to his paper.

Early the next morning John walked back down to the harbor following Mr. Pike's directions to the Fernald and Dyer Wharf. Uneasy that he might run into shipmates, he kept to the buildings and shadows as he made his way. Across the dock from Jordan and Blake's a man stood mending fyke nets in the morning light. An old double-ended sloop lay at berth in the still green water and the finished cone-shaped nets hung from the mast like a lady's hooped undergarment. John stood watching the man as he worked. Leaning against the piling, he fished his pipe from his pocket and searched his vest for a match. He needed time to think. People seemed friendly enough, but he knew there were many kinds of men, some who would not take kindly to being approached out of nowhere, some who would just as easily strike up a conversation and talk all day. From his vantage point he could tell the nets were badly in need of mending, that the man had probably been working alone for hours without taking a break, and that he had a long day's work before him. If, he thought, he could offer the man some of his time, he might find his way forward, a way out of the harbor before too many days passed.

Making his way along the dock, John turned over in his mind what he might say, wary that his accent would give him away instantly to anyone within earshot. Still, he reasoned he had no choice if he were to make good on his plan. He hoped his casual stride and a friendly smile would work the magic he needed. "Looks like you've got your work cut out for you," John said, following through with a smile.

"By Jesus, that's the truth," the man replied, shaking his head. The contrast to the Reverend Pratt caused John to chuckle, thinking the comment might not go down a treat on Sunday.

"I wouldn't object to lending a hand," John ventured.

"I don't have a penny to my name, so I guess it's mine alone to do," he replied. Then added, "but I could use a smoke, if you've some extra."

"Sure, sure, listen, I've got some time on my hands, so I'd have a go."

"You're from away. Sound like a Bristol man," he stated, fishing about for his pipe. "My father had a man aboard some time ago sounded just like you. Where'd you hail from, if you don't mind my askin'?"

"It's a long story," John hesitated, "but if you like, I'll lend a hand here and talk it through as we go."

"Gorry, that'd be fine and dandy. Name's Jim Johnson," he said, reaching over to shake John's hand.

"John Brown. Pleased to make your acquaintance."

The men worked in companionable silence, John reluctant to reveal too much of his story and Jim seeming to like it that way. As the afternoon grew darker, Jim looked up and announced he was bound for home. "My misses will be on the lookout and she'd be some old hoppin 'mad if I didn't ask you to come on down for dinner."

***

The *Target* slugged along downwind, passing the islands slowly as if she were giving John time to know each one. He'd loved fishing with Jim and living on the Island, but he felt he needed to find his own berth before wearing out his welcome. June fishing brought the mackerel fleet to the bay and he was tempted to move on, but Jim had become his friend and the only person who knew the truth about his jumping ship. He'd known that he was taking a chance confiding in him, but he also needed to relieve himself of the burden. In the two months since he left his ship, and England for good, John had come to realize that he could place his trust in some; that good men did give you a chance and didn't question loyalty to country and Queen. He guessed, after all was said and done, that old Victoria

28

probably didn't give two hoots about him. He'd managed to get himself free and he wasn't about to lose that, or the friendships he made fishing with the men from Hope.

Jim Johnson had proven to be a kind and loyal captain to his crew. Most of the men hailed from Hope and as they each trudged home to their families, following the old pathways through their fields, carrying what they could of their catch to waiting kitchens, they were content. Jim's house sat on the eastern tip of the island, a mile or so from his sister's home. Elizabeth and Albert, and their two sons, lived with old Alex and Rebecca in a fine two story clapboard farm house that John guessed had seen a few winters sitting in the middle of the island on the highest point. A generous porch wrapped itself around three sides of the house. Old Alex liked to joke that his father, when building, could not make up his mind which view he liked best, so he made sure he had a choice. Off to the northeast sat little Sand Island and a clear view all the way up the bay. On the west, the view extended across the narrows to Deer Point, and finally to the southwest, out beyond Outer Green to the open ocean. The porch stood out in the bay like a wheelhouse on the island's deck.

John had given himself over to the bay and her people. Not a man had questioned his past, trusting Jim to make the decisions about his crew. John pulled his weight, and those who fished with him knew an able man on the vessel. Approaching forty, his slight frame and quick manner belied his stamina and sturdy feet on the deck. It was family, the feeling of belonging to someone after all the years at sea, that John could not bring himself to leave. When a day's fishing would end and the men walked to their homes, he would walk beside them, tired and at peace within himself. He did not dare to ask for more.

The men fished for cod, mackerel, hake, and if they were lucky, halibut. They set traps around the shores for lobster, and when the herring were running, they hauled their nets from the barns and fish houses and blocked the quiet coves on summer nights. In the spring they shared an ox team, setting the plow deep into the rich, dark soil, steering clear of the ledgy outcrops reaching down to touch the island's core. The winter cellar shelves sagged, laden with blue and green mason jars, lining the earthen walls. Side by side, stacked three deep, they stood in endless variety. If sent on an errand to retrieve a jar, the musty room, caught in lamp glow, pieced a story of the harvest: peaches and applesauce, brick-red beets and sea duck, rose-hip and blueberry jellies, and silver-backed mackerel. The dandelions were a favorite. They floated inside the glass jars, their browning pods mingling with the spring-cut jagged blades. And beneath the stairs, barrels of molasses, flour, and cornmeal carried the promise of sweet tarts and warm bread. The island held them close and centered their lives, often tapping them on a shoulder to remind them. Should a sea break at the bow, or a winter storm settle in, they knew well enough to keep an eye out for the falling glass.

***

On the afternoon of June nineteenth, Jim and his crew rowed ashore from the sloop, covered in mackerel scales, having just sold the lot at Sinnett's. Through their laughs and loud joking they heard Old Alex's yell from the shore. The old man stood waiting at the water's edge, his white shirt stark and crisp in the bright June sun, his eyes not meeting theirs as they landed.

"Thought I'd better come on down before you started up," he said. "Albert, you'd better get underway. Lizzie's waitin' for you."

Albert lunged from the dory and set off across the beach, his hip boots slipping on the muddy shore path. When he reached the elm outside the stonewall, he saw Jane standing in the dooryard hanging clothes on the line. Stopping to catch his breath, Albert leaned over and placed his hands on his knees. Seeing Jane's face told him what Alex could not. She reached down and lightly touched his shoulder.

"There was nothing we could do," she said, softly.

Albert stood and squared his shoulders against the day. "I told her not to go, Jane. She wouldn't listen, would she. She just charged right over there and brought that damn mess back home with her; on her clothes, in her hair, right back. Where is she?"

"In the front parlor. Listen, Al, don't be like that. She needs you to be her aid now. Liz did what she thought was right."

"Is Frank here now? You didn't bring him did you?"

"No, he's at the farm with Mary and Rosy. I wouldn't have."

"Damn it all to hell, Jane, I just can't face her. Damn it all to hell."

Albert turned toward the house and Jane to the shore path. She wanted to give them time alone to grieve together. She knew Rebecca and Alex would make the plans needed, that she could only

30

be a comfort by keeping Frank safe. If Alex needed her, he would ask, for now she needed to walk the shore and breathe some fresh air.

All through the night they had listened to the poor child's struggle, listened to the rasping with each breath, until his last this morning. It was in God's hands now, she thought, as she walked along toward the eastern cliff, catching there a view of home. Sarah's death was still in her heart, lingering in every thought turned over, waking with her every morning to start her day. God knew she could share their grief, only God knew why she had to.

Perching on the stonewall that ran across the point separating the woods from the pasture, she heard the stranger approaching, and turned to greet him, thinking him to be the English sailor and new member of Jim's crew Elizabeth had mentioned.

"Hello! Mind if I join you?"

"Suit yourself," she replied, stiffly. "I'm just getting out of the way for a spell."

"Had the same idea myself," John replied. "It's grand here. I think of home sometimes when I'm up here. You must be Jane?" he asked.

"That's me." She looked toward Bates and could see Mary walking along the bar which she knew meant she'd been to visit Sarah. "I live over there on Bates. Same as my last name."

"Alex mentioned that. Must get lonely sometimes. Though, I'd give my eye teeth to own something that first rate."

"I don't," she said. "It all belongs to Alex. Bought it the year I moved out from the family, from Jim. Guess he figures as long as I farm it, and take care of Jim's children, it's a fair enough bargain."

John shoved his hands into his vest pocket and pulled out his pipe. His gaze followed her's traveling out over the water and back to the woman sitting before him. Jim had not mentioned children. Let it be, he thought. If she wants to tell more she will.

For her part, Jane watched in silence as Mary made her way to the cottage, a basket in one hand and what looked like a bouquet of flowers in the other. It was like Mary to think of wild flowers for the table, she'd know that Frank and Rosy would be troubled. John spoke her thoughts out loud. "They don't know, do they? Over at home, I mean."

"They couldn't. It's too soon."

"You'll be going back in a day or two, I suppose. Can they manage alone?" he asked.

Shielding her eyes from the sun, Jane looked up at him catching a kindness in the shadow of his face and voice. He reminded Jane a bit of her father, tall and lanky, fish scales clinging to his forearms. She warmed to his casual manner. "The children are fine. Mary's old enough to look out. I worry more about Liz and Al, truth be known."

"Frank is their son, then? Al sure does miss him on the boat. Talks 'bout that boy all the time. He's lucky then to have a son to talk about."

"He's lost a favorite in that little boy, I'd say. Frank's his firstborn, and there's a favor in that, but he always talked how William looked just like his own father. They'll be a long time gettin' over this. You don't have children, then...Mr...?"

"Sorry, should have introduced myself straight away, sorry...John Brown, and as you probably guessed by now, a true Johnny Bull," he said, hurriedly removing his cap, causing his thinning hair to fly off in all directions." I'm not usually so dense, but today is not a day when things go the same as usual, I'm inclined to believe."

"That's the truth of it, Mr. Brown, that's the truth."

"John, call me John. I wonder if I might accompany you back to the house? I'd appreciate not having to go in by myself. There's no experience in my life to measure this one by, if you know what I mean. It would be breaking the ice to have you lead the way. I'm that sorry for the family. If I had any sense I'd be rowing for port and getting out of the way."

***

The following Sunday Jane sailed to Hope for William's funeral. She'd gone home the day after he died to look in on Frank and the girls, refusing to hear of them coming back with her as she still feared the epidemic. It had spread now to four families with three children in their graves. Elizabeth's nursing had taken its toll on her own family, yet she felt now more than ever the need help.

Down the hill from the house, in a hollow piece of good ground, stood the family plot. Young elms flanked the outer perimeter and granite stones from Portland held the names of those who brought the family to Hope in 1802. Old Alex's father, James, had purchased

32

the island thinking of a fish drying business, but in the end never left his Freeport farm. Alex had taken possession instead, cutting back the trees and clearing the land with a team of oxen and hard labor, bringing his first wife Betsey to start their home. She now rested under the elms beside their son, Alexander.

After the brief service, the gathering made their way to Alex and Rebecca's for refreshments. A few of the older neighbors came by to pay their respects, but most kept away from the sickness. The epidemic's ruthless killing turned friends into wary strangers as news of those who fell prey traveled to the shore with the men. Neighbors kept doors shut to neighbors. Islanders hurried past, not stopping to wave or chat. Children were confined to dooryards and admonished to stay close by. As with every illness that spread over the island, there were those who speculated, those who gossiped that they knew the one who carried it with them. Eventually, Liz Coffin's name began to circulate. Awareness of that gossip clung to every face, searching the other for a sign of breaking the silence.

By late afternoon the women, watchful of the children, moved to the kitchen to prepare evening meal. Alex made sure that their bellies were full. Rebecca prepared a roast chicken, a Sunday tradition, with dandelion greens, mashed potatoes and rhubarb pies for desert. Albert sat among them in silence, casting worried glances between Jane and Liz. He wanted to rail at his sadness, to reach out and grab the nearest thing to blame by the throat. He could see only his son's face resting as if asleep in the pine coffin Alex had thrown together the night before. He could hear only the pounding of the nails echoing from the barn in the still summer air. He could think only of his beautiful smiling son beneath the earth.

Chapter Six
Caroline and Barnwell

An abrupt crack of thunder sounded off toward the west bringing Jane's digging to a standstill. The black clouds had been gathering since lunch leaving little doubt there would soon be a downpour. In the cove, the dory swung from side to side, fetching at her anchor, as the quickening wind sent erratic warnings across the water's surface. She wanted to fill the hod before it circled around to the island, but the first large drops plunked into the hole flipping mud and salt water, spattering her face. Determined, Jane set her hoe deep into the mudflat and swiftly pulled back, exposing a mess of white faced clams lodged in a neat row. It was satisfying work if one did not count the aching back afterward. Jane was not built for digging clams, her long legs set the distance; the family teasing that she looked like a blue heron as she worked her way across the flats. She laughed, imaging the girls sitting at the window now watching her performance. Be that as it may, she continued in haste thinking she just might get ahead of the storm. Overhead, the gulls stretched their wings open to the shifting currents sailing past the spruce trees on the point. Standing on the low ground, Jane could hear the rain tearing across the water, pulling at its surface, lifting a dark path in its wake. In the seconds before hitting the island she started for the path, turning in time to witness the thunderbolt touch down at Chebeague.

Abandoning her clams to the doorstep, Jane put her shoulder to the kitchen door and burst into the room, shedding rainwater and mud to the braided rug. Mary sat at the table struggling to keep in her smile, trying to fix her expression to her mother's plight. It was in her nature to judge a moment first and speak only if she thought it safe. It sometimes worried her that Jane could seem so certain about things, that she handled her life so directly, without, it seemed, a thought to others' feelings. It troubled her to think that she was too much the other way. Fortunately, Rosy wandered in, unknowingly breaking the tension by handing Jane the dish towel on her way by.

Sitting down beside Mary she glanced over to Jane, then to Mary. "What? What's wrong?"

"Nothing some dry clothes won't fix," Jane replied, smiling. "I thought it might hold off a bit longer. Don't remember when I'd seen the rain come across the water so fast. One minute it was way off to the east end and the next it was at my boots! Sounded just like a freight train."

"And it doesn't show any signs of letting up either," Mary said, relieved to see that Jane had decided to take things in stride. "How'd you do?"

"There's plenty for supper, but I was hopin' for more. Should know better than to wait. Rosy, think you could fetch me some dry overalls? I'll change by the fire."

"Rosy this, Rosy that. Who did you have fetchin' for you before I came along?"

"Oh, don't bother yourself. I'll go," Mary said, tapping Rosy affectionately on top of her head. "Besides, you'll need to keep your strength up for shellin' clams this afternoon."

"See, that's what I mean. I'm a regular slave around here. This keeps up, I'm goin' back to Grandpa's and be done with you two."

"You done with us?" Mary asked, walking back into the room. "Think you've got it pretty snug here, is what I think. And to prove it, I'm making us all a nice cup of tea."

"That would go a treat," Jane smiled.

Rosy frowned, then followed her mother into the front room, waiting while she changed into warm clothes, mulling over whether to bring up a subject that might not go down a treat.

"You know, I was thinkin', it might not be such a bad idea if we was to move over to live with Aunt Caroline and Uncle Barn 'fore winter. We 'bout froze to death up in that open chamber," Rosy said, casting a sly glance in Jane's direction. "I mean, it might not be so bad."

Jane pulled the rocker closer to the fire and stood warming her hands at the flames before sitting down. "I can understand how you feel, Rosy. It gets hard some days."

"That's what I mean. If we'd been there, instead of livin' in this shack, tryin' to stay warm, Sarah'd still be here," she said, defiantly.

Jane pulled the rocker to a halt, feeling the harsh weight of Rosy's words. The grey outside crowded at the windows and spoke into the quiet; each holding the moment, breathing into their separate, soundless thoughts. Hearing the kettle whistle, Rosy stood and brushed a strand of hair from her eyes, eventually walking from the room.

Mary looked at Rosy and sensed a change in her. She had not heard the conversation with Jane, yet she gathered someone had said something cross. Usually, it was Rosy.

"What's the matter? What did you say now?"

"Nothin' bad, I swear. I just wanted to know why we've got to live here."

"That's not so bad. I guess I feel the same way sometimes."

"Well, she don't, and that's the end of it. By the way, you might want to take her tea in to her. Think she wants to be alone."

"Rosy," Mary said, looking her in the eye, "what'd you do?"

"I told ya, nothin', just she gets moody every time you bring up Sarah."

"God, Rosy. You know better than that," Mary scolded, lowering her voice. "She just can't hear her name mentioned and you know it too. It's only been a few months now, and then William. We've had a bad stretch is all. If you want to go live with Aunt Caroline, which I can't imagine myself, why don't you just go. I think it's a good idea. Just think, you could meet other kids your age and go to school too."

"You think they'd make me? I mean, if I go over to live with them. I was kinda thinkin' I could stay 'round helpin' to cook and get some eggs outa the coop now and then."

Mary laughed out loud. "Oh you do, do you? Not only school, but Aunt Caroline's got religion so bad now she'd have you in church every Sunday, and Sunday school, and maybe even take you to the Sewing Circle. Just think of the fun you'd have."

Rosy plunked down at the table and blew across her tea, comparing the two worlds. "I guess I'll have to think on it some. I was doin' fine 'til you got to that church part. She's an awful good cook though. That crosses out a lot of the bad, way I see it."

"Just think 'bout it before you go spoutin' off again," Mary admonished. "I'll take in the tea, then we can get a start on those clams."

By mid-July Rosy got her wish and Jane sailed her over to Caroline's. Mary's prediction about the effect of Caroline's newly acquired religious zeal made sense. Jane was hoping Rosy's stay might not be the tasty morsel she'd imagined. According to Caroline's letters and reports from Barn's visits, the whole island seemed to be possessed by the Holy Spirit. Jane's curiosity about the direction and sincerity of her sister's enthusiasm, she felt, required a closer look. If nothing else, she wanted to assure herself that Barnwell was still in his right mind.

Taking advantage of the light wind, Jane let out the sheet and fastened it loosely around the stern cleat. She wanted to keep the sun and quiet sail inside; in some way store up a piece of the gentle moment so that she might bring it to mind on other days. She wondered if trying to keep it, might cause it to wither in her memory. It was not a longing for more than what she had. She realized it was more a wish to savor the goodness when she had it, to feel it so completely that it became a part of who she was, or who she could be. As if the wind and water had read her thoughts, the dory answered her musings, flipping the main abruptly across the deck. Rosy looked back from her seat in the bow, sending a scowl in her direction, setting the peaceful moments before on a different course.

Sailing into the cove, Jane spied Barn pushing a wheelbarrow down the shore path. Although usually happy to see them, something about his stride, and the fact that he did not wave, sent a warning signal out across the water. As the dory slipped through the eel grass and came to a halt at the bank, Barn and wheelbarrow emerged from the field. Transfixed, Jane and Rosy watched as he recklessly wheeled to the water's edge. Neither said a word as the drama unfolding before them did not allow time for comment. It was no ordinary piece of trash, or broken farm machinery, he now hauled to the brink. It was, in fact, Caroline's new Singer Treadle Sewing machine, which must have weighed a great deal given all that iron work. Standing back, Barn placed his hands on his hips and watched as the Singer sunk into the mud, blowing bubbles on her way down. Whether he intended to explain his actions did not seem apparent. As he stood there, face flushed, sweat beading on his brow, he seemed to be struggling to find just the right words to occasion the Singer's demise. At last, he turned an about face, nodded in their direction and walked doggedly back up the path.

Rosy strolled over to the water and looked down at the submerged Singer. "Well, what in the world did he do that for?" she asked.

"I run of an idea that Barn was pretty mad 'bout somethin'," Jane said. "I also got a good mind to get right back in that boat and sail for home."

"We can't do that now. Uncle Barn knows we're here. Guess that means Aunt Caroline does too. Come on, let's see what's got him so riled."

Jane stood beside her weighing her options. Instinct told her to run. "If Caroline knows about the Singer, then all hell's 'bout to break loose. Company will be the last thing they need."

"Could be you're right, but if I know Aunt Caroline, she'll act like nothins' wrong. Probably just stare a lot at Uncle Barn. 'Sides, I'm starvin'."

"Well, we can't have that now, can we. Come on, let's face the music."

Jane anticipated visits with Caroline with about as much relish as she might putting a clam hoe tine through a new pair of boots. Every stay was filled with venom, along with her specialty, left-handed compliments. Now Jane feared the new wrinkle, religious condemnation. She had successfully steered her life away from the likes of Ladies Sewing Circles and their need to convert others. Jane had always wondered how they could be so certain. If walking the earth and feeling the sun's worth baked in the soil, or watching a child skimming stones across a calm cove on a summer's day, was not enough for them, what could they possibly know? And who was this God who gives life and takes it away so cruelly? It seemed to her that most preachers were more concerned about what came after this life. At least the times she listened to their sermons that was the gist. Jane felt that telling someone else to live in fear, to be rewarded later in heaven, made little sense. Yet, Caroline was so full of certainty that no one better question it. Still, she was her sister and she felt she owed it to her mother and father to try. Walking beside Rosy to the house, she took a deep breath of fresh air and tried to think of Barn.

Caroline pulled her apron over her head and tossed it to the kitchen chair, then pushed her hair back, fixing it into a tight bun.

Since Barn's return, and the news that company was on its way, she had been struggling to keep her composure. It was after all a new machine, a very expensive purchase, and she'd simply asked him to see what he could do about the foot peddle that kept sticking. She resolved to mention this outburst to Reverend Blake. At the moment she'd just have to put a good face on things.

"Jane and Rosy! What an unexpected visit!" Caroline announced. "Here I was just thinkin' 'bout you and in you walk. Isn't that what I just said the other day, Barn?"

Managing a tight smile, Barn nodded agreement, then returned to his reading.

"It is almost that time," Jane said, noticing Barn's newly discovered interest in the Ladies Home Journal. "Looks like we saved you the bother of a trip. But you know you are always welcome."

Over tea and biscuits, Rosy waited for her chance to bring up the subject of her visiting for the rest of the summer. Uncle Barn had not spoken one word since their arrival and Rosy worried the sewing machine incident might spell quits to her prospects. She knew they'd not had time to talk things out, but sailing back to Bates was not what she had in mind either. The matter surprisingly resolved itself with Caroline. "Seems to me, Rosy Girl, you could stand a bit of church goin'. You've been gettin' away with readin' the Bible on Sunday for too long. And, I want you to meet other girls. What if you was to stay on a bit with us and see if you'd like it," she asked.

"What do you think, Rose? Sound like what you had in mind earlier?" Jane offered.

"I guess that would suit me, but I ain't goin' every Sunday."

Jane looked to Caroline for a response, but having delivered her judgement on the subject there was little more to discuss. She knew Caroline would have her dressed in frills and out the door next Sunday morning. "It would be a nice opportunity for Rosy, Caroline. 'Fraid I have a tendency to work her too hard. Least that's what she tells Mary and me."

***

Shipping her oars, Jane sat for a moment in the moonlight breathing in the warm summer breeze, exhausted by her row from Chebeague.

It wasn't until she put the anchor over and looked toward the house, that she noticed a dory sitting high and dry just under the bank. Guessing it would be old Alex come to visit, she hurried on her way. He usually came after a fish trip in the afternoon, causing her to worry about the family, but as she approached, she was relieved to hear laughter from inside.

Mary sat at the kitchen table tapping a red checker swiftly across the board. Between the two players a kerosene lamp cast its yellow glow to the table's edge, abandoning the room's features to vague outlines and evening shadows. John looked up and smiled, evidently enjoying losing the game.

"Look who came to visit," Mary said, breaking the silence. "Since he brought us a whole pailful of mackerel, I thought it only neighborly to ask him to stay and have some."

"John's always welcome, Mary."

John nodded his thanks, then leaned forward on his elbows to study his next move. "Boy, oh boy, I don't know but this girl runs circles 'round me when it comes to checkers. And, I've played plenty on shipboard."

"How long did you go to sea, John?" Mary asked.

"Ever since a boy, I reckon. My daddy sent me out to learn the trade, started up from cabin boy. When you come from a big family like mine was, the older ones had to help out. I kept it up for a while, then went ashore to start a family of my own."

"Mary, John might not want to talk about his past," Jane admonished.

"No, no, that's fine, Jane. Your family's 'bout the only one I've got now, so, you've a right to know 'bout me. I didn't leave because I did somethin' bad, Mary. I left 'cause my wife died while I was out to sea. There was nothin' more for me left at home."

"I'm sorry to hear that John," Jane said. "It must have been a sad time for you."

"Liddy was so young. We'd just started out together. When I made harbor, her momma met me on the dock and told me. Boy, that was it for me."

"I guess you were luckier than some," Mary said. I mean, you had a love of your own…and that's more than some dare to hope for."

"All I can tell you is that I do feel lucky. Tonight there's no place on earth I'd rather be. Now, are you goin' to let me save face tonight?"

"Me? No, I think I'll quit while I'm a winner. But, Jane's a pretty good checker player. If you dare."

"Dare! If I dare? Tell ya one thing, this is what I know for sure. I'm sittin' here with two beautiful women, I've been challenged to a game of checkers, and my boat's out there under that bank grounded high and dry. Seems to me I've only got but one choice to make," John declared.

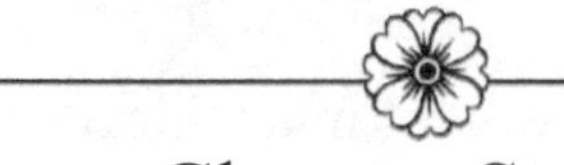

Chapter Seven
Jane and John

Gulls circled over the cove, screeching a wild call into the afternoon, skimming and diving, greedy to taste the tiny herring rushing at the shore. In their wake the mackerel churned furrowed patterns of green waves across the water's surface, flanking their prey. Wading in, Mary tucked her skirt hem inside her waistband, shivering as the silver bodies flipped against her bare legs. She tossed an old seine net out into the swirling mass of fish and hauled back, pleased to see a few on her first try. Jane stood beside John at the bank's edge, laughing at Mary's desperate plunges, before starting down the path to help.

"Thought you'd never get here," Mary said. "Just look at 'em! There must be hundreds in this cove."

"Keep dippin', girl," John said, holding out a bushel basket to Mary's net. "Seems to me this is a might easier than goin' out after 'em."

"I 'magine it is," Jane agreed, "and since they decided to pay us a visit, we might as well take advantage."

Mary stayed with her task, plunging her net deep, lifting and dipping, until three baskets brimming with their catch sat above the tide. Gradually, the school thinned, and as suddenly as they had arrived, the fish instantly moved out with the going tide. The cove's quiet returned with their departure. Offshore, the sea ducks resumed their contented scolding, replacing the gulls' frenzied cries.

Delighted by their good luck, John and Jane carried their catch to the willow's shade and began dressing the fish. Working side by side, they settled into a comfortable pace, each understanding the other, without the need to talk or complicate the task. Their hands fell into a rhythmic pattern following an order and familiarity with the work. In other times they would remember the day Mary caught all those mackerel in the cove. They would remark how many jars they'd put up, and taste the summer day at the winter table; their voices stretching to bring back the moment.

***

August's end brought the work of harvest. Jane clucked the old mare forward as John and Mary pitched the hay onto the wagon. It had been clear weather for weeks, yet the threat of rain kept them working at a steady pace. Getting the hay put up seemed to begin and end the conversations of their days, yet for John, one other thought ran beneath it all. He had been waiting for his chance, and getting Mary off the island figured heavily into his plans. Certain that Jane understood his intentions, he was equally certain that he'd know the right moment. It all hinged on Mary and how he might convince her to take a long walk around the shore, or perhaps go over to Ministerial and get stranded by the tide. Looking across the field now, and the hay mounds scattered before them, he guessed things would just have to find a way to work themselves out. Finally, Jane pulled back on the reins bringing work to a halt.

Mary looked up, then decided not to ask any questions, plopping down exhausted beside the wagon. "You know," she said, "if we didn't have to feed this old gal, we wouldn't have to work ourselves to death. I know we've got the cow too, but think about it. How much hay does she eat in the winter compared to how much work we do?"

"You might have a point, Mary," Jane responded. "Still, I think you'll find she's worth it. Soon's we start haulin' seaweed up from the shore, you might miss her a little."

"I guess so. Just the same, I can't help but think how Rosy always manages to get herself over to Aunt Caroline's when all the work starts up. When is she comin' home, anyways?"

"I haven't heard from them since July, but my guess is she'll be wantin' to avoid school if she can. Maybe we should take a sail over and find out," Jane suggested.

Mary stood and brushed the hay and dust from skirt. "As far as that goes, I could go this afternoon, stay for a visit myself."

"That's a good idea, Mary," John added, looking at Jane to gauge her agreement. "I think your mother and I could finish up here today.

What do you think, Jane? She could fetch Rosy home by herself all right."

Jane smiled, then walked over to the mare who stood by patiently munching her hay. "Tell you what, let's get this last lot in. If you've a mind to go then, that'll be fine."

In the late afternoon Mary sailed out of the cove picking up a light southwest wind. John stood on the bank waving until she sailed past the end of Ministerial, and he was certain she would not bother to return had she forgotten something. Before starting up the path, he made a quick detour to the fish house. Once inside, he eye-hooked the door, pulled a chair from the corner and hauled it to the middle of the floor. Climbing up, he stood on tiptoe and ran his hand along the rafter, until he felt the canvas sailcloth. He had taken pains to keep his plans a secret, and now, clutching the small bag, he smiled and headed for the door.

John quietly lifted the latch and stepped into the kitchen. Jane stood at the stove shucking corn, waiting for the water to boil, greeting him with a smile. "I thought you might be hungry," she said.

"I am, 'bout famished, but while we wait for that corn, I've somethin' I've been wantin' to ask," John said. "I should say, I want to ask, but I'm that afraid you might not take to it. And, if you don't, I'll understand. I know I'm not much of a catch, and worse to look at for that matter, so, I'll just get on with it."

"For heaven's sake John, what on earth's got into you?"

"I don't know. I guess, I don't know how to say what it is I got to say," he replied.

Jane tipped her head to one side, revealing a sly grin, then turned to her cooking. Fearing he'd lost his moment, John tossed his hat to a chair, walked over to Jane, took an ear of corn out of her hand and placed it on the table. Reaching into his pocket he pulled out a tiny canvas bag, untied the ends, and shook a gold band into his free hand. "Jane," he said, "I would be most pleased if you was to consent to be my wife."

"Why, John," Jane said, laughing, "I guess that's just 'bout the first time anybody's ever asked me that question. Seems pretty nice to hear those words, mostly because it comes from you. You think we could make it work?"

"I do, or I wouldn't have asked. I've been savin' up since I met you that day on Hope. You just seemed right to me. How you talked about things so straight. Only thing I worry about is the girls."

"That shouldn't be a worry, John," Jane replied. "Mary's most fond of you. Rosy will grouse no matter. I can't see a fuss made."

"I thought about that too. It just so happens I met this nice fella when I first landed in port and seems like he'd fit the bill. When Mary gets back, I'll sail up."

***

Reverend Pratt reached into his vest pocket and retrieved his watch, impatiently waiting for his first appointment of the day. September first was an odd day to wed, he thought, yet in his experience, the island people didn't appear to pay much attention to the calendar, or time of day for that matter. He supposed they'd be sailing out there in the bay placing their faith in the wind and tide. Leaving his stuffy office he strode down the aisle and out the front door, seeking relief from the oppressive heat of midday. Strolling along Pearl Street he paused in the shade beneath the generous oak at the corner, reflecting on his sixteen years as rector at St. Stephens. Just a year before his arrival, the congregation had provided the means to remodel the old church. The architect had chosen to replace the older square-paned windows running along its side, favoring dramatic arches, and a more elaborate spired entrance towering over the city street.

Overall, the Reverend was well satisfied with his position in the church and with his flock, yet often admonished them for prideful notions by way of a lengthy sermon, reminding them of the promised fall should they forget. Occasionally, a parishioner or two might be overheard suggesting that the Reverend might do well to heed his own words, pointing out his flamboyant manner of speech and dress. As Portland was a modest town, some encouraged the same in a man's character, however none dared bring it forth as a counter argument after sitting through his hellfire orations. Although the Reverend may have on occasion seemed a bit pompous, he was known by all to be a generous man, bound to do God's work, especially with those less fortunate. It was perhaps for this reason that he had consented to marry John and Jane, knowing only the bare details of their past. He was one of those people who could recall by name every man he'd ever met, and it was John's good fortune that he could.

Having consulted his watch for a third time that afternoon, the Reverend Pratt decided that perhaps he had misjudged John Brown and was just about to leave the bench he'd been sitting on, when he spied a couple ascending the steps about to enter the church. If he was surprised by their appearance, one could not judge by his expression, as he straightaway walked to greet them, extending his hand to John. Apparently their voyage had been a choppy one. He noticed the hem of Jane's dress appeared soaked through and her hair tipped slightly askew, having escaped the captivity of a tight bun at the back. John still wore his hip boots, although he had taken the time to roll them down, and it would appear he had forgotten his shoes at home. His white shirt, however, gleamed brightly in the sunshine, only outdone by a brilliant smile.

"Reverend Pratt," John announced, "it seems we've managed to arrive late and I apologize. This is Jane. And she might just be wantin' to turn right 'round and head back home."

"Now, that would be a most awkward circumstance, Mr. Brown," he said, with a grin. "I am more inclined to believe this young woman would be rightly disappointed to have made such an arduous journey, only to discover you've changed your mind. Now, unless I am wrong in my assessment, I believe it impolite to keep her waiting here in the street a moment longer."

"John," Jane said, "seems to me we've got this far, a bit further won't hurt. We should not keep the Reverend from his day." The rector smiled and gestured toward the church steps, allowing Jane and John to lead the way.

Later that evening, the Reverend Mr. Pratt sat with his family half listening to his wife prattle on about her difficulties with the Ladies Sewing Circle. "James," his wife admonished, "you are not paying attention. The very least you could do, I should think, given my duties here, and to your parish."

"I am sorry, my dear. I have had a most agreeable day and do not wish to diminish yours, but to tell the truth, I cannot stop thinking about today's wedding ceremony," he replied.

"Well, it could not be that remarkable, you seem to be amused, or preoccupied."

"Not at all, just amazed. Today, I witnessed the truth of a statement I have oft repeated, yet discovered in my experience how it is possible for one to take new meaning from an old adage. My dear, I believe it must be so, God does work in mysterious ways."

Chapter Eight
Ira Gould

After her chores, Jane walked to the back shore and scanned the clear blue sky, looking past the Cow and Mink Rocks to the thin line of the horizon. The brisk afternoon wind tossed the breakers against the shore, sending cold, white spray against her face. Her father had said, if she started sailing she wouldn't hit a single piece of land until she set foot in Spain. She'd often wondered how he knew, or if it were true, as her father did have stories that she later thought stretched the truth. If the fishermen were any yardstick, she imagined that it was more than likely the truth. She had hoped to catch sight of John who was out fishing with Jim and Albert. She thought they were due to be home soon. Ever since Sarah's death, windy afternoons brought with it Sarah's memory and her guilt. Marrying John had gone a long way toward helping blur the vivid images when she closed her eyes at night. Yet, she was not sure it was altogether proper to dismiss Sarah's memory, she just wished for the living girl to be more present in her thoughts.

Catching sight of the old sloop, she turned from the back shore cliffs and made for the cottage. Jim would pull into the cove and drop John at the dory, then make way for Hope. Jim knew he would not be welcome and Jane marveled that the friendship with John had continued, despite their marriage. She imagined that as they grew older it became more and more possible to forgive. It never seemed to her that holding on to an unexplainable past, especially a grudge, got you very far. Her daydreaming must have caught in the wind, as she looked out to see the sloop just slipping past the bar and Jim turning to wave to her. John would not think anything of it, dismissing the wave as she walked to the greet him.

"You're in early. I've not started supper yet. Have any luck?"

"You know we did! How does a nice fresh pollock sound for that dinner?" he asked, stepping onto the beach holding the fish by its tail. "I've brought mackerel too. We can dress and salt 'em after dinner," he added.

"You must be thinkin' this next winter's goin' to be a hard one, way you're stocking the dirt cellar. How many barrels you got now?"

"Lost count they's so many," he laughed. "I want enough put by."

"Here, let me have that fish," she ordered, laughing along with him. "It's not gettin' any younger hangin' there in mid air, you know." Pulling his fish knife from its sheath, John handed it to her knowing she would gut and dress the fish at the shore, leaving the innards for the gulls who appeared on cue with their demanding cries.

As John stood watching the process, he thought it might be a good idea to bring up the subject of Mary, one that Jane had been avoiding since last night. "You can tell me it's none of my business, and you probably will, knowing you like I do, but we ought to talk about it."

"Nothin 'to talk 'bout," she said, tossing the final pieces to the gulls. "I'll wait for her to come to me. If there's anythin' 'bout it wants tellin', she knows I'll listen."

"Mary's not my daughter, Jane, but it feels like she's not Jim's either, and I feel responsible for her in a way. I want to help if I can, not take over, just be on the lookout for us."

The kindness in John's words resonated with her. He had chosen to contrast himself with Jim, she was sure, not to make himself seem better, but to cast himself in the father's role. John should have been a father, she thought, as she smiled and handed back his knife.

"You know, John, Mary's sixteen now, and if she plans to marry Jacob Frost, then so be it. He's a good boy. I know you are worried and I'll talk to her when it's right." As she spoke, Jane realized that she didn't quite share John's concerns. She knew the Frosts, and Jacob seemed genuine enough in his intentions; bringing over some books for Rosy and Mary. She chuckled thinking about how sly Mary was at first, trying to pretend that the reason for his visiting was for Rosy's sake. Although, it would have been nice if Rosy had consented to sit down with a book, she thought. If John wanted to worry about anyone it ought to be that one. She'd sit for hours and stare at the wall before she'd open a book. Still though, Jane held out the hope that when school started in August she might persuade Rosy, with John's help, to attend. If Mr. Chadwick would give up his summer to teach, then the least she could do is show up. It would mean Rosy would have to stay with Liz for the summer. She had heard that Hope had three students, and if she had anything to say about it, Rosy would be the fourth.

***

Setting the fried pollock on the table, they all watched as Rosy reached for the largest fillet without waiting for grace. Just as Jane wondered at her voracious appetite, John pointed out what usually went unspoken. "Good God, girl!" he exclaimed. "Judging by the food you've got on your plate, I believe it does remove now any doubts your mother and I may have had," he said, passing a sly wink in Mary's direction.

"What'ya mean? she asked, shoveling in a soup spoon of mashed potatoes and peas.

"It's just that we've all been a bit concerned about you, is all. That's right isn't it, Mother? What we'd been worrying about for some time now."

Mary masked her smile, demonstrating her best concerned face in Rosy's direction.

"What was the name of that disease we talked about? Just can't work my way 'round to a recall," John said, looking at Jane for a contribution.

"Let me see," she responded, sitting back and resting her fork on the edge of her plate. "I do recall we talked, something you heard 'bout in England, I think now."

"That's it! We had many cases when I was a lad. Some never recovered, I'm sad to report," John said, shaking his head tragically, with a quick glance in Rosy's direction.

"Well, I've been right here for months and if anybody's brought a thing for me to get sick on, it'd be that Frost fella. He and Mary's thick as thieves, so I guess she might be the one gettin 'your famous old England sickness," Rosy asserted. "Is there any fish left over?" she asked.

Jane smiled, "Over on the sideboard, though I'm not sure where you're goin' to put it." She knew it left John free to finish the tease, pleased she'd thought of it. Giving John the nod, she said, "John do you have any idea where Rosy's goin' to fit any more dinner?"

50

Returning with her seconds to the table, Rosy looked at John. "Well, I'm not worried, if that's what you all think," she argued.

Unable to take it any longer, Mary walked over to Rosy's chair and reached down to pinch her chubby thigh." Yep, I think one does look larger than the other one, now that you mention it, John."

"One what? What are you all talkin ''bout anyway? I'm just hungry."

"That's one of the signs!" John exclaimed.

"What signs?"

"Rosy my girl, I think there's little doubt about it. You've managed to contract that dreadest of diseases that befall girls of just your age. One leg larger than the other, it must be so." Here John paused, letting them savor the moment. "If we can manage, mother, I'm thinking we'd better get Rosy over to Portland, 'cause without a doubt in my mind, she's come down with the holler leg!"

Their laughter rang out into the warm August night, as John, giving up on the teasing, announced he was stepping out for a pipe. Jane and Mary were still laughing about the joke, when they heard John calling to someone from the steps. Drying her hands on her apron front, Jane walked out to greet their visitor, thinking it would be Jacob come calling on Mary, but to her surprise, Ira Gould stood leaning against the railing talking with John.

"Ira. What brings you over tonight?" she asked.

"Just thought I'd be neighborly, is all."

"You've just missed dinner, Ira, but we can probably scare you up somethin', if you want to come in," John said." That is, if there's anything left."

"That's kind of you, John. I wouldn't want to be any trouble," he said, moving to open the door.

"No bother," Jane said, shooting a questioning look in John's direction. John caught her arm and held her back for a moment." I'm keeping an eye out," he whispered.

Making himself at home, Ira eased his considerable bulk into a kitchen chair. Typical of many who fished for a living, his worn overalls were covered in dried salt stains and his boots dripped on the clean floor. John could see that he hadn't bothered to wash and judged by the stubble on his flushed face, that shaving was not part of his daily routine either. Jane knew Ira fished with Jim and John, off and on, but his presence at her table annoyed her in ways she could not explain. She should be welcoming, as with all the men who stopped by their home, but this man's awkward manner made him seem different from the others. It was not her habit to judge by looks, yet he seemed unfinished in some way, as if his broad brow determined all there was to know about him. His hands reminded her of paws, clumsily reaching across the table, carelessly colliding with things. But it was his eyes, grey as ash, that troubled her. Set wide and opaque, as if the light refused to enter them, deliberately following every gesture, setting into memory the measure and worth of each person.

John wanted Ira to feel welcome, but he knew Jane didn't take kindly to her home being treated like a fish house. There would be no room for excuses or explanations if Ira made a habit of coming over for handouts. John knew her limits and getting in her bad books would make Ira wish he'd stayed on Hope. Still, John felt that everyone deserved a chance; he would be kind, until something other than dirty clothes and bad manners presented itself.

Still angry about the joshing she had taken at dinner, Rosy plunked her stocky body into the rocker, picking up one of Jacob's books. Sensing that she'd probably taken enough for one night, and wanting to slip away, Mary grabbed her shawl from the door hook. "I'll be over at Frost's for awhile tonight," she announced. "If that's okay with you and John?" Leaning over the table to light the kerosene lamp, she caught Ira's quick smile in her direction, dismissing his intent as friendly." I'll check in at the barn on my way down, if you'd like me to?"

Jane looked at her daughter in the glow of the lamp and wondered at how she had turned out to be such a beauty. She concluded again that the blonde hair which curled about and framed her thin young face, should not be taken for granted. Jacob was not blind and neither was Ira. Still, she thought, Ira was too old for Mary, judging him to be about 25, or more; he'd not be causing any trouble with John here. Mary watched her mother's expression change from neutral to worry, thinking it to be about Jacob.

"You go along, I'll go down and see to the barn. You and Ira go ahead and talk, I think I'll walk off my supper." John knew she'd be watching to make sure Mary arrived safely at the Frost's; a trip she could make blindfolded. It was just her way since he had known her to keep watch of her girls whereabouts. Tonight in particular, he knew that Ira's presence on the Island would keep Jane awake until she knew Mary was safely home. John understood her overprotectiveness, but he thought she was unfairly judging Ira. He had seen what an able man he was on the boat and that he was kindly toward Frank when he went out with them. He lay the cause of it to Sarah's drowning and he guessed no one on God's green earth would change that.

***

Jacob stood on the Bates side of the bar, swinging his lantern back and forth in the darkness. Thinking that she had been denied permission to visit, he was secretly hoping she would slip out anyway, so he would hold his position until morning if it came to it. Eventually, he reasoned that she'd spot him, whether he was standing or sitting, so he found a ledge near the path and sat. He started to whistle, then stopped, wondering if it would be safe. Thinking it over he decided it would be best to remain quiet, that way he'd hear her if she got off the path, or forgot where to meet. Things did look different in the dark, even if it was a warm summer night and not completely dark like in winter. Jacob thought about her face and soft lips and how he'd love to kiss her. It would be a gamble he imagined. If she liked him, which he thought she did, then she'd surely want to be kissed. On the other hand, if she was shy and he made to kiss her, and she thought him too forward, then what were his chances? Hearing footsteps crunching on the beach coming closer, Jacob called lightly out and was rewarded by her return giggle.

"I'm up here! Mary? Is that you?"

"Course it's me, you silly. Who'd you think I was? The boogie man?" she teased.

Scrambling down the bank, careful not to upset the lantern, Jacob strode across the beach to meet her and without thinking, reached over, pulled her into his arms and kissed her. He'd only kissed one other girl before and he wasn't quite sure if he managed it properly, but the sweet scent of the rugosa traveling on the soft summer breeze and the light touch of her lips carried her reply.

Chapter Nine
A Proposal

Mary Johnson and Jacob Frost sat on their ledge stealing a few minutes together before he would be missed at lessons. With the Lovell's on Ministerial, he now had a total of four students, if he counted Rosy who sometimes bothered to make an appearance. Jacob considered the few extra dollars he would earn this summer and fall a start on what he hoped would be enough to get them settled at the farm. The plan, however unpopular they anticipated it to be with Mary's mother, was to move to the family farm at North Yarmouth and take over a piece of land from his uncle. This afternoon they plotted together, searching for the right words to tell the family of their intention to marry in September.

Reluctant to leave the warmth of the shore, and each other, Jacob stood and held out his hand to Mary. Pulling her close, he kissed her once gently on the cheek then hurried out across the bar, waving when he reached Ministerial. Returning his wave, Mary lingered at the low tide enjoying the summer sun and warmth of the water. Wading in, she pulled her long skirt up to her knees and reached down to collect a quartz stone that caught her eye, recoiling at her own sudden reflection. Since Sarah's death she had found the rush of the tide against the beach stones a continual reminder of that afternoon. She had not blamed anyone for Sarah's death. She knew Sarah all too well; that she had often taken too many chances around the water. She'd always been the one to wade out into the waves without a care, the one to jump carelessly from the cliffs, skinning her knees and then laughing about it. That afternoon, departing for the east end beach, they'd waved to Sarah sitting at the very peak of the bow, laughing and dangling her legs in the water. She had called out to Rosy, waving both arms high into air. It was her last memory of her sister, happy and carefree, her usual playful self.

There had been endless talking to herself and in the family. "If only I hadn't taken that final walk to the east end, if only I hadn't let you go that day, I knew the wind would come up quick, Rosy kept complaining, I didn't know how to make her breathe again". Endless talking and blame taking, until finally each one felt the exhaustion of trying to make sense of it. Until each was simply left to deal with her own demons; the kind that strike when you are least aware, the ones that come to you when you lay your head on the pillow at night, or when you see the dory pitch to a wave, or simply see a stone as the water laps its edges. Mary soon learned that she would have to live with the memory of her sister's death all of her life. She only hoped that in time she might find a safe place to store that memory, at least to have some warning sign when it would strike her. She understood her mother's pain, but not its depth. Even when one of them casually mentioned Sarah, it was like she had shut the door to everything, even the fact that she had shared her life with them. At times she could feel her presence, wanted to speak her name and recall a time together, but her mother would rise from the table and her look would tell them to stop.

***

John stood on the porch washing up, chatting with Jane as she shucked clams for their dinner. He was pleased to summon the day's events to mind and to see her occasional smile in his direction. To be here, with his wife and her daughters, counted for everything that mattered in his world; a world where he could see the boundaries, name the beaches and coves, one he hoped he could prove himself worthy to be in. He considered every breath he took since arriving three years ago as the purest in his life. At fifty-one he told himself that he would never ask for more than this small island and loving family.

Jane reached her hand out to John asking for a hand up, then carried her clams down the path to the shore to give them a good rinsing in the salt water. Preoccupied with the task, she hadn't seen Mary and Jacob walking over from the bar point. Coming into view now she guessed they'd been walking in the woods at the southwestern end of the Island. The trees had been spared the clearing, as her father had pronounced the land too rocky for

55

planting or pasture. Jane had always considered the stand of pine and spruce good protection for the house in the winter winds and a fine spot to cool off in the summer heat.

"Mom!" Mary called. "We're heading up!"

"Be right along," she said, straightening her back, then stooping down again to give the clams a final rinse. As an afterthought she called, "Ask Jacob to stay to dinner!"

Readying to leave, she was surprised to see Ira making his way along the shore, carrying a hod, his hip boots stomping out clam holes. She hoped he'd continue on his path away from her. Putting her head down as she walked, she foolishly kidded herself that she was in some way invisible, as if making eye contact would blow him over the beach.

"Jane! Hold up a minute!" he yelled, taking great long strides in her direction. She stopped short, feeling trapped in her own dooryard, resenting his intrusion into a perfectly fine summer afternoon.

"Ira," she said, greeting him with a slight dip of her head. Oblivious to subtleties, Ira continued, boldly reaching down to relieve her of the clam hod.

"Here, let me take that for you. A beautiful woman like yourself shouldn't be doin' all the carryin'. Where's that man of yours? Likely sittin' down with his pipe while you're doin' all the work, I'll wager. I tell you that man does not appreciate what he's got, that's what."

"Oh, I think he knows rightly enough, Ira. Lookin 'for some steamers?"

"I'd thought some of it, but looks like to me you've plenty here to share with a poor old fisherman like myself," he said, casting an eye to the glistening clams and then to Jane.

"We've got company tonight, Ira. What brings you here? I thought you was stayin' over to Hope these days."

"Nah, I just took myself over to the old Moulton house yesterday, and since there's no lock on the door..."

"Not quite right is it? That's not your place to move into."

Reaching the doorstep, Ira stopped and handed the basket to Jane. "It's not your concern either," he challenged.

"It might be," Jane countered looking boldly into his black eyes. Ira stared back, momentarily considering how he might defend his position, then thinking better of it tipped his cap and bid her good day.

Mary opened the door with the spider in hand, already wearing her apron as Jane entered. "Thought I'd get a start," she said, hoping to set a tone for the evening's news. Rosy sat at the table snapping green beans as John emerged in clean overalls, ready to assist Mary and Jacob with what he imagined might be an evening requiring some reassurances all around. He glanced in Mary's direction and winked, letting her know that he was on her side. Pulling out a chair, he invited Jacob to come and sit. The only person in the room unaware of the tension between Mary and Jacob sat nosily snapping and tossing beans into a pot, occasionally grumbling. Still peeved about Ira, Jane stood with her hands gripping the chair-back, then turned to John with a fire in her eyes.

"That man is a nuisance, John," she declared. Jacob visibly winced, but maintained his position, glancing over to Mary who did her best to smile encouragement.

"What man is that? Whose got you all riled up?" John asked.

"Ira. Met me on the beach and invited himself to dinner, again. Turned him away. Thought he could dig his own clams for once."

"Oh, come on then, that's just his way. You know how he is. Shouldn't let him get under your skin so. He's harmless enough."

"I'm not so sure John. Did you know he'd moved into Moulton's? What's happenin' with that old place? And, he shouldn't, it's not his to move into, now is it?" she demanded.

John raised his eyebrows and shook his head. "He's a brazen one, that's for sure."

"He can be brazen some other place. I don't like him 'round here so much. There's something 'bout the man that sets my teeth on edge."

"Don't worry about him, he's one them that thinks he can do as he pleases with a smile, is all. I'll have a word with him tomorrow. How's that set?" he asked, hopefully." He's more than likely got permission, there'll be an explanation."

Satisfied for the moment, Jane finally sat and acknowledged Jacob presence. "How the pupils comin' 'long? Did this one make it over the bar today?" she asked, glancing over at Rosy.

Not wanting to displease her, yet not wanting to lie either, Jacob settled on a compromise.

"Not feelin 'too well today, hey Rosy? Isn't that what you told your sister?"

Catching on, Rosy pitched a story about some strange ailment that had overtaken her "directly after breakfast" which she allowed made her "right uncomfortable." Knowing a lie when she heard one, Jane just shook her head at Rosy and thought after all, it wasn't Jacob's job to get her to school, but hers. She was beginning to think that Rosy would never learn to read, despite the long nights she's spent reading to her, showing her how to sound out the letters and spell her name. Even after days of practice, she still refused to study, claiming she could get by fine by signing her name with an "x", adding that she knew plenty who did. It seemed an endless battle, one Jane felt sorry to lose, as she watched her youngest idle her days away at the shore. She marveled at the girl's ability to sit for hours and wondered how anyone could be so lazy when there was so much to be done. Letting it drop, knowing that now was not the time to pursue the issue further, she looked over and noticed for the first time since sitting down, that Jacob looked about to burst. Hoping she hadn't put him in a difficult spot she was about to ask him about the other pupils in his class when he stood abruptly and said what had been on his mind since the day began. Unwise, as he judged later, not to have waited until all stomachs were full, he blurted out, "Mrs. Brown, Mary and I want your blessing to get married!" With his sudden announcement, Mary dropped her spatula and hurried over to Jacob's side. All heads turned to Jane and waited. It was, they all knew, anyone's guess how she would react to his announcement. All except John, who understood how fond she was of Jacob.

"Well, Mrs. Brown," John asked, reaching out for her hand, "what have you got to say to this fine young man?"

Jane looked about the table at her family, giving a brief thought to holding them in suspense a bit longer, but catching the look on Jacob's red face, simply said, "I think that would be fine, Jacob."

Chapter Ten
Margaret Douglas

An early snow clustered in white clumps on the field as the sheep foraged in November's harsh afternoon wind. Leaving them to their fate, John took the path across the island's backbone leading him to the old Moulton place. Walking up to the front door he stopped and cast an eye to the gathering black clouds out over the islands and bay. He could just make out a three-master outside Mark Island he guessed would be making for home and a snug cove to settle in. The smoke he had seen the night before from the chimney meant that someone had moved in and he wanted to be certain that it was not Ira back again to squat.

Knocking with his fist hard enough to be heard against the wind's clamor, he yelled out a greeting, then pushed open the kitchen door. The dark afternoon seemed to gather and follow him into the cold room; uninviting and deserted. About to leave, he turned and started for the door thinking he must have been mistaken about a fire, when he heard a frail voice call from an adjoining room. Startled by the high pitched sound of a young voice, he moved cautiously on. Huddling under a blanket he spied the source, and moving closer, discovered a small girl shivering beneath the blankets.

"I didn't mean to barge in, but we got worried the other night when we saw the chimney smoke. Are you all by yourself?"

Pulling the blanket away from her face, John could see that she was shaking, but she sat up and answered him directly showing little fear. "I'm Margaret. Me and my grandfather just moved in. Heard nobody was here," she said.

"Who is your grandfather? Better yet, where is he? You shouldn't be here without a fire going."

"I'm fine. He lights it at night, so we're all right. Told me to stay put and he'd be back before dark."

John stood staring down at her, uncertain as to his next move. "I don't want to interfere now, but you ought to be starting that fire. How about I help you get things going and then you can tell me where your granddaddy might be in this storm that's brewing," he said moving toward the stove to search for kindling and firewood. "Where do you keep your wood? Is it out back?" he asked, hoping that it wasn't.

"Nah, we ran out yesterday. Said he'd bring some coal back to light it with. Who are you, anyway? Granddad said we had nice folks livin 'nearby. That you?"

"That would be true enough, but I've got to tell ya, nobody's sailin 'out there today in a small boat. Maybe you ought to get your coat on and come on over with us for the night."

Margaret looked at John trying to decide if he was the nice neighbor her grandfather had mentioned, wanting to believe that he was that man, then finally asked, "Who all else you got livin' at your place?"

Sensing that she might be wary of him, John struggled with the right words to put her at ease and finally decided that if she was as cold as he thought, and probably hungry, he'd not have much trouble convincing her to come along with him.

"I'm John Brown," he said. "And just across the island is a warm house, some food and water, and my wife, Jane. We've got a girl a little older than you. She's called Rosy. So you haven't to worry. Come on now, get your coat, I'm not gonna 'bite ya'."

John moved to the door and waited for a sign that she understood, yet she did not move. He wanted to make her understand that he was no threat, but hesitated to make a wrong move in her direction, thinking it might frighten her more. Opening the door, letting in the freezing wind, he turned and pleaded with her. "You'll freeze if you stay here, your granddaddy wouldn't want that would he?"

"I guess not," she answered, looking up, her eyes asking questions he could not begin to fathom.

"Come on then. This place is colder than my barn," he said, beckoning with his free hand.

Finally, she stood throwing the blanket around her shoulders. "All right, then, but I ain't got no coat to wear, so I hope it's not far."

Early the next morning, John spied a small catboat sailing into the cove, certain it had to be Margaret's grandfather. Calling to Jane from the bottom of the staircase, he pulled on his hip boots and coat, then hurried to the shore to help the old man secure his dory. The bow sail flapped furiously in the wind as her skipper let go the main and swung her skillfully into the wind, hauling her stern to the beach. Grinding to a halt, the waves continued thrashing at her sides as John grabbed the starboard gunnel and walked along hand-over-hand to grab the bow piece. Pulling to, he hauled her bow to the beach front. Running a line up the beach John made fast the skiff to his beach anchor and hailed the house for help.

With Jane's aid, the old man and John managed to haul the little boat away from the rollers just breaking at her stern.

"Boys, I tell ya, it's some dusky out there," the old man said. "Much obliged for your help. You must be Brown."

"I am. This is my wife, Jane. Your granddaughter is up to the house."

"Hope she wasn't any trouble. I told her to stay put 'til I got back," he explained. "We just got wind the old place was up for grabs and I hauled up stakes."

Jane looked at the old man drenched from head to toe and wondered what story he would tell. It didn't seem right for a man his age to be traipsing around with such a young girl. "Where you from?" she asked.

"Harpswell. Used to anyway."

Warmed and fed, old man Black told his story as they all sat quietly sipping the strong tea Jane had prepared. Hearing his weary voice each listener felt a weight take hold, felt a longing at each turn in the tale to beat it back into its unhappy past, to reset its course. Finished, he rose from his chair preparing to leave." We thank you for your generosity and now we'll be off."

They watched from the front parlor window until the old man and girl cast just their shadows in the November morning, making their way steadily over the pasture path. The images left in their wake sank deeply into their mood, prompting Jane to break the silence between them. "I'm not sayin 'they shouldn't squat there, John, but how's it goin' to be if the Moulton family come back?"

Still standing at the window, John eventually turned to face her. "I've been thinking 'bout it ever since I laid eyes on that girl yesterday. I'm not sure they can make a go of it, Jane. There's no wood, and he's brought back only coal enough to carry in a bucket. We'll have to help out."

"What'd you think the mother died of? He didn't say. She couldn't been that old. That girl's no more than six years old, if she's a day."

"I know, I know, I'm guessing there's more to that story. I'll get a fish day when this weather clears, see what I can find out. He's on the up an up, but I can't see that boat of his making it out of the cove, let alone back over to Harpswell. There's not much we can do I 'spose, but give them what we can. If he can't fish, they'll likely starve. Can't have that now, can we?"

***

For two days the wind screeched out of the northeast leaving a foot of snow before the storm headed out to sea. John paced the pine boards and grumbled after shoveling, generally complaining about needing to get out to fish. It was uncharacteristic for John to grouse about bad weather, or complain, and Jane knew the source of his discontent to be more about the new squatters than he wanted to let on. Every other day, one or both had diligently made the walk to the old house taking what little they could from their own larders. Seeing themselves in a more fortunate situation they thought it little enough they could do; learning while visiting that the Wainwright's and the Wallace families on Ministerial had also pitched in what they could. The islanders would not see a family starve, if they had anything to say about it.

On the following Monday, John got his wish and set out that morning to fetch Frank to set his gear. He hadn't mentioned to Jane that he would be taking the catch this time to Portland as he'd some business which he hoped would please her. Since meeting old man Black, he had given considerable thought to the Moulton house and the remaining acreage on Bates. He intended to investigate the deed.

John usually avoided selling in Portland due to his unwarranted fear that someone might catch sight of him and send him back to England. He knew that no one much cared where he might be, yet he still felt his stomach churn whenever he sailed into the port. Now, on his approach to the harbor, he noticed a flurry of activity around Hog Island. Under a mile away he could see two large sloops dumping grout and off loading granite blocks at the shoreline. Against the sky, a tall boom worked steadily moving the heavy stone while men climbed the cliffs yelling to one another. He wondered who would want to build a wharf on Hog Island. He guessed there would be a reason and hoped he would remember to ask once in the city.

After tying his dory at Dyer's Wharf, he started for the new Court House where he knew he would find a deed, or some evidence of ownership, for the land he hoped might be for sale. He thought again how pleased Jane would be, but told himself to keep his excitement down until he knew for sure.

The idea had come to him quite out of the blue one day when he and Charles Moulton had been chatting while baiting trawls. Charles had just finished building his large two-story house on Ministerial and he'd let it drop that he might someday like to see what his family planned to do with the old house on Bates. He guessed that it would have to wait because he'd spent about all his savings on his house, but still thought it was such a damn shame to see it fall down like that. At that very moment, John's plan began to take shape and continued to grow as he considered the extra food tilling more land would bring. He even thought he could keep old man Black on the land for his remaining years helping out on the farm.

Searching for the deed, John found Henry Moulton's name listed as deceased. It was then he knew, a simple matter to check probate and find out who inherited. He had already made up his mind that if Charles would agree he would make him an offer. How much he wondered would roughly one-third of Bates and that old house be worth? He borrowed a pencil and copied the information from the old deed which left the land of Henry Moulton to his heirs and assigns forever. As far as John knew that was just one man.

Chapter Eleven
Ira's Pitch

The August heat beat down on their backs as they walked through the high corn stalks, pulling the ripe ears and tossing them into the bushel baskets. Garden soil clung to her bare feet as Margaret worked her way along the rows, her head barely reaching the brown tasseled tops. Humming one of his customary English ditties, John reached the end of his row and peeked through the stalks to surprise her. He thought of them as family and cherished the very ground she walked on. Jane would say she could do no wrong in John's book. She liked the smiling girl, who unlike Rosy, poured over her reading primer and tried her hand at reading every newspaper John brought home to her from Portland. Since their arrival on the Island, old Black and his granddaughter had found a home with John and Jane, pitching into the work at hand with gratitude.

Placing their baskets in the wheelbarrow, John headed for the barn where they would all spend a long summer night husking and telling stories until the last ear fell into the crib. Some of the harvest would go to feed the cow and pigs, the choice ears saved for canning and their afternoon picnic. The old man had been to his traps that morning keeping back the biggest lobsters in his catch. He did what he could, and did not fool himself into thinking that he could ask for anything more than what they had here on Bates Island.

Hitching a ride to the barn, Margaret pitched from the wheelbarrow and ran to the beach, throwing herself headlong into the cold water. Following along behind them Jane envied the girl's freedom, seeing her own girls at that age, then quickly dismissing the memory. There would be no bringing back those early days on the island when she and the girls first arrived. Sometimes her mind would wander further back to similar occasions when she and her sister were young and living in the same dream world, yet she blocked her memories as surely as she stood breathing the warm summer air. She wished to be different, to be more like others, willing to take the good and bad together, but she lacked the sensibility for it. Even as a girl she had shunned ribbons in her hair and the long dresses her mother had made for her, deciding long ago to let it be. She guessed that the island did not ask her to be more than she was from sun up to down; it was good enough to get by on. Even so, she and John had made what they could of life and did not want.

Making her way to the water's edge, she called to Margaret swimming out into the cove. Lifting a hand to her brow, Jane caught sight of a dory's sail just making the point heading in to shore, recognizing the skillful handling of the skiff. Not the most welcome of sights. Putting up with his visits became more and more of a common occurrence lately and this time he had company. Hauling up, practically at Jane's feet, Ira let go of the main and stepped out leaving his companion to deal with the dory.

"Mrs. Brown! Fancy meetin' you here!" he said, pulling his cap and bending at the waist, mimicking his habitual dramatic bow. "Been thinkin' 'bout your pies ever since I left."

"Ira," she said, nodding in his direction, then added, "John's up to the barn if you want him."

"I do," he grinned, then went on to add fuel to his fire. "You know Mrs. B, I do believe that you get better lookin 'with every visit."

"Ira! Stop pesterin' my wife," John yelled, coming to join them on the beach. "If it's a meal you're lookin 'for you"ll have to take it up with Jane, and I'd be damned careful about choosin 'the right words in the askin'."

"Well now, I wouldn't mind a mug-up, but I wanted a word in private."

Pulling his pipe from his pocket, John nodded toward the barn, then walked up the beach to sit on the bench beneath the willow. A favorite spot for afternoon, the massive old tree invited sitting. It's great wide branches provided the shade one needed for talking things over, which John suspected would be some great Ira scheme. Ira marched up behind him leaving his friend standing by the dory to fend for himself. Jane shook her head and walked over to meet him, feeling sorry that he had to endure the likes of Ira, yet considering he'd chosen to sail over with him, she guessed he'd made his choice.

"He's not much for standin 'on ceremony, is he?" she said, by way of introducing herself.

The young man reached out his hand and said, "Mrs. Brown, is it? I'm Moses Dyer, glad to make your acquaintance."

Jane stood looking at the young man standing awkwardly by the dory's bow, judging his claim to family true by his slight frame, dark complexion and eager smile. "Any relation to Asa over on Stave?" she asked.

"Probably, but I think you'd find most of mine over on Chebeague," he replied politely.

"I've a got a sister there, Caroline, Caroline Johnson. Married to Barnwell, know them then I 'spose."

"Gorry, I'll say! Nice folk. Nothin 'wouldn't do for ya'," he said.

"That's Barn. My daughter Rosy's over there now."

"That so. Don't think I met her yet. She live there does she?"

"Back 'n forth, mostly between the two. I've been hopin' she's keepin' busy attendin' the school, but I haven't put much stock in it to tell the truth."

"I finished up ages ago," he said. "West end school it was. Had to fit it in 'round fish trips with my father, but mostly got what was needed. Listen, I'll just go on up and see what Ira's chawin' 'bout," he said, tipping his cap.

As he approached the barn, Moses could hear Ira's strident complaining voice followed by the even tones of the man in his company. He began to have second thoughts about his decision to accompany Ira. From what Ira had told him these people were his friends, but it seemed now, like so many other Ira stories, this one too didn't quite ring true. He wished he could get back in the boat and sail off, but it was Ira's dory and he wouldn't want to get in his bad books for love nor money. Apparently arriving in the middle of things, he stood off to one side, then noticing the spring, bent down, cupping his hands together to scoop up a cool drink. Walking past the gathering, Jane and Margaret sought refuge in the barn listening as Ira raged on.

"If you'd just hear what I got to say, John," Ira shouted around his cigar. "It's a good deal for you and you know it. What can that old man pay you for rent? They're just a burden, that's what they are, a burden to you and Jane. I'm working now on the fort up there in the harbor. Makin 'good money."

John drew deeply on his pipe, then looked directly at Ira, pacing back and forth, pulling at chin stubble and raking his hands through his hair. He felt pity for the Ira so desperate to have his way. John wanted to treat him fairly. He had the idea from other encounters with him that Ira's life must have been hard in some way he didn't know about, but he just didn't see how he could do what the man asked. He knew Jane would never consent to Ira's plan and that was all there was to know in his book. He watched as Ira wiped the sweat from his brow and pounded the ground beneath his boots.

"I'm sorry you wasted your time, Ira," John said, calmly. "I guess you thought since you fished with Alex and Albert and me, that the family might owe it to you, but the house and land belong to me and that girl and old man need it more than you do."

Pulling back his shoulders Ira scoffed his reply. "That's just plumb crazy, is what that is. Mose, did you ever hear anything so crazy in your life? That old man's 'bout ready to kick and whose gonna 'take in the girl? You think of that? I say ship 'em back where they came from and let me move in over there."

"You have my answer, Ira. Now, I think you and your friend ought to be catchin 'the tide 'for it goes out."

Listening from her vantage point in the hayloft, Margaret pulled a length of dry straw from her hair and wondered if what the man said about them could be true. She loved John and Jane, they were her family now. It was true about her grampa she thought. Poking her head out of the loft, she watched as the big angry man stomped down to the shore, his scrawny friend keeping a few paces back. Picking her way down the ladder, she walked out to John and Jane standing beneath the willow, watching the two men launch the dory and set the bow sail. Coming up between them she reached out to take John's hand, leaning against his sturdy frame, finding a child's comfort in its warmth.

***

Their dory made slow progress, tacking back and forth through the calm waters of the bay. Sitting at the tiller, Ira sulked, occasionally lifting his whiskey bottle to take long deep pulls and cast accusing looks at Moses. Mose guessed that his role in the day's events had not measured up to Ira 'expectations. Taking advantage of Ira's brooding silence, he kicked off his hip boots and stretched his short legs across the middle seat, propping his back against the gunnel. Judging that striking up a conversation might be ill-advised, he pulled his cap over his brow and closed his eyes, enjoying the lap of the water slipping beneath the hull. Ira would have no need of a second hand given their slow pace. He thought about the letter he'd received that morning before leaving his father's house, about the things he had read in the paper, about the fighting, and about the guilt he'd felt not signing up when it first started. As his father had said at breakfast, he now had his marching orders. The question he pondered now was what it meant. He had only known life in this small bay, fishing with his father and playing with his brothers and sisters on the shore; always at the shore, free as a gull.

Since morning, Moses had a restless feeling. He needed to escape, to just run as fast as he could away from the news his father handed to him, the news now sitting in his front shirt pocket making more noise than any gale he'd ever heard. He smiled to himself, supposing that was why when he met up with Ira, he had agreed to sail along with him. Even though Ira's slap on his back greeting had almost knocked him off his feet, he'd known that whatever they'd get up to there was no escaping what sat at the back of all his thoughts.

He wondered if he'd get back some of those feelings he'd had a little over a month ago when the *Forest City* came sailing into the harbor towing that boat load of Reb prisoners off the *Caleb Cushing*. He stood that day on the dock waving his cap, while others shot their pistols into the air whooping and hollering. Caught up in the excitement, he'd felt like going right over to Ligonia, to Camp Lincoln, and putting his name down to help the Union cause, but instead he had followed the rowdy crowd of men up Fore Street aiming to drown the thirst of their patriotism. The war had been going on for two years, at twenty-five he had convinced himself to wait and see. Now at least he had an answer. His future, he guessed, would be planned out for him by some stranger wearing a blue uniform far away from this beautiful bay and a life he hadn't yet planned beyond the edge of the shore.

Chapter Twelve
Caroline's Visit

Reaching into the flour barrel, Jane measured out two cups, then broke two eggs into the bowl. Although the day promised to be hot, she planned to bake a cake for her company which needed to be perfect, or at least she had convinced herself that it did. Sister Caroline's visit required sweets and patience, the first she felt she could probably manage. Each August she'd spend days dreading the visit, wondering if she should just be herself, or please Caroline. Yesterday, John announced at breakfast that he had run into Barnwell at Hamilton's selling his clams and he thought the weather would hold for their summer jaunt.

Flying into action, Jane had spent the better part of the day on her hands and knees scrubbing the floors until the old pine glistened in the afternoon sun, and now she was up early putting a cake together. Dinner would be a cold ham, and potato salad with garden peas. She hoped it would do.

"Rosy, trot on down to the barn and see if that old cow has any more milk left in her. And bring up some eggs while you're at it."

Rosy looked up from the letter she had been puzzling over, finally tossing it onto the chair. "Why do I always have to be the one to do everything around here? Where's golden girl? Can't she go for once?"

Placing her wooden spoon carefully back in the bowl, Jane took in a deep breath and turned to face her daughter. "The golden girl, as you want to call her, is down at the shore digging clams with John while you've been idlin' away in that chair moonin' over that letter. When you get back with the milk you can tell me how he's gettin' on."

"That's just it isn't it? I can't say now, can I?"

"Rosy girl, we've been all around this and back, if you want to read you have to go to school and that's the long and short of it."

"I know, I know, but right now I need to know he's not hurt, or nothin 'bad."

Jane walked over to the rocker, picked up the letter and started to read it out loud.

Dear Rose,

Hope this letter finds you hearty. We just made Camp Sickles near Potomac Creek and will stay for a night or more, unless some Lieutenant comes at a gallop through here, then it will likely be off in the morning. Sure like the rest tho, my feet are raw from marching all day. Captain Sawyer says it won't be long cause we got old Johnny Reb on the run. Proud as punch of the old 17th. Maine boys put up a fight. I'm sending along my months pay to you so if you get to town you can put it down on something pretty for yourself, just save some out for when I get back. Say hello to everyone there at home and if you get over to see my folks to.

Won't be long before I'm sailing into the cove.
Until then,
Moses

"Didn't make a promise of any sort that I can tell, Rosy. Shouldn't put too much stock in it," Jane said, handing the letter back.

"There's plenty stock there and if you can't see it you're blind. Or maybe you just don't want me marryin' Mose, is that how it is?

"No, that's not it Rosy. He's alright, just I think a might old for you is all."

"I'm eighteen and can make up my own mind on it. Mary was just sixteen and you didn't kick up a fuss when she married Jacob, now did you?" she pronounced, hastily stuffing her letter back into its envelope.

"I suppose we can talk more about it when he gets back," Jane responded, then added, "and at the moment, I'm still in need of that milk, so if you can spare me a few minutes out of your day, I'd appreciate some help."

"You're just mad 'cause Aunt Caroline is comin 'over and you have to bake all day," Rosy announced, straightening her blouse and secretly stuffing Moses 'pay into her skirt pocket. "I don't know what you'll do when I'm livin 'on Chebeague and you've got to do without me. You'll be callin 'over the water to have me back, I wager." Pausing at the door, Rosy cast a wise smile in Jane's direction." 'Sides, you've got more than me to worry about, guess who just sailed up into the cove!"

Hurrying over to the sideboard Jane grabbed a tea towel and tossed it over her cake bowl, then slipping her apron over her head, stopped to tuck her hair back into its bun. "Foolishness," she said to the room. "Just plain foolishness," she said again, turning in time to see Caroline waddling up the path.

She put a smile on her face and stepped out onto the porch to greet them, thinking that she would be lucky to make it through the day without falling down, given her fancy button shoes and a slippery floor.

"Hello the house!" Caroline called, waving as she approached.

"Caroline, Barn, come in! How was the sail over? Not too choppy, I hope."

Stopping to help his wife negotiate the steps, Barnwell gave a slight shake of his head, warning Jane off the subject of their trip, knowing as he did, it would do little to dissuade his wife from holding forth on the perils of the journey. Settling her into a chair at the table, Barn patted her on the shoulder, then turned to leave. "I'll just go on down and help John with the boat while you two catch up."

"Go on then, attend to your business, don't want to swim home, do we?" she said, waving him off with a flip of her hand in his direction. "I tell you Jane, sometimes I wonder these men have the sense to come in out of the rain," she commented, inspecting the house. "The old place hasn't changed since we were girls. I'd of thought you'd taken that old face off the mantel by now. But I see you've put up some new curtains since I was here last. They look nice. Now, where's my girl?" she asked.

"I sent her down to the barn, and she's takin 'her sweet time about it, is where she is. I swear she dawdles on purpose to get my goat."

"You're too hard on that girl, Jane. I told Barn that just the other night. I thought you should send her over to live with us again this summer, but I guess you had need of her here. You ask me, she was makin 'progress and could have made good use of the extra schoolin'. 'Magine how we would have done if we'd had the chance. But then you was always one for goin' out to the traps, or down to dig clams! Then, some things never change. I 'magine you know that Rosy was keepin' company with that Dyer boy. And, Barn thinks it might be why you called her home. Not too far off are we? Well, here we are! Speakin' of the devil! Come over here and give your Aunt Caroline a big hug!"

Knowing that she had the perfect audience in her aunt, Rosy planked herself down next to her aunt Caroline. Grinning widely, she gave the milk pail a quick shove with her foot across the floor to her mother. "Mother's makin' you a cake, Aunt Caroline," she said. "Says it's your favorite with that boiled frostin' you always make. 'Magine it's not up to your standards, but we'll make do, I guess."

Jane grabbed the pail handle and hoisted it to the sideboard. Busying herself with her cake, she listened as Rosy twisted her Aunt's favor in her direction. As Caroline had not been fortunate to have had children of her own, Jane found her lacking in her understanding of their cunning ways. Mary's tack had always been to play the innocent little girl, who managed to return from visits to her aunt's with ribbons and lace. Rosy preferred the sweets bulging in her pockets, which Jane found later stashed in a pillow case. She never felt the need to compete in the battle for their affections, guessing that little doses of Caroline enough for anybody. She shook her head, hearing now the harangue of sly insults assaulting her from the table.

"Jane, how is that poor little orphan, livin' over in the cove? Did you ever find out who her mother was? I just can't 'magine it. Whatever was that old man thinkin' of, startin' out with her like he did? He's still kickin', I assume, or somebody would have told me by now?"

"Yes, he's still kickin', Caroline. Say, how are things with the Ladies Circle?" Jane asked putting her cake in. "I've been meanin' to send over a few doilies, but the farm keeps us so busy, I'm that tired at night."

"You shouldn't worry 'bout that when you've got your hands full here takin' care of that girl, and Rosy," she added for emphasis. "You know we made three dollars on that last sale, and if old Mertie had done her bit, it might of been more. 'Member mother used to say Mert was like the old cow, gave you a pailful of milk, then would kick it over just to spite? I've had the sciatica pain somethin' awful. That new doctor tells me I have to rest, but I told him there was no rest for the weary, and do you know what he said? He said that I shouldn't worry because only the good die young! Well, I nevah! Barn says he was just jokin', but I don't think so. He's not like old Doc Wilson, not by a long shot. Now there was a man who knew what he was 'bout. None of this nonsense 'bout gettin' more exercise and eatin' better. Old Doc Wilson, rest his soul, knew his medicines and wasn't shy 'bout dispensin' 'em either. Land! Is that your cake I smell? Better have a look see, don't want burnt cake, do we Rosy?"

"No we don't! Mother!"

Dutifully, Jane checked the cake, which promptly sank into its middle when she opened the oven door. Sighing, she walked to window to gather in the sanity of the field and cove.

***

Waving her goodbyes from the beach, Jane took in a deep breath, giving silent thanks for the long year standing in the way of their visits. She knew she should love her sister and be grateful that she had one, but if she had to choose she had to admit it would not be Caroline. Quickly admonishing herself for the thought, realizing it might damn her down the line somewhere, she started back to the house to face the cleanup which she would bet Rosy had not begun. Barnwell and John had played scarce after dinner, choosing the fish house and each other's company to the endless woman talk. She hadn't blamed them, thinking that it would be her choice as well.

Waiting for John to walk up from the shore, Jane caught sight of the old man's dory bobbing in the waves just beyond the cove's ledges. Calling out to John she pointed to the dory, then hurried down the path. The wind had come up out of the southwest and they knew he would reach the ledges long before they could launch and row out against the rollers. Still, John cut the oars in deep, hauling back again and again, frustrated by the lack of headway, relying on Jane to direct their course. Pulling along side, Jane reached over and caught the bow line, winding it tightly around the stern cleat. Hauling hard on his free oar, they swung clear, jerking the half swamped dory away from the ledges, the weight pulling them backward in the swells. With the rollers now forcing them in to shore, each pull on the oars, thrust the tow forward, almost along side, then back, taking more water over the side. John hoped old man

Black might still be alive, but he knew when they'd reached the dory, when he did not stir, that it was wishful thinking.

***

John stood back surveying the crude pine coffin he had pieced together that morning. It would have to do he thought, wondering if there was family to notify in Harpswell. In all the years they had been together, old Black never mentioned family, with the exception of that first night when he told them his daughter had passed and he was Margaret's only kin. Many times John had started to ask, but something in the pure sadness of their lives seemed to keep him from it. He thought of how they got by with his small gang of traps using alder branches for his buoys. He knew that if it hadn't been for the kindness of neighbors, and John's offer of the house, they would have probably moved on, but he was certain that it would not have ended well if they hadn't found Bates when they did.

They made a small gathering at the family grave site. Their Ministerial neighbors, Charles and Sarah, walked down from the house in company with Henry and James. Margaret stood at John's side listening as Jane read a passage from the Bible, hearing the final words spoken over her grandfather's grave. The strangeness of the verses somehow did not seem to fit the old man she loved. Searching each face she sought a reassurance in their eyes, a telltale glance that might escape to reach her, but they stood as still as the quiet and somber cove. Overhead the gulls called, breaking the silence and weight of the moment, then swooped low over the clearing, angling off toward the sandbar, pointing the direction home.

Chapter Thirteen
Ira and the Fire

Ira leaned against the wharf piling, smoking, gazing out on a quiet morning, waiting for a fishing schooner or mackerel sloop, hoping to scare up a day's pay. A hot dry wind out of the west promised another scorcher and he really wasn't feeling much like working, yet he waited, not having much else to do. Wiping his hands over parched lips, he was just thinking of leaving for the saloon when Jim's sloop *Leader* coasted in to tie up. Tossing his cigar stub into the harbor, Ira hailed to Jim, then hurried to take up the bow line.

"What are you doin 'hangin ''round the docks today, everybody's on the island at a picnic! It's the fourth you know!" Jim announced.

"Fourth or not, a man's gotta eat, Jim. Lookin 'to pick up a little somethin 'to get by on. `Sides, there's gonna 'be fireworks tonight and I'd hate to miss 'em."

"The kids are that excited to see them and it looks to be clear. Came up to sell off this last haul, but I'm thinking there's more money in clams to tell the truth. Lend a hand here why don't ya. We've got plenty of grub at home, is all I can offer."

Ira looked down into the hold and judged by the scant catch that Jim wouldn't be sharing any profits, still, he hated the heat and the thought of getting out of the city held an appeal. Jim hoisted the bushel baskets onto the wharf and with Ira's help lugged them into Dyers. It was a poor catch, almost rotten from the intense heat in the sail up from the Island, but he'd managed to put a few coins in his pockets.

Weighing his options, and still thinking of that drink, Ira walked back out to the wharf's edge. He needed a drink and Jim was not going to go along, even if it was the Fourth and they could hear people's celebrating shouts from the streets along the waterfront. Having made up his mind, Ira grinned down at Jim. "You know, Jim,

I think I'll try my luck here in town. Might be I find some pretty young thing lookin 'for some fun tonight. But, I'm glad of the offer just the same. Be sure and remember me to the family," he said, then walked off in the direction of Brown's Wharf.

In his experience on the fishing vessels and mending nets on the docks, Ira had become an expert in finding ways to convince himself that hard work could be just too much a waste of good time. He preferred the excitement of the city to the quiet of island living that Jim and Albert loved. Settling down to support a house full of kids did not seem to him all that life had to offer. Strolling along India Street he tipped his cap to a young lady passing by, giving her his brightest smile, then slipped through the door of Duffy's Pub.

Duffy stood behind the bar drawing off drafts of beer and chatting with one of his regulars when he spied Ira coming through the door. Ira headed for the bar tasting the cool beer before he'd made it half way. "Hotter than Hades out there," he said, wiping his brow and sitting down next to Tommy Flaherty. Leaning on the bar, beckoning Duffy to come closer, he whispered low. "Now, Duff, you've got a fine establishment here and, as you know, I've always been a good customer, but it just so happens today, I'm a bit short. But knowing you to be a generous man, I was hopin' you'd extend a hard workin ' fisherman a bit of credit."

Duffy looked at Tommy who shrugged his shoulders taking a long pull on his beer, then to Ira, who hoped he'd worked his magic, still wearing confidence in his big grinning face. "It's credit he'd be wantin 'Tommy. Do you ever recall me handin 'out free beer to any that comes through that door?"

Tommy laughed and slapped a few coins down on the bar. "Now that you mention it Duff, I can't think of a single solitary instance, but being that it's a holiday, I'm inclined to think that this man here at my side is in need of libation. So, set him up on me and we'll hear no more of it."

Ira leaned over and slapped Tommy on the back, heaving a huge sigh of relief. "You see Mr. Duff, there are still decent folks in this world and I guess it was my luck to run into one today."

Duffy stared at him for a moment, then turned his back on the two men, leaving them to whatever fate might befall them under his roof. He was not long in wondering, as a young boy dashed excitedly through the door and announced that the parade was about to line up.

Duff nodded acknowledgement of the news, then wished him a good time, knowing that very few of his customers would be joining the boy out the door. The Fourth of July was a big day for him and he'd be pouring drinks all day and into the night, especially he thought on such a hot, dry day as today.

The saloon door opened and closed, bringing in new customers until the place was packed to the gills by four o'clock. Men dressed for the festivities, had by afternoon, loosened their ties and shed their coats, sitting at tables telling stories of other Fourth of July celebrations. In their white shirts and tweed vests, blurred syllables slurred out across the tables, while cold beer slipped down their throats.

Outside the city celebrated. Firecrackers snapped in the sky and shouts rang throughout the streets, while mothers and children waited for the parade on Congress to commence.

Having worked all morning and into the late afternoon, Duffy gave the bar top one last swipe, then stepped outside for a bit of air. Standing on the corner he inhaled the hot July air, thinking of the long night ahead, when a strong whiff of smoke caught in the afternoon breeze. He thought of Walter Corey's fire last week, just the next street over, and wondered if there could be another. In the seconds he stood pondering if he should call it in, he heard the rattling of the horses 'hooves hitting the cobbles and someone calling," All out! All out!" As men ran past the pub, chasing the fire steamer, patrons flew out onto the street, just as the roaring flames from Exchange Street gained height and burst over the neighboring building.

In the confusion, some ran down the street seeking the source of the fire, while others stood dumb struck in their wake, the terrible heat assaulting their faces as cinders and blazing fragments of wood flew above their heads. Within minutes the fire lurched to the opposite side of the street, sweeping through Middle, Union, Cross and Plum, gaining strength, engulfing all in its path.

Ira stumbled out onto the street, facing the suffocating clouds of smoke, showers of broken slate and glass, pulling Tommy behind him. "We've got to move, boy! Where do you live?" he shouted into the blasts of heat and flames, instinctively turning to run not waiting for a reply. Reaching the foot of Congress Street he stopped to check the proximity of the fire. Unable to catch a breath in the smoke clogged air, Ira pulled his handkerchief from his pocket and tied it over his mouth. Hearing a scream, he saw Tommy pointing to the flaming cinders arching toward North Street.

"Come on! We've got to hurry! he yelled. "That's my street!"

Reaching the top of the hill they paused and looked back to the waterfront. Brown's Sugar House was now completely engulfed in flames, as was Staple and Sons, and the Richardson Foundry. They could still see the spire of First Parish church. Men shouted into the inferno pulling furniture and anything they could lay their hands on out of burning buildings. Boys stood at curbsides struggling to still frightened horses while women hauled mattresses and trunks from their homes. Cinders filled the blood red sky, swirling and diving on the quickening wind. Men climbed ladders hauling buckets of water to douse their smoldering roofs. Searching new fuel the flames hungrily worked steadily up the hill like a mindless predator.

Reaching North, Tommy burst through the door to find his mother calmly packing a trunk with clothing and a crate with items from the kitchen pantry. As he entered she looked up and asked him to lend his father a hand. His younger brother and sister stood at the door shuffling boxes out onto the sidewalk, apparently unimpressed by the flames licking at their heels. Seeing his family's calm, Tommy wondered if they were in shock. In his confusion, he thought perhaps they understood something he did not about the nature of huge uncontrollable fires.

"Where is dad?" he finally asked.

"Outside somewhere. Said he'd organize a wagon to haul this lot out of here."

"Mom!" Tommy pleaded. "There's no time! I just ran up the hill and everything below us is on fire! We've got to get a move on! He reached over attempting to pull the kettle she was now placing into a crate from her hands, but she shrugged him off.

"I'll not be leavin 'the good china, or my kettle, so you can either give us a hand or find your father," she said, turning back to the kitchen.

Exasperated, he grabbed his mother's arm and pulled her forcefully out onto the sidewalk hoping she would see the danger with her own eyes, just as his father burst through the door. "It's no use, Mary! Tommy, take hold here! We've got to make a run for it!" Grabbing his brother's and sister's hands, Tommy yanked them out the back door, mother and father following at his heels, his mother incredibly still clutching the tea kettle. It hit him as they ran, that he would likely see the scene for the rest of his life. What he did not see in this vision was a glimpse of Ira who had made a run for it himself.

Throughout the early evening of the great fire people moved their belongings from one place to the next hoping to salvage what property they could, only to turn in their flight to see the house they'd departed in flames. It had come down to running for your life and many residents of the Munjoy Hill neighborhood ran to the water. Many gathered in the Dumps, a clearing near the east end beach, the only shelter they could find away from the blasts of smoke, flying cinders and scorching winds. Sitting together, huddled in mass fear, the children looked into the worried faces of their parents, now homeless, who looked themselves into the faces of neighbors and strangers for someone who might tell them what to do. Among the crowd, Ira too sat listening to the explosions from the city below the hill. He knew they would be falling the great buildings to make a fire break, hoping to stop the fire from taking the entire city.

Finding a hollow in a bank, below the Dumps, Ira curled up and slept until dawn, waking to the clinging damp of the cold clay. Stretching, he looked out over the bay and cursed at the state of his affairs, briefly giving a thought to Tommy's family and what end they'd met. Driven by his hunger and thirst, he set out among the crowd hoping to beg enough food to keep him on his feet, yet moving through the gathering, those who did look his way just shook their heads. There was nothing to do but join a few men now making their way slowly down the hill into the city. He tried to follow the streets, but could not recognize a single one. Where one landmark should be, piles of smoldering bricks scattered the landscape. He looked into the cellar holes and saw them glowing like coal furnaces and passed charred house beams still flaming in the morning light. Kicking his way through the ankle deep ashes, he reached a place that looked familiar. Guessing that he was on Middle Street, he walked in the direction of the waterfront not knowing who or what he would find. An eerie silence claimed the city dressed in black and grey. Everything was gone. Not a single building stood against the perfect blue sky.

***

The morning of July 5th, Jane sat at breakfast with John, and waited for the news from Portland they knew would come. It was not possible to imagine how a fire that immense, seen so far down the bay, could now be left unreported.

"It must have started in the fireworks," John commented.

"We'll hear soon enough. I've just been thinkin' that it must have been terrible trying to escape those flames, John. There'll be folks homeless and without food or water."

"Still, there's nothing we can do until we know more. If they set off those explosions we heard, then it would have been to build a firebreak to stop it. I've seen it done once. They blow up a building right in its path and that keeps it from moving on to another. If that's what it was, then you can be sure it was one awful fire. Think I'll have a walk down to the shore."

"Don't be gettin' any ideas of sailin' up there. Knowin' you, you'll bring home half the city, or what's left of 'em," Jane announced.

"I know. There's nothing for us to do, still I'm curious at that."

Late that afternoon old Alex and Albert sailed into the cove.

"Seems he was right smack dab in the middle of it," Albert reported. "'Course you have to take it with a grain 'a salt, knowin ' where it's comin 'from. I've never met a bigger liar in my life, I swear," he concluded.

"Be that as it may, from the noises I heard last night comin 'from that direction, I got to say, I'm inclined to believe him," John said. "How'd he get out?"

"Found a punt adrift and rowed. Still, to believe him, there's not a place left standin 'from Brown's right straight up the hill and over to Congress where she died out. He said it was a good thing the wind shifted or it would of been worse. Took the old hotel right down to ashes, old John Sturdivant's House, and the St. Stephens too, John. Boys, hear Ira tell it, not even a wharf left to tie up to!"

"That's us out then," Albert noted.

Albert pushed his chowder bowl off to one side and leaned back in his chair, looking in Jane's direction. "That's the best damn chowder I ever ate, but don't you be tellin 'Liz or I'll be sleepin 'in the barn! You know, I was thinkin' on the sail over here, might be some work

80

in town, if Ira's on the up 'n up. They'll be needin 'workers to build it back up I 'magine."

Old Alex stood and thanked Jane for the chowder, then wandered over to the door. Pulling out his pipe he walked out on the porch and looked up the bay toward Portland. He could see the smoke clouds rising above the landscape and then it dawned on him that the trees were missing. He shook his head and lit his pipe, giving the devastation there consideration, thankful for his Island home. He knew what damage fires could do and it was a constant worry to him. Albert and John joined him, each man thoughtful in the peace of the quiet afternoon. Reaching down to pound the dead ash from his pipe on his boot heel, Alex looked at Albert and nodded in the direction of the dory. "She'll be groundin 'out on us pretty quick," he said, knowing that Albert would be the one to run down the path and shove her off into deeper water. Before leaving Old Alex popped his head back into the kitchen. "Jane, my girl, I think I ought to be tellin 'you the rest of the news, just so's you can kind of get prepared for it."

"Oh?" she questioned, turning to face him. "And what might that be?"

"It seems that this ought to be comin 'from somebody else, but Liz got word yesterday at the picnic on Long. Seems our Rosy girl's in the family way," he said. "I know how you felt 'bout her marrying so young, but all in all, I think it was for the best. She never seemed happy livin 'here."

"Perhaps you're right, Alex," she said. "I'll put some things together and sail on over when John's free."

Turning his cap over in his hands, Alex looked up into her eyes and read the worry he guessed all mothers felt when they knew a baby was on the way. Still, he wanted her to be glad for Rosy and Moses and the boys. They were young and deserved a chance at a life of their own making. He finally started for the shore, leaving Jane to make what she would of his message. He'd always admired her, but he'd never been able to fathom what went on inside. She was just one of those women he guessed who didn't always let you in.

Occupied in clearing the chowder bowls from the table, Jane heard John kick his boots off on the doorstep. She hoped that Alex had shared Rosy's news with him down at the shore. Her girls had always been her girls, and she knew John loved them dearly, still Rosy had managed to rub everyone the wrong way. Despite Jane's desire to see Rosy ready to live her own life, she faced the fact that her daughter would find any way she could to avoid hardships. Now she would find that life had thrown an obstacle in her way she would have to face. Another child would dictate the terms. It was too bad, she thought, that Moses had not settled them on Chebeague nearer to his family. With Lemuel and Wealthy they'd fair better, but Moses had chosen to live on Long and it was not for her to say. She guessed she would wait to hear John's thoughts on the matter and keep on as she always had done.

***

John hauled in the dory's sheet as they tacked back and forth into a stiff afternoon breeze between Hope and Chebeague. It had been a week to the day since the great fire and news had gradually found its way down the bay to the Islands. There was talk of work to be had clearing away the rubble for any able bodied man willing to lend a hand, and the talk suggested that the pay was worth their trouble. Many from the islands rowed or sailed into the harbor daily. Since the fire they carried baskets of potatoes and fresh vegetables, blankets and what clothing they could spare for those living in the tents along the hill.

Jane waved from the beach, as John pointed the dory toward the city not five miles off. Greeting old friends as she walked toward her daughter's home, she wondered who she might rely on to be there when the baby came. Not familiar with the ways here, she hoped she'd remember to ask Rosy about any plans for a midwife. Knowing Rosy as she did, she figured she hadn't thought of it.

The tiny cape stood at the head of a tree-lined lane, a straight walk up from the beach. The chimney smoke told her that they were up and about, and hopefully ready for company. Stooping as she entered the low entry door, Jane placed her basket on the nearest chair and removed her shawl. She had taken pains that morning to wear her skirt and her best blouse thinking to make a good impression on any neighbors who might drop in and find her visiting. Although she felt a proper fool in her city clothes, as she dressed that morning, Jane managed to think of it as a city day, thus convincing herself to act accordingly.

Rosy scuffed into the kitchen and plunked herself down into the nearest chair. She looked over at her mother, not with an expression of surprise, but rather one of disbelief that it had taken her so long to show herself. "Well, mother, what do you think of my news? I 'magine you're none too pleased about it," she said.

Not answering right away, Jane rose to put the kettle on, finding the wood box empty and the fire almost gone. "Where do you keep the firewood? I'll start some breakfast, if you're hungry."

"Go on out the back door, it's in the little shed out there. Mose was spose to bring some in before he left this mornin', but sometimes he forgets things."

"How is he managin'?" Jane asked.

"Good's can be expected, I guess. Still has bad spells. Wakes me up yellin 'and hollerin 'nonsense. Can't see as that war did anybody any good. What did you think about that fire they had up to Portland? Mose says you wouldn't believe it to see it, with everythin' gone. Lost that new courthouse and that's a fact too. All the hotels and places along the docks to buy food and clothes. We sent up a package yesterday."

"Can't say as I want to see it," Jane said, leaving for the wood. Returning with the kindling, she turned to Rosy who brought up the subject of the baby again.

"I was plannin 'to have it there, but Mose says we'd be better off here, or take our chances over with his folks. I think there's a new doctor on the island."

Jane replaced the stove lid and pushed the kettle over, then joined Rosy at the table. "I think that would be a good plan. You might think of gettin' yourself off early, just to be sure things go right."

"Don't worry, I'll not be knockin 'on your door. 'Magine havin 'a baby there!"

"Your grandmother Bates did just fine with me and Caroline, you know," Jane said, then laughing added, "though to hear your Aunt tell it, she wasn't born on the island."

"Maybe she wasn't. She should know where she was borned, shouldn't she?"

Jane left the question unanswered choosing to return to Rosy's decision.

"I'm glad you're plannin 'on Chebeague, but you might want to give some thought to what you might do if it comes early."

"That's a long way off, we'll think of somethin'."

"Still, do you know of a midwife here? Someone to call on for help if you need it? You need to think of how much work this new baby will be. Bringin 'it into this world is not the hardest part. Might want to send the boys over with us."

Rosy peeked out from under her stringy bangs and laughed. "From what I've been hearin 'that's not likely the truth. Mrs. Henly stopped by the other day and I felt like I'd given birth to everyone of her five kids before she left. That woman could talk a seagull out of his dinner!"

Laughing together, Jane could imagine hearing Martha holding forth on the perils of childbirth, hoping she would not be the one to come to their aid when the time came. "I brought you over some things from the house, that old quilt you like and John packed up some vegetables and such. We didn't think you'd had much of chance to put a garden in. I'll have John stop in once a week, if that's all right?"

"That would be just fine and dandy. With Mose workin 'now we've got some money comin 'in, but he's had to sail over to Sinnetts for groceries, it's that bad in town. When John does come again ask him to stop up and see Mose. We was talkin 'the other night, and what with this one comin', we thought John might want to buy us out."

Before saying something she might regret, Jane stood and poured herself another cup of tea. It seemed that Mose had been doing a lot of thinking about money lately and how best to lay his hands on some. In the end Jane kept her thoughts to herself leaving Rosy to puzzle over her silence.

"Cat got your tongue?" she asked, leaning back in her seat extending her tea cup out for a refill. "You know what land I'm talkin ''bout, don't ya'? It's the woods just to the southwest of the stone wall, you know that's my piece from grandpa. I don't see how you think I'd have any other land to sell."

"I know. I'm just surprised, that's all. John will leave the island to you and Mary, so why would he want to buy?"

"Just ask him to talk it over with Mose. Four and half acres more or less it says on the deed, could be he'd like to cut down some them trees and plow it over. I don't know, but if he doesn't want it, we might sell to someone who does. Thought we'd give you first stab."

Jane sighed deeply, thinking of the little girl she remembered when they first moved to the island; the little girl who laughed so freely as she played on the back beach gathering the round, rosy quartz stones. In that moment, she recalled her sisters' endless teasing about her name. Looking over now, she saw a girl about to have a child of her own, one who bore little resemblance to the chubby girl of that summer.

Chapter Fourteen
The Dinner Guest

Ira stomped over the beach hoping to find John in his fish house. Jim had dropped him off at the cove on Ministerial that morning with a final wave and a shake of his head. He knew that Jane would not be happy to see Ira coming over the bar and hoped that Ira would not tell her who left him at her door. Ira was becoming a nuisance around the shore as well. It was growing more and more clear to the men that he had little intention of working if he could help it.

Spotting John baiting up his mussel trawls, Ira saw his chance and picked up his pace. If John would give him a few hours work and a decent meal, he thought his plan might work. His planning going no further than an invitation to stay the night.

Engrossed in his work, John did not see Ira until he was standing at the fish house door. About a third of the way through the trawl tub he was working on, he turned to face Ira, just thinking a break would be welcome in the oppressive August heat.

"Ira. What brings you over? They finally kick you off Hope?"

"Is that any way to talk to a man in need of company?" he asked, grinning.

"Just joshin 'with ya, Ira. What can I do you for?"

"Nothin', wanted to see how things are. Heard you might need a man with your trawls, maybe go a trip or two."

"You know how things are Ira. I'm just scrapin 'by as it is. Bottom's dropped out of the clammin 'and, well, it's tough all the way around."

"So I hear. No harm in askin', I guess," he said. Leaning against the fish house wall he removed his cap and brushed away the sweat with his forearm. He mulled over an idea he'd had on the way over and then decided to try it out. "You know, I've been thinkin 'about gettin 'into the hotel business."

At first John thought he was joking, until he saw the earnest expression. It seemed to elicit a certain sadness, or maybe it was pity. Deciding he was serious, John thought it would be a kindness to talk it over. "Well, I tell ya, you've come to the wrong island if you're lookin 'for hotel work, son." Then realizing that he'd seen no boat in the cove asked, "Say, how'd you get over?"

Ira kicked over a bucket and sat down, expecting if he stayed under foot long enough John would offer him a drink, or at least a meal. "Came with Jim. Dropped me off in the cove across the way, said it was easiest on the half tide," he responded, waving a hand in the direction of Ministerial. "Don't have any hooch around do you?"

"No, 'fraid not, but we can probably rustle up a mug-up if you've a mind to stay, which I am assuming 'you do as you've got no boat I can see."

"If it's not too much trouble. I could use a bite to eat now that you bring it up."

"There's no trouble, Ira, with me anyway. Just tread lightly with Jane. She's a tad prickly this mornin'.""

"Don't you worry, I can handle that old gal, she likes me underneath it all, I can tell.

Always can tell when a woman takes a shine to me," he bragged, pulling himself up and starting for the house.

John shook his head, mumbling under his breath that Ira had no idea about the storm he was striding into.

Jane took one look at Ira coming up the path and threw her dishtowel at the cat who skittered out the door as Ira walked through. "Boys, I could smell those pork scraps fryin 'all the way to Hope!" he announced, looking to gauge her expression. "If I was a bettin ' man, which of course I'm not, I'd say you're fixin 'to make a corned hake for dinner. And that is, without a doubt, my favorite."

"Seems there's no end to your talents, Ira, at least when it comes to knowing when I'm ready to set the table," she said. "John's down at the shore," she added, hoping he might gather her meaning in and turn back out the door.

"We've just been talkin'. On his way. Say, what do you know about that hotel on Little Chebeague?" he asked, changing the subject.

Jane set her mother's granny fork on the edge of the spider and turned to stare. "What are you talkin ''bout? As if I'd know 'bout any hotel. I'd say if you want to find out you'd best inquire there."

"I will, I will, just wonderin 'what kind of work somebody might do is all. It's been that hard. Since I escaped that fire I've been hard pressed to find a speck of work."

Jane turned back to her cooking deciding that she'd leave John to deal with Ira. Opening the door quietly, John walked in, edging his way closer to where she was standing at the stove, searching her face for signs of softening toward their guest. "That's lookin 'like a tasty dinner," he prompted.

"It should be I'd 'magine," she replied, not giving up an invitation.

Not one to pick up on subtle hints, Ira walked to the table and sat down.

"Ira's been out of work. I took pity on the poor sod and asked him to stay for dinner. Hope that's okay?" he asked.

"Never turned a poor sod away in my life. I'd invite him to pull up a chair, but I can see well enough he's already done that!" she replied, staring at Ira.

Wanting to break the tension, John searched for a safe topic and managed clumsily to find the one subject least safe of all. "You probably heard Ira, Rosy and Mose are expectin' a baby. We are that tickled. Aren't we mother?"

Before she could reply, Ira jumped in. "Well, by God, if that doesn't call for a celebration, I don't know what does! Seems a drink would definitely be in order, John."

"Not under this roof, Ira Gould. If its drink and celebratin 'you want you'll have to hop right back in your boat and sail right on over to Chebeague for it, 'cause that's where the new baby will be."

"I guess I forgot you're a tea-totaler, Jane. Didn't mean nothin 'by it," he said, hoping to simmer the mood.

"Where's Maggie?" John asked, changing the subject.

"She'll be along soon, I 'magine. I left her puttin 'fresh hay down for the cow."

"Maybe I should go on down and see if I can lend a hand," Ira put in. "A little girl like that shouldn't be doin 'all that hard work."

Jane cut a sharp look in his direction. "You'll be doin 'no such thing, just sit yourself back down and John can give her a call when dinner's ready. She's just fine on her own."

"I meant no harm. Just tryin 'to sing for my supper," he said, thinking a little joke might carry him through the meal and an evening invitation to stay, at least sleep in the barn. He really didn't have a way off the island and he knew better than to ask to borrow the dory as it was John's only means of transport and livelihood.

"Who didn't mean any harm?" Margaret asked, walking in. "I'm sure it's not Ira talkin', 'cause we all know what harm he can get up to. Don't we Ira?"

"Whoa! That's no way to talk to your elders! You've turned into a right sassy little miss, I'd have to say," Ira exclaimed. Then looking her up one side and down the other he added, "You're quite the young lady now, aren't ya? She used to put me in mind of a colt, with them long legs runnin 'through the field, yellow mane flyin 'out the back of her. She's growin 'up, John. You'll be chasin 'them off with a shotgun pretty soon!"

Jane flung her apron over her head and tossed it down in the empty chair next to Ira. Dispensing with etiquette, she planked Ira's plate down in front of him. "I wouldn't be making too much about it, Ira. We can take care of Margaret just fine without you puttin 'your oar in."

Margaret settled into her place at the table and looked over at Ira trying to decide how to respond to his comments about her and why he was here. She decided he was just being friendly in the way that her uncles teased, still he made her nervous grinning and making jokes all the time. Since Rosy's marriage, she had relied on Jane and John to be her family and she hoped Ira wasn't planning to stay on the Island. As if reading her thoughts Ira gave his chewing a rest and gazed in her direction. Something was on his mind and he was taking his time planning just how to say it.

"I been wonderin', John, what you might have in mind for that old Moulton house now that nobody's livin 'there? Might be I could move in for a spell." His plan out, he followed quickly with a compliment. "Jane, that was the best damn meal I've had in a good long time. Not sure when I've ever tasted a better dinner, and that's the truth of it. My dear old mother, rest her soul, used to make it for the family. Father used to bring a hake in from his nets and we'd make it stretch, never felt as full though as I do right now," he said, leaning back and loosening his belt. "I guess you'll think I'm just sayin 'that to butter you up, but it's the God's honest truth, by Jerusalem." Finishing up his speech, Ira stretched out his beefy arms, revealing his paunchy stomach hidden beneath a stained shirt front.

"I believe you know what I think, Ira," Jane said and rose to clear the table.

"To answer your question Ira, I've had a few inquires about the old place, but its goin 'to take some considerable attention. Water got in through the shingles last winter and I've not had the time to make it fit to live in."

"Now, you see, that's just what I'm gettin 'at, John. I could move in and work on the old place. I'm not of a mind to stay there forever, just through the year and we'll see how it goes. What'd ya say?"

The thought of Ira underfoot day and night held little appeal. Each understood that Ira was looking for something for nothing and that John would regret letting him in. John felt sorry for Ira. He saw a man who could not come to grips with making a decision about his life and sticking to it; a man who took the easy road in any circumstance and left out how it might affect others. Jane's penchant for a swift judgement left no room for guesswork which explained why all eyes were on her as she stood staring down at Ira. Straightening her shoulders to the task, she pulled her almost six foot frame taller. Margaret knew the look. It was the same look she put on when Rosy disappointed her, the same one she used when the old cow got into the garden, or John spent too long explaining a night in town. There would be no room for Ira to wiggle, as Jane's thin lips tightened and her hands clenched into fists. A master at the silent treatment, at waiting out her victim, Jane stood there poised to strike. The room waited, John holding his breath for what would inevitably follow. "Guess you'll be off in the mornin' then," she said, weighing each syllable equally, never once breaking eye contact with Ira.

Ira brought his chair gently down to rest on all fours and looked to John for sympathy. "You know," he said, slowly, "I've met many a woman in my day, John, but this one of yourn takes the cake. She invites a man in for a meal, then before it's even digested, she's usherin' him out the door! How you ever live with her is beyond me!" he announced, shoving back his chair and searching for his coat and cap. "I'll just go on down to the fish house tonight, if that meets with madam's approval?" he asked, bowing at the waist and sweeping his cap to his head. At the door he turned to deliver his farewell. "Someday you'll be sorry for treatin' me this way. I've always watched out for John 'round the water and one day I might not see so well. I might just be lookin' in the other direction, if you get my drift? So if it's all right, I'll sleep in the fish house tonight, or do you think it might be I'll do it some big harm?"

"Go on down then. It'll be warm enough tonight, but you'll not be welcome again, Ira. I'll have no man under my roof speaking ill of my wife," John replied.

His welcome worn out, Ira closed the kitchen door and headed for the shore. Watching him go, Jane returned to her washing up. In her mind the subject of Ira was closed. She understood too well John's kindness toward others, but Ira was one man she could not abide. She was glad to see the back of him. To her way of thinking, Ira always brought trouble as his companion and she wanted no part of it for her family.

Chapter Fifteen
The Birth

John settled his oars back into the thole pins and resumed rowing into the thick fog. Jane sat in the stern, her auburn hair fringed in dampness, listening as the oars dipped gently into the cold bay, watching the circles disappear. The islands had been shut in for over a week now and today was no different as they slowly made progress toward Chebeague. Despite the warmth and promise of an early spring, the fog carried a damp chill that surrounded each one it touched, unconditionally holding a person in one place. Even the dory's bow was lost to sight as she peered into the blanket of white, hoping to see the Island's shape come into view. She imagined that the men would have a fire going on the shore below the bank in case they arrived at nightfall, which would be of little use to them now. In the thick fog, sight let sound and smell take the lead. Straining to hear any sound that might guide them, John pulled in the oars and rested, turning in his seat to face the bow as if it might tell him where they were since they'd left home that morning. The dense fog had not lifted and they were drifting either toward their destination or out to sea. The compass that he always kept in the hold, had gone missing, along with a box of ganging and hooks he'd rigged a week ago for a new trawl. It was up to him to navigate without the most valuable tool he needed, even so, he was angry at himself for accusing a man of stealing without any proof, yet he continued his internal dialogue leaving Jane to continue hers.

The only thing to do was to keep rowing and hope that he had gauged their direction true. By his reckoning, John guessed by the time, and direction of the tide running swiftly past the random buoys they passed, that they were somewhere in the vicinity of Bangs Island which should put them near either Johnson's cove or out in the sound. He hoped that the latter was not true as that could take them past Deer Point and out to sea. They could sail right past home and be none the wiser he thought. Yet, in the stillness surrounding their small dory, he fancied that he heard a crow call which meant island and an end to their journey.

"Listen," he said, touching an index finger to his lips. "Did you hear that?"

Adjusting her shawl more tightly about her shoulders, Jane sat still and looked a question in his direction.

"There, there! Did you hear it that time?"

"Crow," Jane whispered. "Hope he's not going the wrong way."

"Not by a long shot, we're almost there," John said. "Hello! Hello!" he yelled.

Eventually, they caught the faint return call prompting John to adjust the dory's heading. "Keep yellin 'back old girl. They'll keep me straight."

"Jane!" John!" came the reply from the shore followed by the directive, 'hurry, hurry! Jane! Hurry!"

John pulled hard on the oars, two, three hard pulls, then stopping to listen, felt seaweed slip under her bottom and heard the gentle scrape of her planks on the barnacles. Shoving off with his oar, John smiled knowing he'd hit Uncle Joe's ledge just outside Johnson's cove. Running now along the shore they could just make out the vague shape of the beach head which they followed along to Coleman's. The crunch of the beach beneath the hull was the most welcome sound they'd heard all day, yet the joy in that moment was soon erased by the sight of Mose and Lemuel standing forlornly to greet them.

Stepping out of the dory, Jane stretched, then reached out to take Mose's offered hand. "You'd better come up quick, my mother and the doctor are with her," he said.

"She's havin 'trouble with the baby?" Jane asked, quickening her step.

Catching up, Mose grabbed her arm and pulled her along with him, heedless of his tight grip. "She's not good. Went into labor last night. Not like with the boys. I sent for Doc Hale an hour ago."

"You waited to call him?"

"I'm sorry. She'd not have him. Said to leave her to mother, that she'd be fine. I didn't know what to do. I hoped you'd come when I sent word last week with Barn. She was plannin 'on you being here this time. I don't understand it, she was feelin 'fine just like always."

The dimly lit bedroom was crowded when Jane walked in. Rosy lay on her back writhing in pain, clutching at her stomach as Doc Hale stood to one side talking quietly with Mose's mother, Wealthy. Stripping off her wet shawl and moving closer to the bedside, she looked down at her daughter and instantly knew what the others did not want to tell her.

"Where's the child?" she asked.

Wealthy steadied herself against the bedpost, crying helplessly, wiping her eyes on her apron. Ignoring the old woman's tears, Jane reached out to take Rosy's hand, but she jerked it away, looking beyond her mother's face into her own fear, recklessly tossing her head from side to side.

"I think it would be best for you and Wealthy to go on down now and let me see what can be done to make her more comfortable," Doc Hale suggested.

"What does that mean? Has she lost the child then?" Jane asked.

"Yes," he gently replied, taking her arm, urging her to move.

"I'll stay right here, if it's all the same, doctor. What can I do to help?"

Reluctantly, the doctor nodded, affirming her decision, then prepared an injection of morphine to quell Rosy's thrashing and ease her pain. "It will be a few moments now, Mrs. Brown."

Jane caught Rosy's arms and held tight. "Rosy," Jane said softly, "Rosy, girl, I'm right here. You go on and get some rest now. Listen to me. The doc is here with us and he's goin 'to help with the pain. Let him do what he needs to. It'll be all right. Baby's been born. You hear me. I'm right here now, just..."

Rosy lashed out, her body convulsing as her leg muscles constricted and her head arched back. Moses burst into the room, but stopped suddenly. In the now quiet room he saw the doctor listening to her heart and knew that it had stopped, just as her screaming had. Jane turned her head toward Moses, then patted the bed and called him to her. Lifting the quilt to Rosy's chin, she reached over to smooth matted wet hair from her staring eyes, then left Moses to sit beside his wife.

Noticing the small basket sitting on the bureau, she paused to lift the sheet. Cocooned within, the infant's dark hair still damp from birth, gave the appearance of life. Lifting the baby into her arms she took a tiny hand in hers, savoring the simple act in her grief. Turning to carry her from the room, she heard Rosy's boys calling to each other outside the window, and thought it only right that they should see their sister, at least to say goodbye. It was Mose's place. Mose looked to Jane holding the child, then to his wife, weariness hanging on his small childlike frame." She wanted to call her Sarah," he said. "I'll just sit here with Rosy for a bit. Be down directly."

"You take your time Mose, I'll go on down then and let them know. John and I will stay the night, be what help we can," she said, gently, not knowing if he could hear the sadness in her own voice. Mose had lost a wife and child. She had known how it felt to lose a child once, now she'd need to find a way to live without another. Turning to leave, the child still cradled in her arms, she hesitated, unsure what she should do, in the end she placed her tenderly back into her basket thinking Mose would want to say goodbye to her too.

***

May 10, 1871
Dearest Jane,

This death has been such a shock to all here on the island I do not know where to start. Everyone has been such a comfort tho. I only wish you could have stayed longer after the funeral. I do think it was sensible under the circumstances that Mose purchased his own plot with so many in his own family. Even if it is way over in the new part. Barn is beside himself with worry for you and John. He stays at the shore for hours just working on his traps and won't hardly eat. It has bothered my digestion as well, but the doctor has taken pains to give me something for it. I keep telling myself if only Mose had gone sooner for him, it might have turned out better. He might have saved her. I just can't think of how the boys will manage without their mother. And that poor infant. I've seen only one funeral like it, but it seemed only right to see her resting in her mother's arms, buried together for all eternity. I do wonder how God chooses who will live or go. It seems so cruel to take our girl from us at such a young age, especially after Sarah. Barn plans to sail over soon so I will send such provisions as I think you'll need. Unfortunately, as things are now, I think it best that I not come along for our visit. I know you will not be pleased, but you of all people must know the

95

toll this has taken. I simply cannot face that trip this soon. Send word back with Barn if you get a chance. I hope you are still reading those passages I told you about. They will bring great comfort. Place your trust in God, his love will not falter.

Your loving sister,
Caroline

Part Three
1876 -1877

Margaret

Chapter Sixteen
The Sunnyside and the GAR

The sun was just showing through the trees when she'd left Aunt Caroline and Uncle Barn's. Luckily, old man Ricker, just passing the farm, offered her a ride in his wagon. Margaret had felt fortunate to find work at the Sunnyside House on Little Chebeague, yet she supposed she would be lost in a sea of people today, more than she had ever seen in her life. For her the challenge was not in the work, Bates had sheltered her for eighteen years, now facing the prospect of this hot July day, she squirmed in her seat.

"I'm not sure what kind of a shindig Joshua's gotten up to this time, but I've been haulin 'his clams over there for two days," Stephen said. "Seen you walk down the road sometimes a 'mornin'." Taking a quick sideways peek, he noticed her knee jiggling up and down and sweat beading at her brow. He envied her youth and thought what he'd give to have his own back, yet knowing there wasn't too much good to come from wishing for things you couldn't have. Life had been a matter of taking a day at a time and he supposed it was true for everyone the same. Still, this day was full of promise and the excitement of the GAR encampment was sure to attract all manner of fun. He gave the reins a quick shake to quicken the mare, and pull himself back into the present.

"So far it's just been a few guests here and there," she was saying, "but today I'm that worried if I can take it on. Live up to expectations, I suppose I mean."

Stephen pulled the horse up to the barn and hopped down, walking around to lend Margaret a hand, but she had slipped easily from the buckboard's seat and was now stepping off toward the path waving her thanks with her hat.

"Hold on a bit," he called. "You'll be needin 'somethin 'to take with you for good luck, I 'magine." As he spoke, he reached down and plucked a daisy holding it out to her.

"Why thank you, Mr. Ricker, that's very sweet of you. I only hope it works!"

Watching her light step on the path he shook his head and laughed, prompting the mare to turn her head and nuzzle for the expected ear rub and sugar cube. "Well, old girl, what do you make of that, I wonder? 'Magine she'll be run ragged 'fore the day's out. Joshua will have every hand on the island turnin 'to today," he said, reaching in his pocket. "Couldn't help but notice how nervous she was though. Put me in mind of father's old sayin ''bout somebody bein' as nervous as a long tail cat in a room full of rocking chairs. Boys, always liked that one."

***

Ira had spent the last two days pounding nails into the long boards which would serve as tables for the clam bake. Today, as he helped to carry them to the back shore, stumbling down the hill and over the beach to the bake site, he wondered why they didn't just sit on the beach and eat their clams. People made so much work for themselves he thought. It seemed such a bother to make a few dollars, still he had found work on the island since arriving in April, and Joshua was a generous fellow with the rum when the day's work ended. He guessed he shouldn't complain. Today there'd be plenty to go around. If it was to be anything like Joshua promised, it was sure to be something for the history books.

It had been eleven years since the war's end and the Grand Army of the Republic had formed to assist the veterans and their loved ones left behind. Their encampments provided the opportunity to tell their war stories and sit around a campfire again, sing familiar songs and listen to the old vets deliver their glory speeches. Today was Portland's turn to show the country what patriotism really looked like. The GAR committee had been down twice that summer to make sure all would run smoothly for the event. It was up to Joshua Jenks, proprietor of the Sunnyside House, to execute the elaborate plans.

Charles Sawyer too could not have been more excited on the morning of August tenth. The sea was glassy calm and the cicadas hummed high in the trees as he sat down to his breakfast. Their song promised a hot day, and if they were lucky, they'd get through it without an afternoon thunder storm. Even so, his barge, *Island Belle*, was up to the trip, thunder or no. It would be his biggest haul yet, ferrying almost two thousand men from the Portland pier to Little Chebeague before the day was through. It meant a huge profit for his company, and himself, as the steamer *Henrietta* had also been hired for the day.

A week ago the tents had arrived on the towboat, *Uncle Sam*, and the crew, including Ira, had lugged them to the east field closest to the sand bar and set up a tent city. Every piece of lumber had been hauled to the barn where they'd constructed enough tables to seat nineteen hundred. Men from all over the islands had supplied four hundred bushel of clams, and they all turned out to pick enough corn for every man to have two ears each. Ira had heard Jenks say that he had purchased four hundred dozen eggs for the bake and the next morning's breakfast, which meant every man could expect to enjoy the meal and would have more than enough to keep him happy. It was bound to be the biggest event Casco Bay had ever seen and those islanders who had helped with the preparations, were invited to attend as well.

The kitchen crew consisted of Mrs. Barker, head cook, Nellie Soule and Esther Hamilton, the two table maids, dishwashers and general clean-up detail. Margaret, last to be hired that summer, took her orders from Mrs. Barker who had been with Jenks since he started work on the old Osgood Hotel. With financial backing, he had signed a five-year lease with the Cleaves brothers, the island's owners, to farm the land and rebuild the hotel business. All agreed that his first year was to be a grand success. He even hauled two Civil War cannons to the island for the occasion to mark the celebration's grand finale.

***

Having traversed the bar, Margaret stood for a moment, wondering if she should walk through the field and tent city, or stick to the shoreline and take the walkway. Deciding to stay clear of the tents

100

and possibly encounter someone who might slow her down, she hurried on her way across the sandy beach to the bank. At the top, her gaze followed along the clamshell promenade, past the fields and tilled land, to rest upon the Sunnyside. The substantial, two-story hotel stood gleaming in the early sunlight, boasting a fresh coat of white paint and wide verandas running across the front and sides. It was the biggest house she had ever seen. Every time she approached the walk, the realization that she had a role to play in its success, caused her nerves to run amok.

Greeting Margaret as she hurried along, Mrs. Jenks wheeled her baby boy along the clam-shelled promenade. "Good morning," she hailed.

"Morning, Mrs. Jenks. How's little Harry?" she asked, poking her head in for a polite peek.

"I'd like to say he's sleepin'", she replied. "Been up all night with him. And, Mr. Jenks has not slept a wink with the preparations. Everybody's in a hurry today, but me, I guess."

"I'd count my blessings if I were you, Mrs. Jenks," Margaret said, smiling. "I wish I could join you, to tell the truth. I'm that scared of making a mistake on the big day."

"You needn't worry dear, there's plenty to help. It's lookin 'to be quite warm, so you should pace yourself and take the lead from Mrs. Barker, or one of the girls. They'll be helpful to you."

"That's so kind of you to say. I guess I really should be off now, or they'll think I'm already takin' a break!" With one last bye she hurried up the road. Bursting through the kitchen door she spied Nellie sitting on a stool humming as she peeled potatoes.

"Thank God you're here," she said, tossing an apron in Margaret's direction. "Thought I was going to have to manage with just Esther, and you know 'bout how much help she is."

"I'm here now, so what should I be doing?" Margaret asked.

"Well, I don't know, do I?" Nellie glared. "I'm just the hired help, like you. So, I guess you'd better go on out back there and see what's what."

Margaret heard Nellie's derisive laugh follow her out the back door, but she was determined to keep a steady keel today. Nellie would not unbalance her, or her good mood. In the dooryard Esther and William were sitting on the back of the buckboard tossing ears of corn into large crates. Esther's scrawny arms glistened in the sunlight, her body dwarfed by William's bulk. William stopped mid-toss, not hiding his regard for the girl who now pitched in to help.

"You're a welcome addition, If I do say so myself," he said, smiling at Margaret. "I always say if a man's gotta 'work, he can at least have two beautiful women by his side."

Esther paused long enough to land a playful punch to his shoulder, then winked at Margaret. "I guess we know who the beauty is to you, Will. You haven't taken your eyes off her since she showed up. Better keep an eye out, Mag, he's got designs on you, or I'm not standin 'here beside this horse's behind in the hot sun!"

Despite Esther's humorous quips and laughter, they were relieved to hear William announce it was time to take the load down to the pit. The girls stood watching as the wagon made its way out through the field, readying for the next job, when Nellie flew through the door. "Didn't you two hear the whistle? Steamer's comin 'in with the first load! And, I for one am hightailin 'it down to the wharf. Well, aren't you comin'?"she asked sharply.

"What's to do down there?" asked Esther.

"What's to do? Do I have to tell you everything! To do is a whole boatload of men ready for some fun, and I don't plan on workin 'all day!" she announced.

"Whose not plannin 'on workin 'all day?" asked Mrs. Barker, appearing on the doorstep. "I'd of thought you'd be appreciatin 'the work, Miss Nellie. There's plenty 'round that would."

Nellie stopped in her tracks, then turned to address her boss. "I'm just goin 'down to wave and welcome the soldiers, any harm in that, I'd like to know about it. We've been workin 'our fingers to the bone for weeks and I judge we deserve a bit of fun today."

Mrs. Barker's smile grew larger as she tossed her hands up and laughed. "Go on then, the lot of ya', just get back here in half an hour, or you'll have me to answer to!"

The girls laughed with her, then set off at a run for the wharf.

***

Late afternoon found Joshua Jenks sitting comfortably in the shade of a giant elm beside his friend Nathan Cleaves. The men drank lemonade and laughed together as the old and young soldiers lounged across the beach, jumped in the cold Atlantic, or gathered in

102

small groups to share their war stories again. Many had not seen each other since the war and the reunion brought nostalgia for their fallen comrades, as much as it carried remembrance of their days in the camps.

Since the day began, the girls and Mrs. Barker had not had a moment to relax or enjoy the day's festivities. The work was demanding and they'd managed to catch only glimpses of the fun here and there. They looked forward to hooking their aprons on the kitchen door and joining everyone at the campfire and listening to the cannon blasts scheduled for early evening.

"Well, thank God that's over," Mrs. Barker announced to the girls.

"What else can we do?" asked Margaret.

"Just the tables to see to, but for the moment let's catch a breath. You three can finish up tomorrow mornin', I think Mr. Barker has the men washin' them down with salt water. They'll haul them up here and we can give them a good scrubbin 'tomorrow. I've a mind to put my feet up, not as young as I used to be, and those old cannons out there are not my idea of fun."

"So, we're through for the day then?" Esther asked, eagerly. "'Cause I got to say, Mrs. Barker, this has been the longest day of my life. And, if old Mr. Jenks thinks he can keep parties like this up next year, he's gonna need to find us some extra help. That's my opinion on the subject. Now, I'm goin 'down that lane for the shore. Anybody else for danglin 'her feet in the water?"

The girls looked to Mrs. Barker for the go ahead. Giving them the nod, she smiled brightly. "Go on then, you deserve it. But, mind you, I expect to see all three of you bright-eyed and bushy-tailed first thing tomorrow mornin'. We're to send them off with a big breakfast under those shiny belt buckles!"

A gentle warm breeze blew off the land, providing a little comfort from the day's heat. The girls pulled their skirts above their knees and waded at the shoreline, now and again reaching down to splash their faces and arms. In the field they could hear light laughter as the men settled in after the long day's activities, resting up before the bonfire and cannon rally. Across the field Joshua's hired men lugged the tables up from the shore to the waiting wagon. Trailing along behind, Ira caught sight of the girls and waved his cap.

"Ira!" Nellie yelled. "Come on down here and soak your feet! That's Ira," she said, turning to her companions.

"We know," Margaret and Esther said in unison.

"What on earth did you do that for?" Esther asked. "He's nothin '
but an old wash up and you know it. 'Sides he's got to be three times
your age, if he's a day. Ought to soak your head instead of your feet,
what I think."

"Oh, he's right enough, just wants to have some fun and God
knows there's little enough of that around here for us working sods,"
Nellie said, looking to Margaret for assurance. "Your folks know Ira,
don't they? Heard he was livin 'over there for a spell."

"We know him," Margaret replied. "But that doesn't mean my
folks like him much."

"Why? What's he done? Made your make-believe daddy mad or
somethin'?"

"That's enough, Nellie, leave her be. You're always makin '
trouble. You can see Mag doesn't like him," she said, hoping to stop
an argument before it started.

"It's okay Esty, Nellie can talk to anybody she likes to. I don't
have to stay and listen."

"Well, make up your mind quick, 'cause here he comes."

"Ladies," Ira said, sweeping his cap. "What a lovely vision you
make this fine afternoon. Hope you're stayin ''round for the cannon
firin'. I'm to be the torch man," he announced proudly.

Straightening her skirt and tucking in her blouse, Nellie tidied her
hair, flashing her brightest smile. "Oh, go on with ya', all them big
soldiers on hand and they've got you doin 'the honors. I swear, next
they'll have old Esther here loadin 'the cannon balls!"

Ira laughed, giving a nervous nod to Margaret, who had moved
further down the beach. Edging his way past Nellie and Ester, he
walked slowly in her direction, catching up with her as she reached
the lane. "Maggie girl, don't be that way, now. Just bein 'friendly.
Anything wrong with a man bein 'friendly?"

Margaret turned abruptly, causing a near collision between the
two. "I don't recall you bein ''round the Island too much lately Ira.
I'm thinkin 'it's 'cause you know how my family feels about you.
So, I'd just as soon you not try to pretend."

"Just been busy, is all. I think the world of you and yours. Nothin '
John wouldn't do for me, and you know it too."

"I know nothin' of the kind," she said, continuing to walk along
the lane toward the house.

"There's plenty of fish in the ocean, girl, so I'll not be castin 'any net in your direction, if that's what you're thinkin'."

Unable to believe his words, Margaret stopped and turned to stare at him. "You really don't understand, Ira. I've kept to myself all summer and I'd not like to talk ill of you to John. He has been fair with you and you know it. But, Jane will feed you to the dogfish as soon as look at you, and you can't deny she'd frown on you steppin ' foot so close to me. The others are comin ''long," she hesitated, "don't you have big important work to do? I think you best move along and do it."

Catching up with Ira and Margaret in the lane, the girls saw the tension between them and both recognized trouble, yet each saw in the standoff an opportunity. Nellie wanted to see it brew and boil over, while Esther sought to protect her friend.

"Guess I'll be shovin 'off," he said, at their arrival. "Maybe see you later tonight at the bonfire."

"What got him all up 'n arms?" Nellie asked. "Think he's mad at you, Maggie."

"Leave her alone, Nell, it's nothin 'for you to stick your nose into," Esther scolded. "We'd better get back up to the house before dark," she said, urging Margaret along toward the house, leaving Nellie to follow on her own.

"Don't pay her any mind, Mag, she's just lookin 'to start somethin'. You can't walk into the pantry without she'll say a nasty word. And, as far as Ira goes, I'd be mighty careful if I was you. I don't care for the way he looks at us and I don't mind sayin 'so either. Besides, I'm puttin 'my money on William. He's got eyes for you so don't try to tell me otherwise. Come on, admit it, you must be puttin 'somethin 'down it that diary of yours. I can hear your pen scratchin 'away over in the next bed."

Margaret blushed, she couldn't deny that she favored him, but she still felt uncertain. Jane and Aunt Caroline had not really been helpful about men, and since Rosy's death, she'd worried about having children of her own. William had been a perfect gentleman, yet she wondered if Esther might be thinking along the same lines.

"You know, Esty, I think I'll stick to workin 'hard and keepin 'us good friends for the time bein'. For now, that seems enough for me," she said, giving her a quick hug. "Come on then, let's go on down and see what big brave Ira does with those old cannons out there."

Esther laughed and grabbed their shawls from the door hook. "Ask me," she said, "he'll probably have the whole damn field afire before the night's over!"

Chapter Seventeen
Ice Walk

John pulled the door quickly to and stomped the snow from his boots. The wind howled from the northeast and January had turned bitter cold freezing the bay from Portland to Birch Island. For weeks men walked from island to island, pulling sleighs carrying their supplies from the mainland. John had just returned from Orr's Island, judging the walk to be shorter than to Chebeague.

He stood now warming his hands at the open fire, his beard dripping melting snow on the pine floor. "Boys, I tell ya', Janie, that's the coldest I've been in a good long while. You forget how cold it gets. Anybody been down to the barn?"

"Margaret went earlier. Had to break the ice out the buckets. Good thing there's plenty of hay. How'd you find things?"

"Just the same. Old Harry's grousin ''bout the cold and lettin 'the heat out every time somebody comes in the store. Usual gang sittin ' around the stove tellin 'lies as fast as words can shape 'em. Though, I did run into a fella that knew Colonel Chamberlain there. Said he was fixin 'him up a place over to Chebeague. Name's Tozier. Seems like a good sort. He was right there on that hill and saved old Joshua's life, by godfreys. He didn't tell it though, one of the other fellas did after he left."

"'Magine that," Jane said, only half interested in John's war stories. To her way of thinking men started the wars, shook off all the horror they could, then twisted out enough of the bad to make it sound like they were out for a camping trip together. She'd read enough of it in the papers, and heard enough from Mose, to know the truth of it. Numbers told the story. Too many young men in this country had died. Whether it was for a good cause, or not, she could not decide. What she understood at the moment was, that John, who had not been, should not be so pleased about an old war hero living near by.

Oblivious to her disinterest, John continued." Guess he's got the old place right up the hill from Lemuel's place. Got a family too. Luck was with 'em that day, near as I can tell."

"It's a wonder you made it through, John," Jane quipped.

"It's a wonder I made it home, you mean," he countered.

"Well, you did and I was thinkin', now that you're all warmed up and still dressed, how you might want to fill up that wood box over there," she said, unsympathetically.

"You're all heart woman, remind me how it is I came to be so fortunate."

"You found your way down the bay, is all I can think of," she said, pulling his cap down over his ears and giving him an affectionate pat on the shoulder.

"All heart," John said, stepping through the door as Margaret rushed in.

"It's so cold out there my eyelids is frozen!" she exclaimed.

"Get on over by the fire and get warmed up. All shipshape down there?" she asked.

"Should be until morning, I think. I stayed while they took a good long drink. They got their hay and I gave the horse a taste of sugar. She likes a bit of attention too."

"You'll spoil her," Jane said.

"I just like the way her muzzle gets all thick in the winter time. I think she rather enjoys a break like we all do. But, she'll be some frisky when it is a chance to let her out. I think it's one of things I love the best, when John gives her the go ahead and she goes runnin' up through the field."

"I know what you mean, they all seem so glad to be out and free. Guess everything alive wants that," Jane said.

"I know I do," Margaret said, looking into the fire. "I think I've got a bit of feelin 'in them now," she said, rubbing her hands together. "How much longer do you think this cold will last? John says it's the worst he can remember."

"Hard to tell. Still, while it's here, let's take us a walk out on the ice tomorrow and go over and see the boys. If we start out early we can make a day of it. What'd ya 'say old girl? Want to go sleddin'?

"Do you really want to? I mean, once you get out in that wind it's terrible. I wasn't sure I even wanted to go down to barn!"

Jane walked over and tapped twice on the glass. "Looks like a steady glass," she said. "Might be calm all day. Wait and see."

***

With their sled in tow, Jane and Margaret set out early for Chebeague. The sensation of walking over the bay, on top of the frozen water, created an odd feeling to those who spent their lives in boats gauging tides and wind. Today the sun glared on the ice blinding them in its brilliance. Pulling John's cap low over her eyes, Jane stepped carefully watching the ice for possible breaks or clear patches. As a precaution they carried tall poles and stored a length of rope on the sled. Jane had heard stories of people falling through. Those who managed to live through the ordeal had said that once you were under, the hole you had fallen through disappeared, leaving only the broad expanse of ice above you. She also knew that the bay had been frozen over for weeks and seeing others out walking from island to island signaled that it was safe.

The walk seemed to go faster on foot than by boat, and they marveled at an early arrival. Mose and the boys were at the shore readying their sled when Jane called to them from the ice. Johnny, now eleven and Gus just nine, spied Margaret and Jane, both starting at a run to greet them.

"Johnny!" Mose called. "Get on back here and bring your brother."

"Why? It's okay," he called back. "Granny's comin'!"

Hurrying over, Mose reached out and pulled them back to the shore. "Just hold you horses, boys! They'll be right along."

"But why can't we go meet them? It's just a little way off shore."

"Because, they've got a sled, and poles, and rope, and if they fall through the ice, we can get them out. Now, just stay put a minute."

Reaching the shore Jane hauled the sled onto the bank and tied it to a rock. Hearing their laughter, she shook her head at her own stupidity. "Guess I needn't have done that," she chuckled. "Old habits!"

"Never mind that, you never know," Johnny said, taking her hand, "some old thaw might show up while we're up to the house and there'd she be adrift, Gran."

"Glad to see someone's got some common sense around here, Mose. How's the family? Everyone keepin 'well in this cold?"

"We're all just fine. Come on, let's get you two warmed up. Glad you came over, I was thinkin 'some of payin 'you a visit, so you saved me a trip, I guess."

Warmed and full of Wealthy's fried donuts, the family gathered at the kitchen table visiting and catching up on the news. Jane still felt Rosy's presence in the room, forcing herself to visit over the years for her grandsons. Mose had been generous with their time and made sure they spent a few weeks in the summer with Jane and John. They loved going out to the traps with John and working on the farm with the animals. Young Johnny especially liked the water. There seemed little doubt that it would be his calling, and Gus did everything in his footsteps. Wealthy had taken on Mose's children as her own as the only sensible arrangement.

As the afternoon approached, Jane was anxious to return home before dark set in, mindful of the danger it could bring.

"Looks like it's gettin' on out there," Jane announced. "What's ya' say, Maggie, we hit the ice road?"

Mose scraped back his chair and walked over to the window gazing out over the icy bay. "Might be a good idea, it is gettin 'on. Don't want to do any late night rescues. Here let me walk you down, just had somethin 'in mind to talk with you 'bout," he said, helping Jane into her coat.

Margaret pulled the sled out onto the ice, then turned to wait while Jane and Mose chatted on the shore. "I've been meanin 'to talk to you and John for quite some time now. Just been offered a schooner berth soon's as the weather breaks. It's gettin 'harder on the folks, what with my brothers and sisters still home," he ventured, leaving the door open for her to walk through.

Knowing there could only be one possible meaning in his words, Jane looked along the shore, then up toward the bank where Johnny and Gus waited to wave goodbye. "You want us to take the boys," she said. "Do they know?"

"I wanted to talk it over first, 'fore I said anythin'," he replied, avoiding a direct look. "It's just be while I'm out fishin', then I'd collect them after my trips. I've got to find some work, Jane. I can't keep livin' at home like this, it's too much of a burden to the family."

"I understand, Mose. Send them when you're ready. They're always welcome and I 'magine will be a big help to John."

Mose nodded." That's good news. I'll be in touch, soon's I hear word."

"I'm just worried 'bout their schoolin'," Jane said. "Don't want that to pass 'em by. It's too valuable as things are now."

"I know, I know, we'll just have to sort it out somehow. Maybe they'll start the school up again over on Ministerial?"

"Not sure I know," Jane said.

"Listen, if it's too much for you and John, I had thought some of askin 'Mary and Jacob to take 'em at the farm, but I hate to take them away from the water. They'd not like it so far away from home."

Jane started toward Margaret patiently waiting. "I'll talk with John, but don't think of Mary. She's seven children to look after. Her last just this month. I can't imagine how she'd cope. She'd not turn you down, but you can see it'd be difficult. Come over in a day or two and we'll sit down with John."

Mose waved to Margaret, then headed back toward the house. Jane watched for a moment as he walked away. Mose would need help to find his way, she thought, and if she had a say about it, he'd be a father to his boys. They deserved better in life than the isolated world she and John had chosen. Margaret was finding a life off the island and settling the boys in would be making a mistake, one only Mose could mend. If he couldn't see his way around it, he might be tempted to leave the boys. There had to be a better solution than the one at hand.

Chapter Eighteen
Return to the Sunnyside

Margaret was pleased to see Mrs. Barker sitting on the bench at the head of the promenade as she walked toward the big house. Wondering if the others would be back, she hurried her step and flounced down beside her.

"Gracious girl, almost knocked me off my seat, but I'm that glad to see you comin 'up the walk," she said, moving over to give Margaret room beside her.

"I'm so happy to be back, Mrs. Barker. It was one long winter out there, I can tell you that right now. Times when I thought I'd go crazy listening to that old wind howlin' through the open chamber at night. If I didn't love Jane and John so much, I swear I'd ask Mrs. Jenks if I could stay on."

"She'd probably welcome the help with that little one all over the place. And, if I didn't know better, I'd say she's probably got another one in the oven!"

"Mrs. Barker!" Margaret exclaimed, surprised by her forwardness. "If that's the case, then maybe I will ask her," she said, doubting herself even as she spoke her thoughts out loud. She liked her boss, and judging her to be a fair woman, Margaret ventured further into their chat. "I don't suppose you've seen the others yet?" she asked.

"Not hide, nor hair, of any of 'em yet, unless you're talkin ''bout William?" she added slyly. "'Magine he'll be hangin' 'round the barn this mornin'. Joshua's got 'em exercisin' the horses. Mind you take care 'round 'em, the horses I mean," she smiled, catching Margaret's blush.

"William! I'd not be talkin' 'bout William. It's Esty I've been waitin 'all winter to see!"

"Oh, I see," Mrs. Barker said, grabbing the tree's trunk with both hands in an effort to pull herself to her feet. Noticing the struggle, Margaret rose quickly and offered her both hands. "Landsakes, if I get any fatter, Mr. Barker will have to put me out to pasture," she said, taking the offered help. "I just can't seem to keep the weight off and you think how hard I work all day. Runs in the family. My grandmother was heavy, my mother too, so I guess I'm no 'ception. Sometimes I look at you young girls and I wonder when it happened. I can't blame it on children, 'cause Mr. Barker and I have not been blessed, still, I'd like to find somethin 'to lay the blame on, I'll tell you that right now. My old granddaddy always said that weight was an awful curse and I'm inclined to believe him."

Walking along the lane together, clamshells crunching beneath their feet, Margaret thought about what she had said and couldn't help but think of Jane. She was practically the only woman she'd known in her life who hadn't seemed to be in Mrs. Barker's predicament. Even in her fifties, Jane was all muscle. She stood head and shoulders over John, which hadn't seemed odd to her when she was growing up, but now that she'd been out a bit, she saw that Jane was not like other women. For starters, she'd always worn men's overalls, which she guessed made sense given the work she did. Sometimes she'd wear her skirt. It just seemed to Margaret that she dressed to fit the day ahead. She wondered what Mrs. Barker would say if she met Jane. She knew what her Aunt Caroline had to say, which was why she supposed Jane made few trips to visit her. Margaret thought she understood. When she was younger she feared that her aunt would die young because of her many ailments, then she once overheard Uncle Barn saying that Caroline enjoyed poor health. She'd had to think about it for a long time before she realized what he was saying about his wife. When she did, she vowed never to be like her. She wanted to be like the woman she admired and loved, although she had to admit she did like her dresses, so maybe she'd draw the line there. Still and all, Margaret had begun to make sense of other people, she knew the ones she didn't have to give in to, likewise the ones who could be your friend. It seemed that truly it boiled down to being that simple.

That afternoon Margaret walked down to meet Uncle Barn hauling her trunk for the summer across the bar with his team. Given the tides across the bar connecting the two islands, daily travel was impossible with her work day, which meant she would live in one of the cottages on the hill Joshua had completed the past winter.

"Where we headed?" her uncle asked. "Doesn't seem possible another year's passed us by. Your aunt wanted to come along today, but she came down with 'nother one of her headaches this morning. Seem to get worse in the heat."

"It's just you and me then. Mrs. Barker says to come up to the big house when we're finished for some refreshments before you leave."

"She's a good sort, Maggie, glad you have her here to kind of keep an eye out. Jane would approve, I think."

"I think so. She's here most of the time, 'cept when she and Mr. Barker sail over to Long to check on the house. He's Mr. Jenks right-hand man, I'm told."

Pulling up at the house, Barn tethered the horses and pumped fresh water from the well into the trough, then hauled Margaret's trunk to her room on the second floor. Joshua had taken pains to lath and plaster the walls which pleased her. She had grown used to sleeping in the unfinished chamber and this was luxury. Mrs. Jenks had even found the time to hang curtains. Taking a peek out the window she noticed Ira walking into the yard. "Oh no," she said, "there's Ira pokin' 'round down there. I'd been hoping he'd gone off fishing, or found some place else to haunt," she said.

"Isn't he the fella John kicked off a while back?" Barn asked.

"You heard 'bout that? He can be a nuisance. Mostly, I just ignore him."

"Better go on down and see what he wants," Barn said, leaving her to unpack. Barnwell had heard stories of Ira's penchant for walking off with things he might not properly have a right to, and the back of his wagon held plenty of items a man might find useful to sell. Through the screen door he saw Ira circling the wagon, lifting crate lids and nosing about under the seat. "Need a hand there?" Barn called, causing Ira to bump his head.

"No, no, just wonderin 'whose buggy it was, is all," he replied, rubbing his head.

Barn stepped down from the porch and walked over to calm the agitated horses. "Funny thing about that isn't it?" Barn asked.

"Don't quite get your drift," Ira replied, feigning ignorance.

"It's not too complicated, Ira. I always say, if it isn't yours to begin with, then you ought to know it belongs to somebody else."

"I knew it warn't mine, Barn. I'm supposed to keep an eye on things here 'bout. Part of the job."

"That so," Barn said, looking over his wagon. "Didn't know you come up that far in the world."

"None of your concern who I work for as I see it. Ah, now here comes somethin' to brighten the day," he said, as Margaret bounced down the steps. "Back for more punishment again, I see. Thought maybe last summer you'd had enough rough times."

"Ira, I was just thinkin' the same of you."

"Me? Nah. Know a good thing, don't I? And since everything's shipshape here, I'll just be moseying along," he said, leaving the two standing together, Barn watching him closely until he disappeared down the lane. Turning to Margaret, he asked the question he knew an uncle should ask. "Does he bother with you? Because if he does, I've a mind to go right back up those stairs and pack up your things. Don't know but I should, Mag. There's somethin ''bout him turns me wrong side out."

Margaret tipped her head away, not wanting to look at him directly, then thought better of trying to evade the question. She knew that everyone felt the same about Ira, everyone that is, but Mr. Jenks, who only saw a man who apparently did his work. Still, she answered truthfully.

"I know you're worried, but I've got the other girls livin 'here with me and we watch out for each other. Come on then, he's gone, let's go get that lunch and I can introduce you to Mrs. Barker. If she doesn't ease up your fears, I don't know who would."

***

The expectation of success, after last year's, made the Sunnyside House a popular place with young and old alike. Guests hailed from as far away as Philadelphia, New York and Boston, with steamer trunks packed for a month's stay at a time. Still others came from Portland for day picnics, swimming, and enjoying the fine dining with fresh produce from Joshua's farm.

Margaret discovered that her old friend, Esther, and the cantankerous Nellie, were there and the three stepped seamlessly back into their roles as kitchen and chambermaids. They spent their days laughing together at work and afternoon breaks strolling the beaches, occasionally taking little Harry along. Mrs. Jenks rewarded them with a few added coins which meant a little extra for each.

115

The summer saw the finest weather of any they could remember, and with the sun, came droves of visitors making their days fly by. By the time they had reached July's end, each girl could boast a fine savings to help their families through the winter, with a little left over for occasional trips into the city.

Their luck ran out when the first two weeks of August ushered in foggy days, reordering life on the island. Many of Joshua's picnic goers rescheduled their dates, sending their messages by steamboat, however today, he expected a large crowd. As Mrs. Barker's liked to know for certain how many would show, she'd sent the girls for a head count. Listening intently for the sound of her whistle, Nellie claimed she could hear the steamer rounding Deer Point.

"Tell you, I can hear her out there," she said, adamantly stating her case." Listen a minute, hear that, she's just inside now."

"What are you on 'bout?" Esther asked. "If she's inside the cove, I guess we'd know it. They're not comin 'today."

"Maybe you're right. Perhaps we should walk on back and see what's to be done."

"You go on ahead," Esther said. "I for one, plan to stand here and wait, 'cause I sure don't want to miss seein 'what a boatload of Oddfellows looks like!"

Margaret laughed, giving Esther a friendly nudge knocking her sideways. "You go on then, I'm for takin' a walk."

Esther poked her back, then continued her listening with Nellie. "I'll catch you up as soon as we're sure they're not comin'", she said, waving her on.

The thick fog penetrated Margaret's clothing as she walked along the low tide shoreline, listening for the steamer, hearing distantly Esther and Nellie's chatting diminish as she drew nearer to the southwest end of the island. The ledges loomed ahead of her, seeming larger in the dense light, sending an unwelcome shiver through her limbs. Still she walked on, seeking a quiet, sheltered spot. All day the fog shut in around the island, isolating objects in a ghostly scene, holding her thoughts to fixed boundaries. Sitting down, she reached for a piece of driftwood, swirling circles in the sand, pausing when she heard the crunch of boots along the beach. Thinking it must be Esther, she waited, but instead of her friend, a man walked out of the fog. It took just seconds for her to recognize the shape and bulk of him.

Ira clumsily stepped around a boulder, then threw himself down on the beach to sit beside her. "Well, well, well, out for a little stroll are we?"

Margaret's mind sought a reply, knowing that what she said next should get her to her feet and moving back to her friends.

"I was just waiting for Esther and Nellie to come."

"Esther and Nellie's over on the wharf waitin' for a boat, that ain't comin 'in today."

"All the same then, I heard 'em comin', so I'll just go to meet 'em," she announced, standing to brush the sand from her skirt.

"Here, let me walk you back," he said, taking long strides to catch up.

Margaret hastened her step, picking her way carefully over the seaweed and beach stones, yet Ira continued along beside her. As they approached the wharf, Esther waved, then leaned on the piling eyeing each visitor departing the steamer as Margaret joined them.

"Only two!" she called to Nellie.

"That puts paid to that then. You wanna go or not?" Nellie asked. "I think we should catch this one and stay at my folks tonight."

"I'll go if Mag does," Esther replied.

"Go where?" she asked.

"To visit Nellie's, silly. Come on, Mrs. Barker says it's okay as long as no visitors show up and we're back in the mornin'. What'd ya say?"

"Make up your mind, Mag, they're not goin' to hang around here all day," Nellie ordered. "I swear gettin 'you to make up your mind to do somethin 'is a job all by itself. I for one am goin', with or without you two."

Margaret stared out into the fog bank, shifting from foot to foot, catching the pleading look on Esther's face, convincing her that sometimes she needed to embrace adventure, even a small one like deciding to step onto the steamer.

"Well, all right, but you're sure 'bout Mrs. Barker?"

"We are! Come on let's get on, I've brought along the fare and you can pay me back tomorrow."

The *Magnet's* whistle sounded as the girls hopped aboard for the short trip over to Western Landing on Chebeague's west end.

Captain Abner stood at the wheel slowing the throttle to an idle, listening for the breakers crashing off the Old Prince. The bay's half submerged ledges, and the danger for his boat and passengers, were one thing when it was clear sailing, but thick fog advised further precautions. Satisfied, he'd navigated outside the ledge, he cut the wheel and followed the compass heading until he was safely inside the sound between Hope and Chebeague. Following the shoreline along, he was relieved to see the island's wharf taking shape. Sounding the whistle he brought her in, thinking he might lay over for a few hours before making the final day's trip back to Portland.

Passengers below deck, worked their way topside and along the gangplank single file, searching the wharf for anyone who may have come down to greet them. The excitement of each boat's arrival meant news. Many strolled down to meet the boat on the off chance of learning something new about the goings on in the city, or other islands. With a nod to the few islanders standing about, Nellie took the lead and started down the road toward home. Passing by Lemuel's house, Margaret paused, spying Johnny and little Gus playing in an old punt in the backyard.

"Hi boys! What ya 'doin'?" she called, walking over to greet them.

"Just haulin 'some gear back," Gus said, seriously, pulling his cap tighter over his eyes. "You wanna 'come?"

"I'd love to hun, but my friends are waiting for me," she said.

"Ah, come on then," Johnny said. "We're more fun than 'em guys."

Margaret laughed, considering his invitation. "You know boys, you're probably right, but I've made a promise and you can't break promises, now can you?"

"Break 'em all the time," Johnny replied. "Sides, Gram'll be mad, if you don't come in and say hi." Looking across the yard, Margaret caught a glimpse of Nellie standing impatiently in the middle of the road getting ready to send out a holler in her direction.

"Hold your horses! I'm comin'," she yelled, preempting her directive.

"Well, hurry up then!" Nellie called back.

"I just want to go in and say hello," she said, catching up to the girls who had started on their way. "They'll think it's odd if I don't. You go on ahead and I'll be along after a visit. That okay?"

"Have to be, won't it," Nellie said, picking up speed." Can't vouch for how much pie we'll have left over, but suit yourself."

Margaret stood undecided, then turned and walked toward the house. In the brief encounter with Nellie, she noticed the fog had lifted enough to see out beyond Sand Island and the vague outline of the southwestern tip of Bates beyond. It would be a simple enough job, she thought, to get Mose to row her over. Then, deciding it was a poor plan with the fog setting in and out, she turned and walked toward the house only to discover that Gram and the boys were off visiting themselves. "Well, that's gratitude for ya,'" she said, hearing Jane's voice in her head. Sitting down on the front steps, she resolved to wait, then thinking they might all be down at the shore, she turned and walked to the shore path. Now, more determined than ever to see her family, she spied Mose just stepping through his fish house door.

"There you are," she said pulling the door open to surprise him, "I thought you'd all gone off to live on Stave!"

"I don't know 'bout them," Ira said, "but I wouldn't mind it much."

"I, I, thought you was Mose," Margaret said, edging her way back.

"Didn't ya 'see me aboard the boat? Came over same time you did. You girls was yacking it up down below, thought I was in the hen house."

"You was on the steamer? No, didn't happen to notice. Seen Mose?" she asked.

"Nope. Lookin 'for him myself. Everybody gone off then?"

"They're probably back by now. Probably at the neighbors or somethin'."

"Well that's too bad, isn't it? Why don't you stick around here 'til they get back. I was just thinkin', Mose must have a bottle of hooch 'round here somewhere. I don't suppose you have any idea where he hides it?" Ira asked, hopefully.

"No, I don't, and I wouldn't tell you if I did. You shouldn't be so free with other people's things, Ira."

"Share, and share alike, I always say," he offered, continuing his search. "You know," he said, turning to face her, "You've been a little hard on old Ira. What'd ya 'think harm will come if you was to be nice for a change?"

Staring back, Margaret thought about the man standing in her uncle's fish house and about herself. Had she been unkind to the poor man who really had not been unkind to her in all the years she'd known him? He was just a man who worked hard all day long and was looking for his friend to share a drink. Maybe she had been harsh when it came to Ira. After all, he had been a perfect gentleman on the beach that morning, offering to walk her back. He hadn't said or done anything out of the way that she could see. Looking at him now, hoisting himself onto the workbench, she laughed out loud, noticing he had put both hands in wet paint pooling at the edge.

"What's so damn funny?" he asked.

"Oh, nothin'", she smiled, "just that you've got paint all over you!"

"Damn, damn, why didn't you warn me off?"

"I didn't have time, you was up there too quick!" she laughed.

"Hand me that rag," he ordered, shaking his head, laughing at his own predicament. "You're probably thinking serves me right in here snoopin ''round. Say, where are the girls? Thought you was goin ' with 'em?" he asked, scrubbing at the paint.

"Changed my mind. I wanted to visit with the family, but now I'd just like to go and see John and Jane. Haven't had a chance all summer with work. Sometimes I wish they'd move here."

It was Ira's turn to laugh." You'll not find Jane livin 'on the same island with that sister of her's."

"Never thought of that," she said, toe kicking the dirt floor.

"Listen, you want to go see 'em that bad, why don't we borrow Mose's dory and I'll sail ya 'right into the cove in jig time? What'd ya say?"

"I say John would tar and feather you the minute you stepped your boots out!"

"Don't think I don't know it too. He's mighty prickly when it comes to that woman. It might be gratitude for takin 'him in like she did."

"What do you mean? They're married, Ira. If anyone was taken in, it was me, and I've not shown thanks enough," she said, stopping to think about his offer. "Did you mean it? About takin 'me over?"

"Surely did. Still want to go?"

"Why not. I'll tell them that Mose said it was okay with him and that should get you as far as the door at least," she said, smiling at him. "What about the fog?"

"Never let a little thing like fog stop me, girly. I could sail that rig out there all the way to Europe before dark, now I want to tell ya'."

"All right then, let's go, but Bates Island will be quite far enough for me."

Chapter Nineteen
Dusk Settling In

The morning's fog sifted through the spruce branches off the southwest point, enfolding ghostly arms about the ledges and coves, tracing each arc of green blade in its watery invasion. Stepping out into the white stillness, John blinked, squinting his eyes against the glare. It was not the morning he had hoped would greet him. Jane nudged his arm holding out a canvas sack she'd packed that morning with salt fish and bread for his tea, knowing it would take him most of the day to row to the rock, set his trawl and pull back his catch.

"I know what you're thinking," he said. "Probably best to wait for it to clear, but if I do that I'll be old and gray. Looks like it's got a mind of its own."

"I should come with you. Spell you on the oars."

"No, you're all right. You've got your own to do."

"Let me at least see you off then. If the sun does break through, It'll be some muggy when it does. I'll see about canning those beets. Most likely be all speckled red by the time you get home," she laughed.

John smiled, pleased that she did not insist he hold off his fish trip. "Don't worry about the fog, the others will be out there in company and the fish don't care what the weather's up to."

Jane waited on the shore until the dory faded from her sight, listening to the oars' grousing against the thole pins as John dipped his oars, casting diminishing circles on the glassy surface.

She had walked by the bushel basket sitting on the back steps for two days, always finding a good reason to put the chore off for another day. They seemed to taunt her, like sullen, red-faced beggars waiting for the inevitable skinning, just bruising for a fight. The once leafy green tops had collapsed and now slumped, fringing the basket's edge, emphasizing her neglectfulness. She had to stop herself from giving the basket a good kick, however much she knew pickled beets were John's favorite. Although thinking about a thing made it seem more of a drudgery than it really was, she wasn't so sure that the wisdom of her observation actually applied in this case. Beets were messy and would take up most of her morning. Nevertheless, she pulled her apron over her head, set the kettle on to boil, grabbed the paring knife and headed back out to face it head on. Cutting away the tops, leaving a measure of stem and tap root, she plopped them one by one into a bucket of cold water. After boiling, peeling, and slicing, then adding the vinegar and onions, she would tap them snug into the glass jars. Later, when winter held her frozen grip, she would open the kitchen cupboard and regard the bright red jars lining the shelves and wonder if, sitting next to the faded dandelion greens, they didn't just manage to have the last word after all.

By late afternoon, she'd shelved the last jar, cleared the counter and kitchen table, finally settling in for a cup of sweet tea. Fortified, she pulled her shawl from the door hook, grabbed the empty water pail and started down the path for the well. She looked toward Ministerial, its profile lost to her view, willing it to appear out of the dense white shroud. The field path was well worn, still she watched her step, mindful of the loose stones and shale outcroppings, unnerved when the black-faced ram stepped in front of her. Reaching the barn she lifted her head and crossed to the well, standing still for a moment to assemble the pieces of her world. She marked the tide's gentle swell at the shore and strained to hear John's dory, her ears tugging at the dampened silence, as if she could haul in a wish from the spectral realm. It was useless to try. The fog would lift when it made up its mind, and in the meantime, she had chores to tend to in the barn.

She left the full water pail on the well cover, glancing toward the barn, wondering why John had closed the doors. He had not been down to the barn that morning and she knew there had been no wind to blow them to. Inside, the jersey kicked impatiently at her stall, yielding a series of hollow thuds resonating deeply within. Usually a docile creature, it was not like her to be making a fuss, prompting Jane to move with haste. Removing the braces, she pushed the pine doors wide against the barn's face and entered the dimly lit interior.

In the retelling, she would struggle to recall the moment clearly. She could not say for certain how long she stood at the entrance, listening to the odd creaking sound, punctuated by the cow's hoof striking erratically at the stall. She could not say when she finally looked up, or how long she stood staring at the rope fibers rubbing at the beam, while the body's weight arced, slowly twisting, inches above the barn floor. Instead, she began with the moments after, circling her arms about the legs and lifting. Later she would hear her own voice wailing out into the fog drenched stillness, shouting into the blank impenetrable white, as if she might summon a single living creature from a breathing world.

Dusk was settling in when she stirred, felt his arms about her shoulders and looked up into eyes blurred with tears. She felt his hands gently covering her own, taking care to loosen her grasp about Margaret's wrists. He had found her sitting with her back to the barn door, stroking single strands of hair away from the girl's face, muttering about the cow and damp.

***

In the morning John made tea and set to work in the kitchen hoping that a good breakfast would bring her out of the silence she'd adopted since he'd tugged the covers about her shivering body the night before. He needed her to come to her senses, to talk to him about what she knew of Margaret's death. He had never known Jane to withdraw from reality, no matter how destructive and cruel, yet he worried about this time, this death. He saw it one way only; she had suffered enough for one woman and he wasn't about to stand by and see her suffer more. To his way of thinking, they needed to find out who was responsible for her death.

That night, soon after Jane fell asleep, he'd walked down to the barn. Retrieving a canvas sail he judged sufficient for a shroud, reluctantly, deciding to leave her body in the barn for the night, hesitant to take her to the house. Lighting the kerosene lamp he'd surveyed the scene, walking through what he thought might have happened. It was impossible to miss the ladder leaning against the beam. He climbed to the top, set the lantern on the beam and studied the half hitches. Although securely fastened, he thought whoever tied them was in a hurry. Reaching down he'd pulled the end loop closer, hand over hand, to the light. He imagined a simple slipknot, yet saw instead the familiar three wraps, affirming his suspicions. The knot he held in his hand could only have been fashioned by a man who had some familiarity with gaff rigging; a skill he knew could mean almost any fisherman in the bay, but the knot had at least ruled out the worry that she'd taken her own life. Margaret would likely not have knowledge of a more intricate knot; a running bowline would make sense, as he had taught her himself, but a hangman style knot would have been beyond her skills. Besides, however much proof the knot could provide to those who would investigate, it still did not explain why she was dripping wet from head to toe.

***

Returning to the house, he paused, lighting his pipe to think through for himself what next steps should be. He couldn't leave Jane alone for long, that much was certain. The authorities would need notification and he would see if Jim would sail to Portland. His courage in place, John found Jane seated at the kitchen table, dressed for the day ahead.

"I've been sitting here going over and over it in my mind, John. I just can't seem to make sense of it. She knew she could come to us if she was in some kind of trouble. What's to be done?"

John sat close beside her and reached his arm about her shoulders. "There's more to it, if you are able to talk about it."

"What more could there be? I thought we did right by her, gave her what we could. God only knows what happened over there."

"No, Jane. Listen to me. You're thinking about it all wrong."

Jane turned to him, her eyes granting a willingness to listen.

John held the moment, measuring her expression against enormity of the knowledge he would not be able to take back once she heard the truth. He knew he would not be able to keep it from her. In the days ahead, she would face trials of recrimination, ultimately return to herself, fronting each blow as it landed with her head held high. It was his knowledge of her pride and strength, that belief in her, that gave him strength.

"I've looked things over down there. Been up the ladder. Put things together. There's no doubt in my mind but someone else had a hand in her death. She could not have known how to tie that knot. It

125

was the kind we use on gaff rigs. I'd taught her the basics, but this was different."

Jane nodded once, taking John's words in, slipping the information about inside, trying to balance what her heart had felt to be wrong with what the world would judge to be true.

"I didn't want to believe it, John. But, we have no proof. Why would anyone want to harm that girl?"

"I can't pretend to understand it, but the facts are there for anyone to see. We knew her, she was happy working for Jenks, had her girlfriends and making a bit. Mostly, I know how facts line up, how to read them. I didn't see a dory and she sure didn't swim from Little Chebeague. That adds up to someone bringing her over and leaving."

"Might be it drifted off," Jane added.

"Might be. We can find out who was missing a boat. Most likely, she came over on the steamer, then got a ride from there."

"Mose should know. I can't see her striking out in all that fog, neither."

"She'd been overboard. No one would be that wet from a row in the fog. We can't keep this. I'll have to sail up to Portland and tell the authorities. I don't suppose you'd go over to the island today, maybe stay with family until I get things ironed out here."

"Can't go off and leave her here alone, John. We should go down and bring her up to the house. I can manage until you get back."

"Are you sure? Might be a spell. I was thinking some of asking Jim to go on up, then sail right back. Don't matter who tells them. That way I wouldn't be so long."

"Wouldn't do him any harm."

"It's settled then," John agreed. "I'll go on down now and see to her."

***

By mid-morning the fog had lifted, promising an afternoon breeze out of the southwest. John had sailed for Hope soon after he'd carried Margaret's body to the house, leaving Jane to tend to her. He knew Jane would wash the body and lay her out in her finest dress, a sight he thought never to see in his lifetime, causing his mind to work at the image again and again, splintering apart only long enough to mend anew. The sooner he informed the right people, the sooner he would be able to tell them what he knew. Everything now depended on making sure whoever had taken her life was brought to justice. He knew enough about the law to understand that a coroner would be dispatched without delay and weighed the idea of sailing directly to Portland himself, against leaving Jane alone.

The dory made slow progress, tacking into the wind. Once inside the gut between Hope and Chebeague, he threw over the tiller and beached the dory in the cove below Jim's house. He would tell them what had happened and return to Bates.

They waited throughout the afternoon with no word from Portland. John paced the floor and kept a constant vigil at the window, finally announcing he would walk down to the shore. He wanted to revisit the barn in daylight and retrace his steps; he could not dismiss the sensation that something wasn't right, that he had missed something in his search the night before.

The afternoon sun had begun its descent, lingering about the barn's entrance as if it had been waiting for him, balancing out some of the dread he carried with him. He stood just inside the door and surveyed the interior, trying to imagine the scene, reluctantly considering how it might have happened. If Margaret had been carried up the ladder, he reasoned she would have been unconscious. It might explain how she came to be wet. There could have been a struggle in the boat. She would have been lugged into the barn set down on the floor while he climbed the ladder and rigged the line and noose. John paused to gather in the scenario playing out in his mind, then walked to the ladder. Looking up he reconsidered the knot and half hitches over the beam, mentally climbing back down, unconsciously glancing at the bottom rung. He could not think how he had missed it. The answer was at his feet. The ladder had not been dragged into position, the only signs of disturbance were his own, Jane's footprints and the man who staged the hanging. Whoever carried her up that ladder had been strong, or there would have been drag marks leading from the outside where he'd left the ladder himself the week before. It was all the proof he needed, the missing link. Margaret could not have carried the heavy wood ladder from the outside into the barn. She would have had to drag it along.

Taking care not to disturb the scene more than he already had, John closed the barn doors and walked along the outside until he reached the site where he'd left the ladder. He was sure now that he had the right of it. It just remained now to find him, because as sure as Margaret lay dead in his house, a murderer was walking free, pretty certain he'd made it look like she'd taken her own life.

Chapter Twenty
The Coroner

Jim took off his hip boots, propped them against the railing and waited outside for John. He had agreed to sail the coroner and his assistant to the island, having spent a good deal of his time in Portland the day before explaining that access by steamboat was not possible. He wasn't entirely sure of his role beyond this gesture, knowing that he'd provided what he could, and that his measure of the man thus far left him wondering how he managed to get himself out of bed in the morning. He knew Jane would not stand for any foolishness where Margaret was concerned and guessed he might be just as well satisfied to wait.

Jane leaned against the kitchen workbench cradling a cup of morning tea in both hands, listening to the men's muffled conversation from Margaret's room. She had declined the offer from Mr. Shepley to be present, leaving it to John. Pulling the door to, John kept a hand on the doorknob, worried that Jane might change her mind and try to enter, while keeping a close eye on the two men as they approached the single bed. The assistant drew a notepad and pencil from his satchel and stood by, ready to record Shepley's remarks. Next to Shepley's rotund frame, the young man appeared waif-like, hinting at his character compared to Shipley, who seemed to dominate the room. At odds with its meager setting, taking possession of what remained of innocence. He stood quietly for a moment taking in her overall appearance, then removed his pocket watch, reciting the date and time in a businesslike tone, adding the location of the examination. Eventually, he lifted Margaret's hands, remarking that they appeared to be without injury. Leaning in, he reached behind her neck and ran his hand along the vertebrae, halting for a moment before continuing along her back. Standing upright, he pushed his glasses back, nodded to his assistant, then to John.

"I have concluded my examination here, Mr. Brown. Now, if you would please lead the way, I should like to investigate the scene of death."

John returned his nod and stepped back, allowing the men to pass, leaving the door ajar, knowing Jane would want to make certain all was left in proper order.

"We're just going down now," he said softly. "Perhaps you could invite Jim in for tea while he waits."

Shepley followed John along the path to the barn, his attendant trailing behind them. "This is not where we landed, Mr. Brown? I wonder if you could inform me as to how many such landing sites are available to this island? That is to say, if one wanted to gain access?"

John thought for a moment realizing the import of Shipley's questions. "An able man in a boat could land most any place along the shore, some places better than others. The backside is ledgy and a far distance from the barn. This beach and the one just below the house would be best suited, I should think."

"Right then, let's move on. Barn doors, open or closed, when your wife found her?

"Closed tight."

"Do you usually leave the doors open?"

"Open in the good weather. It was foggy, but there was no need to shut the barn up."

Shepley waited while John removed the braces and stepped back for him to enter. So, this girl, Margaret, I understand is not your natural child. How did she come to live with you?"

It was a question John had not expected. He rushed through the retelling of Margaret's story, feeling the words he'd chosen to describe their love for the girl wanting. He briefly wondered how the assistant would translate his speech and do it justice. He hoped it would be enough to satisfy the man who seemed to move on in a hurried manner from question to question.

"Now then, I'm going to ask my assistant here to climb up and take this down. No need to leave it any longer," he announced, craning his neck backward. "I want a look at that noose."

John held his tongue, judging that Shepley was a man who did not take kindly to suggestions or theories, waiting for him to form his own opinion about the knot. However, he also knew he would not let the man off the island without telling him what he thought. It seemed to John as if Shepley almost admired the handiwork as he examined the three turns forming the slip knot. "Not many bother to do it this way," he said, turning to face to John. "Yet, I suppose a fisherman would know how."

John understood the implication. He had surmised as much himself. "Just about any man on the water could tie that knot, used a lot in a gaff rig."

"I don't suppose, the girl knew," he hinted.

John shook his head. "She knew some to get by on, but that was beyond her."

"She'd been working at a hotel as I understand your wife to say. Is it possible a young girl like herself could have been broken-hearted? Some fella toss her over?"

"If there was, she never said, Mr. Shepley. We was pretty close knit and I guess she'd of said. I just don't know about that, but what I do know is you're thinking about it wrong-headed. I didn't realize it myself until I took another look. Now, I know we've scuffed it up pretty bad in here, but you need to hear me out. That fella you got with you, you think he could lift that ladder and carry it outside this barn?"

"That's an odd question, Mr. Brown. But to supply an answer, truly, I would be most surprised if he could."

"And," John replied, "if he might have a go, how would he go about it?"

"Why, I'm not sure. Harry, come over here a moment. Have a go at that ladder, would you?"

Harry handed the note pad to Shepley, then marched to the ladder. "Where would you like me take it, sir?"

"Just outside a bit, if you please, Harry."

John and Shepley stood back as predictably Harry was no match for the ladder, losing the balancing act at the outset. "I'm sorry, sir, but I think I'll need some assistance. This is a very heavy ladder."

Shepley looked John in the eye and asked his question. "What are you driving at here?"

"That ladder was outside the barn, Mr. Shepley. Margaret did not have the strength to move it. And if by some odd chance she tried, don't you imagine there'd be drag marks along outside and in the barn? Now, I know we walked all over in here, but outside is different.”

After close scrutiny of the barn area, Shepley sighed and pulled his handkerchief from his pocket to wipe his brow. “I’ll have to think about it Mr. Brown, but at the moment, even though you moved the body post-mortem, it appears that the circumstances regarding this girl’s death will require an inquest. I will send word down to you as to the date and time. In the meantime, you may wish to supply my assistant with the name, and whereabouts, of any man she may have been in contact with. Preferably, one strong enough to move that ladder.”

Chapter Twenty-One
The Inquest

Coroner Inquest into the death of Margaret Douglas
City Hall Portland, Maine: September 30, 1877

Silas Shepley, City Coroner:

Please state you name and residence:
My name is Minnie Barker and I live on Long Island, that's in
Casco Bay.

Q: Mrs. Barker, good afternoon. I understand you are in the
employ of Mr. Jenks proprietor of the Sunnyside House at Little
Chebeague?
A: Yes, that's right.

Q: And, how long have you been working for Mr. Jenks?
A: Goin' on into my second year now.

Q: Please describe the nature of your employment?
A: Head cook for the house.

Q: I understand that in your capacity as head cook, the deceased,
Margaret Douglas, worked under your direction?
A: Yes.

Q: How long had you been acquainted with the deceased?
A: She came to work for me summer before last.

Q: And did she stay the entire summer season at the Sunnyside?
A: Yes, 'cept when she went home to visit.

Q: Did she do that often?
A: Only when the work slacked here and there.

Q: When the work slacked, as you put it, where was her home?
A: Why, she lived out on Bates with Jane and John Brown. They were kind of like parents to her, I suppose. Poor girl was an orphan, I think.

Q: On the day in question, August 29 of this year, did you see and converse with the deceased?
A: Yes. She worked in the kitchen that mornin'.

Q: That was the last time you saw her?
A: That's right, she went with Esther and Nellie down to the meet the steamboat.

Q: And, approximately what time was that?
A: It was the 11:00 o'clock boat.

Q: Why did she go down to meet the boat?
A: There was supposed to be a gang comin 'from Portland, but they didn't come.

Q: When the gang, (checking notes) the Oddfellows, I see here, did not come…why was that incidentally?
A: Thick a fog and drizzlin', wasn't it.

Q: I see. So, when the planned guests did not materialize, what did the girls keeping company with the deceased do?
A: I heard from Nettie, that's Mrs. Jenks, that they put their heads together and hatched out a scheme to go on over to Nellie's for the day.

Q: And did they?
A: That was what they told me they was goin' to do.

Q: What time did the next steamer depart the island?
A: I wasn't there, so I'm not too sure 'bout the time.

Q: Doesn't the steamer run on a regular schedule?

A: Thick a fog. Anybody's guess when she might make an appearance, sometimes they don't bother to stop at all. Makes folks mad. I guess she finally did come though.

Q: If I am understanding you correctly then, the girls took the afternoon off, left on the steamer that came in sometime after eleven o'clock with the intention of traveling to Nellie's home.

A: That's right.

Q: And Nellie is, Miss Nellie Soule, who lives on the neighboring island Chebeague?

A: That's right too.

Q: Just one more question, Mrs. Barker. Did the deceased ever give you reason to believe she was unhappy or sad; that is, was she the sort of girl who might be apt to take her own life? I am just trying to establish her state of mind.

A: Good Lord, no, whatever kind of nonsense is that? Maggie was most content. Always had a smile. Poor girl.

***

Please state your name and place of residence:

Esther Johnson, Chebeague Island in the winter and Little Chebeague in summer.

Q: Esther, I understand that you and Nellie were friends with Margaret Douglas?

A: Yes, we was good friends.

Q: Mrs. Barker has testified that you three worked together that morning and then left the island on the steamboat sometime after eleven o'clock. Is this correct?

A: Yes.

Q: What was your intended destination?

A: We couldn't work, so we planned a trip over to Nellie's for the afternoon. Her mother makes the best pies and we thought it'd be kinda fun to do somethin 'different. Mag, that's what I called Margaret, she was for it.

Q: Did you stay together the entire time after you arrived at Chebeague?
A: We planned to, but Mag got homesick when we got there. She kept talkin ''bout seein' family and said she'd catch up with us.

Q: So, she did not accompany you and Nellie to Nellie's home?
A: No. She said she'd go on over to Lemuel's for a visit.

Q: Is Lemuel a relative or friend?
A: Well, 'course he is, he's her grandpa, kind of, I guess.

Q: Did you see her go into his house?
A: No, when we got there, me and Nellie started down the road, then she came out and talked to us.

Q: Was that the last time you saw her?
A: 'Fraid so.

Q: Just one last question before I call on Mrs. Brown. Did you ever have reason to think that your friend would want to take her own life?
A: Never thought much about it. But, I'd say Mag was mostly happy. She just liked to get off by herself sometimes.

***

Please state your name and place of residence.
Jane Brown, wife to John Brown, Bates Island.

Q: Good afternoon Mrs. Brown. Could you please tell the court your relationship to the deceased, Margaret Douglas?
A: She wasn't my own, came to live with us when her grandfather, Mr. Black, died.
Q: How did she come to live with you, where was her family?
A: We don't know. Mr. Black told us when they first came that they was from Harpswell.

136

Q: How long had she lived with you?
A: Since the old man passed away.

Q: Could you be more precise?
A: July or August of '65.

Q: I see. Why did you and Mr. Brown take on the responsibility of raising someone's child? Had she no relatives?
A: John asked around, but no one came forward. Her grandfather said her mother was dead and he was the only one left for family when they came to the island.

Q: On the day in question, I understand that you found the deceased?
A: I did.

Q: Could you elaborate?
A: I went down to the well that afternoon. We didn't expect her home.

Q: You did not expect her to arrive then?
A: No.

Q: Mrs. Barker has testified that she often went home on her days off. Can you verify that to be true?
A: Yes.

Q: Then why didn't you expect to see her that day?
A: We never knew when she might be comin'. It depended on when she could.

Q: The fog that week did not make you think she might arrive home?
A: I may have given it a thought. She didn't have a boat of her own use.

Q: Did she not arrive by steamer then?
A: No.

Q: Can you explain?

A: We use our own boat to get on and off the island. The steamboat lands over to Chebeague and stops some days at Hope.

Q: I see. So the only way to travel to Bates Island then is by private boat?

A: That's right.

Q: When you went down to the well that day, approximately what time was it?

A: Afternoon. Probably gettin' on to three o'clock.

Q: You cannot be more precise?

A: No, not in the habit of lookin 'out for the time of day.

Q: For what purpose did you go down to the well that afternoon?

A: To fetch water for the house. I'd been canning vegetables and used up all the water.

Q: When did you discover the deceased?

A: The barn is right there and I noticed the doors were shut. I thought it was strange as we usually left them open.

Q: What did you do then?

A: Climbed the ladder and cut her down.

Q: You mean, you thought she was still alive?

A: Yes, I thought she could be.

Q: When did you realize the truth?

A: Not long after. She let out a breath and I thought there'd be some hope, but she was gone.

Q: What did you do then?

A: I sat there for awhile. Held her head in my lap.

Q: Could you tell how long she'd been in this condition?

A: I couldn't.

Q: Did you think at the time that she had taken her own life?

A: I can't recollect what I thought. It may of run through my head, but in the end John and me thought somebody did it to her.

Q: Your husband was away that day?

A: He was. Talked it over when he got home.

Q: How soon after you discovered the body did your husband arrive?

A: Not long, perhaps an hour or so, gettin 'on toward dark.

Q: Did it not occur to you at the time that your husband may have seen her earlier?

A: No. He was outside of the island fishin'.

Q: Could he not have come in without you knowing?

A: He could have, but the boat was full of flounders.

Q: How can you be certain?

A: Mostly because he told me. You're not a fisherman are you Mr. Shepley?

Q: What I am, or am not, is not the issue here Mrs. Brown. I'll ask you more directly if you are certain your husband could not have inflicted this harm?

A: I am.

Q: Could anyone else have been on the island?

A: I 'spose.

Q: You've stated that the only way on and off the island is by personal craft, isn't it possible that someone, a stranger, landed on the island, took her life, then left?

A: I 'spose, but it don't seem likely a stranger would come to the island meanin 'harm.

Q: So, you did not see any person on the island that day then?

A: No.

Please state your name and place of residence:
John Brown, Bates Island.

Q: Mr. Brown, your wife has testified that she found Margaret Douglas, the deceased, hanging in your barn and that she cut her down from the beam. Can you support her testimony?
A: I can take her word for it.

Q: Where were you on the day in question?
A: I left home that morning to go fishin' off Half Way Rock.

Q: Were you gone all day?
A: Most of it. Got in just at dusk.

Q: Please describe what transpired when you arrived.
A: I pulled the dory into the shore with the intention of gutting fish there. Jane was there at the barn with Margaret.

Q: What did you do then?
A: As I told you when you came out to the Island, I settled Jane in and walked down to the barn.

Q: Did you think Margaret Douglas had taken her own life at the time?
A: No, I did not.

Q: Can you tell us why?
A: Because she was all soaking wet from head to toe.

Q: I'm not sure I follow you?
A: Stands to reason that she'd been overboard before.

Q: Before? Do you mean before she was hanged?
A: That's what I mean.

Q: You are of the opinion that someone hanged her to make it look like a suicide?
A: Yes.

Q: Is it not possible that she swam earlier, then hanged herself?
A: It is possible, but I don't believe so.

Q: Can you explain why?
A: That next day, I knew something was bothering me, but I couldn't think what it was. That's when I saw the ladder had been moved. You couldn't see where it'd been dragged along the outside or inside. Somebody stronger than Margaret had to have moved it. You see, there'd been no drag marks made.

Q: Are you sure the ladder was not inside the barn already?
A: I'm sure of it. I'd been workin 'on some shingles at the other side, week or two before, and I know where I left it.

***

State your name and residence:
Ira Gould. I live on Little Chebeague.
Q: Mr. Gould, Mr. Jenks has testified that you asked for the afternoon off to travel to Chebeague Island on the day in question. What was your business there?
A: I did. Left on the same steamboat as the girls and stopped off at Western Landing. Went to visit friends I have there.

Q: And is that friend present today?
A: Yes. Mose is here.

Q: At approximately what time did you arrive on the Island?
A: Boat was a bit late that day 'cause of the thick fog, I'd say sometime after noon.

Q: Did you go directly to your friend's house?
A: No, he was down to the shore in his fish house.

Q: How long did you visit with Mr. Dyer?
A: Not rightly sure we were kind of talkin', not payin 'attention.

Q: Is it safe to assume you spent two or three hours visiting with Mr. Dyer?

A: Could of been.

Q: You have said that the girls; Nellie, Esther, and the deceased, were on the same steamboat that afternoon?

A: Yes. They was up on the bow.

Q: When the steamer landed did you see them?

A: I might of noticed. I recollect, they all walked off together.

Q: To be clear, you walked to Mr. Dyer's fish house and they walked off in another direction. Is that correct?

A: Best I can remember.

Q: Mr. Gould, could you tell me if you know how to fashion a gaff rig for a vessel?

A: Mr. Shepley, any fisherman in this bay knows how. Hell, I'd lay odds that Jane even knows.

Q: Is it my understanding that you worked at the hotel with the girls?

A: I did.

Q: Let me be more blunt, Mr Gould. Did you form any sort of romantic attachment with Margaret Douglas?

A: She was a pretty little thing, but she was just a girl who worked there to me. They all were too young for me to take notice.

Q: What did you do when you concluded your visit with Mr. Dyer?

A: I walked over to Joel Ricker's to see 'bout using his ox team for Mr. Jenks.

Q: And did you talk with Mr. Ricker that afternoon?

A: I stopped by, but he warnt home, so I hung there a little while waitin', then took myself back across the bar. Tide was comin 'in.

Q: Where did you take yourself back to, Mr. Gould?

A: Went home across the bar. I had work to do.

***

State your name and residence:
  Moses Dyer, Chebeague Island.

Q: Mr. Dyer, Mr. Gould has stated that he visited with you on the day in question. Is that your recollection?
  A: Ira visited quite often and I'm fairly certain he did that day.

Q: Fairly certain. Could you not recall more clearly as to the exact day?
  A: I'm not the best at keeping track of that sort of thing, so it would have to be a guess.

Q: I see. Tell me, Bates Island is directly across from Chebeague, is it not?
  A: It is. You can see it plain as day.

Q: Do you travel often to Bates Island, Mr. Dyer?
  A: Often enough. My wife was Jane's daughter. So my boys go over some.

Q: And, you have been a widower for some years, I understand.
  A: That's right. Lost Rosy in '71. Not likely to forget that day.

Q: I also understand that you are a fisherman. Meaning you own a vessel.
  A: I do.

Q: Although you say you do not recall the date clearly, wouldn't you be likely to know if your vessel went missing?
  A: I would most likely know, but then again it would depend on whether I went down to the shore that day. If I went out. If it was as thick as they say, then I might not have checked on the dory.

Q: Do you have any reason to doubt Mr. Gould's testimony here today?
  A: I 'spose not. Always known him to be trustworthy on my account.

143

Chapter Twenty-Two
No Free Moments Left

Jane laid the last dress in the cedar chest, smoothing the fabric's surface, prolonging the moment when she would close the lid and surrender Margaret's scent to the darkness. Her hands recognized the common chore, yet her mind resisted each movement, belaboring the task long into the afternoon. October's blue sky had faded to gray outside the attic window, pressing a somber light into the room. She had been waiting for John to return. She knew she should light the lamps and prepare a meal, but she held the lid open, keeping the ties unbroken between herself and the girl she loved. It was not her way to leave a chore unfinished, even after losing Rosy, she'd taken hold and done what needed to be done. This time it was different. She could not shut Margaret out of their lives until she understood how. Rosy and Sarah were deaths she could understand, even as she railed against them, she could turn toward accepting each as a measure of natural causes. With Margaret's death, suspicion lingered in her mind, affecting the common passing of each day.

A single lantern perched in the center of the table, shared its space with two large soup bowls and a kettle of stew when John returned. He hung his coat on the door hook, reaching into the pocket to remove the paper. He dreaded this moment from his first reading, searching for answers during the sail back to the island.

"There isn't much there," he said. "Enough to tell us what he decided."

Jane sat and shifted the paper to the light, reading the report under the title "Brief Jottings".

"He could of sent word before now, John. What kind of a man lets a family grieve for weeks, then find out like this? There was nothing about that hearing to make a person think this," she said, tapping her finger against the offending type as she read it out loud. 'The

Telegraph learns that Miss Margaret Douglass, aged 19 years, residing on Bates Island, committed suicide by hanging. Disappointment in a love affair is assigned as the cause.' There's no sense to it. What's to be done?"

"I hate to say it, but there's an end to it. We got the inquest and I wasn't even sure he'd do that much."

"We know the truth, John. We can't just let it go like this."

"We know some of the truth. Not all of it."

"I think Mose knows more than he's letting on. Thought so from the outset."

"You know I faced him out on it. Skun out of it, except for the look on his face. Short of beating it out of him, I don't know what we can do."

"Maybe I could talk some sense into him. He owes us that much."

"And then what? Do you think the coroner will listen to a man who thinks he remembers, a man who has already vouched for another under oath. If he comes clean about Ira and the dory missing, if he knows that much, then we can go over there and roust the man out. Take Jim and the others," he suggested.

"I don't know, John. We don't have much proof unless Mose actually saw him rowing off into that fog."

John thought for a moment. "I'll ask around the shore, it may be that someone else was down there that day and saw something. We need that proof before we confront the man. I just can't see Mose keeping something like that from us. He knows what the girl meant to us. Perhaps he'll come around in time."

"That's true. We have to mean more to him than Ira does."

John reached over and withdrew the offending paper from beneath her hands. "Let's put this away for a bit, shall we? I'll think of something. I promise I won't rest until I know."

***

At daybreak John set the dory's main and sailed out of the cove. They had talked over the outcome of the inquest, concluding that finding the truth would begin with Mose. John hoped to find Mose alone, wanting to avoid the boys and Lemuel when he confronted him. He did not have a plan beyond looking him in the eye. If Jane was right about him holding back, then John thought be might persuade him to do right by the family.

Just outside Sand, John let out the main, catching the light wind from the northeast, sighting Mose's schooner at anchor. Coasting into the cove, he marveled at the morning sunlight conveying a reddish glow to the white-faced houses perched at the bank's edge, their rippled images reflecting across the water's surface. Beneath the high bank, the maple trees had dropped their red and orange leaves to the fish house rooftops and settled into the ledgy crevices above the high tide. It seemed the world was taking a moment to remind him, practically shouting for attention, calling out for sanity. How, he thought, could life turn about so abruptly, throw the wind across your bow and toss you off course so completely? Did it offer up this perfection to balance it all out? He could not pretend to understand it. He just knew it had happened to his family and despite how unjust it seemed, he was there for a good reason.

Wading out, John tied the anchor line to the painter and shoved the dory off into deeper water, adjusting the length of his stay to the tide, then walked along the beach to Mose's fish house. He thought it unlikely he would find him at the shore this early, but he wanted to make sure. Unlatching the door hook, he stepped inside, noting the mound of seine against the back wall and a pile of freshly tarred ganging on the workbench. A splotch of yellow paint smeared the work top and appeared to have been hastily wiped with a rag, then tossed to the floor. He could not say why, perhaps his inclination to tidiness, but something prompted him reach down and pick it up. It may have been the contrast of yellow and blue that caught his eye, however oddly out of place it seemed, he'd chanced upon a pale blue ribbon floating freely to the floor.

John leaned against the workbench, trying desperately to recall Ira and Mose's testimony at the inquest. Had they mentioned where they met? Specifically, did they say the fish house? He couldn't say for sure, as so much depended on his own words that day, he would have to rely on Jane's memory. His hand closed over the ribbon, holding it as if he were protecting a tiny bird that had fallen from its nest. He knew in his heart that it was Margaret's. He thought to use it when he talked with Mose; it would give him some proof that she had left from the cove. He wondered how Mose could explain its presence in his fish house. Although accustomed to the stench of fish and tar, the discarded clutter of the interior seemed so foreign to the soft ribbon he now tucked inside his vest pocket.

Stepping outside, he glanced down the beach and decided to move the dory out to deeper water before she grounded. He swore he would keep moving it down the beach, if it came to it. Moments later, he spotted Mose slowly making his way down the path to the shore, pushing a wheelbarrow with what appeared to be a bundle of loose shingles bouncing about inside.

"John! What brings you to this neck of the woods? She finally get sick of ya?"

"Wanted a word, Mose, if you got a minute."

"Sure, sure…what can I do for ya?"

John walked over to the wheelbarrow and guessed that Mose was about to do some patching up. "Why don't I lend a hand here, Mose. We can talk as we go along."

"That'd be great. I hate this job, but the rain's getting in and I want it snugged up 'fore winter trawling. I'll just fetch the nails and some hammers. Won't be a tic," he said, then turned to face John. "You're not here to patch up my fish house, so tell me straight what's bothering you. Is it Jane? She's not sick is she?"

"No, Mose. Unless, you count being upset about Margaret."

"Thought that was settled, John. Don't see what more I can add to it."

John weighed the moment, seeing in Mose an attitude of denial before he'd had a chance to ask a question. "You know the coroner ruled it suicide and laid the cause to an unhappy love affair. What do you know about that?"

"Not one blessed thing. How on earth do you imagine I would? I'm over here living to home, minding my own business, got nothing to do with that hotel and what might go on over there. I 'spose there might be some young man she didn't tell us about."

"You think it's likely Jane wouldn't know about it?"

"Probably not. But, it's more unlikely I would. What are you getting at here? You don't think I had anything to do with her do you? Because I can tell you straight to your face that you are barking up the wrong tree there. God, John, don't know how you could think such a thing."

"Jane and I keep thinking you know something about that day, even if it's something small, something you may have forgotten when you testified."

Mose shook his head, then started for the fish house. "I'll just get started here then, unless you want to keep yammering away at me some more."

"I do," John said, reaching into his pocket, holding the ribbon out to Mose in the palm of his hand. "Know anything about this?"

"What's that? A blue ribbon. Now, what do I know about that?"

"Found it in your fish house this morning. Wonder if that doesn't put Margaret there as well. If you talked with Ira the day she died, like you said, seems to me, that she was in there at some point before she got herself over to the island. And, since Ira doesn't have a boat of his own, it stands to reason you might of loaned him yours."

"You're doing an awful lot of supposin', John. You know damn well I'd of said if he took my dory. And that ribbon could of got there any time. You and Jane just need to settle to it, is all. She was just an orphan girl that you put up over there, and as far as I can tell, that's the end of it. Let it go. No good will come of it if you keep digging. Now, I got work to do."

"All right, Mose. I'll go, but you would do well to search your recollection of that day. If you say you didn't lend him your boat, I'll take your word on it. As far as you having a chat with Ira, Jane and I both think you made a mistake, thinking of another day. If you don't believe Ira is capable of harm, then you don't know him. Why do you think it took us so long to get here the day Rosy died? I didn't tell you then, because you was hurting. Ira had been through my dory, helped himself to things. We could of used a compass that day."

Mose brought his head up and stared at John for a long while, mistrusting the story. "Listen John, I know you've got Jane to contend with, and I feel for ya that way. She's a stubborn woman, and you've been good to me and the boys, helped us out and I'm grateful. But I can't believe either one of you would think I'd ever lay a hand on that girl. And, I don't believe Ira would neither, despite what you think of him. That's all I've got to say on the subject."

John listened to his justification, thought to say more, but he could see that Mose would just level another argument in Ira's defense. He did not fully understand why Mose felt he had to shield Ira from the truth, but he knew as sure as he was standing there, that was exactly what he was doing. He looked down the beach toward his dory, almost aground in the falling tide, then turned to Mose. "I know I said I'd go, but tell me one thing before I do. Where is he now?"

Mose pushed back his cap and squinted into the sun, tipping his head against the sudden glare, finally nodding toward the curve at the Sandy Point. "He's staying up at the old Johnson farmhouse, working for Joshua. Guess you could find him there."

John fixed his gaze on the shoreline, then on Mose. "He alone then?"

"Think so. Digging a cellar hole. Jenks got some idea of building a hotel, bought the place outright, so I hear."

"I'll be off then, Mose. But, don't suppose this is the end of it. I'll have my say with you both."

***

Ira swiped a sleeve across his brow and looked over the edge of the cellar hole. He and Joshua had been hauling rock from the shore below the fields for two days and he judged they would begin the footing by afternoon. It would serve as a root cellar for the hotel, providing just enough room for storage. Joshua had taken his plans for the foundation dimensions from the old Sunnyside. It would stand two stories tall with wide covered porches running along the front and two sides of the building. It seemed a lot of work to put into a gamble on the tourist business, but Ira guessed Joshua knew what he was doing.

The sun had begun its climb overhead, warming the fields and releasing the dampness from the soil in steamy clouds along the rim of the pit. Ira leaned on the shovel handle and surveyed the area, hoping Joshua would pronounce it deep enough for his cellar when he appeared with another load of stone. He took a last look around and decided that it was about right, allowing for headroom, then adjusted the ladder against the bank. With each step, he felt the gravel grinding beneath his boots, conscious of his weight loosening tiny fragments of soil scattering into the pit. He dipped his head toward the sound, correcting his balance, taking a firmer grip. Satisfied, he continued to climb until his eyes were level with the top. The boot heel struck his face in one blow, pitching the ladder sidewards, launching him to dirt floor. Stunned, he pulled himself to sitting position, shaking his head as if to summon a sensible sequence to the seconds before his fall.

John stood at the edge glaring down into the cellar hole, his eyes carrying the fire of his anger. "I'm sorry it didn't kill ya," he yelled. "Get up on your feet."

Ira stared for a moment, trying to focus on the face looming at the edge. "I know you're mad about the girl, but you're hunting the wrong man. I don't know what happened and that's the truth of it."

"That's odd Ira, second time I heard that today. You and Mose work that lie out together?"

"You can't just come around here and knock people all over the place. I'll have the law on you. It's best to leave before Joshua gets back, too. He's got law friends on his side."

"The law does not worry me, Ira. If they was worth their salt, you'd be in jail. I'll leave when you tell me the truth. If it was up to me, I just as soon shovel that dirt right back over your head and walk away."

"I'm sorry, John, but there is nothing for you here. Nothing to tell, but what I told in Portland."

"What you told was a lie and I'll find the proof. I know she was in that fish house before she left and I put you in Mose's dory with her. Far as that goes, you ought to be worried about Mose. Blood's thicker than water, they say. I don't know what happened, but I know you don't deserve to walk free. I hope her death eats away at you. I swear, I'll be watching. Sooner or later you'll trip up. No man can live with what you did."

"I'm not going to fight you over this, John. If you hadn't taken advantage, you'd be in rough shape right about now. Don't be a fool. It's over and done and I am not the one you ought to be mad at. Plenty of other ways to see it, but I can tell you and that woman have got me in your sights and there ain't a damn thing I can do about it. No matter how you rant and rave, there will be no ending to this story that'll satisfy you, or her. I'd be obliged if you'd leave me to hell out of it. If it comes to blows, next time you won't be so lucky."

***

John spent the remainder of the day letting the wind choose his direction. He'd let out the main and followed the shoreline of Chebeague to the east end point, listening to the quarrel within constructing the reasons for letting go, or hanging on. He knew where Jane would side. He knew how he thought about it would have to be settled before sailing home. He had taken what revenge he could. The man responsible for Margaret's death had shown his guilt and John had given notice. There would be no free moments left to the man. For all his days he would carry the burden with him. Every time he heard his name called out by another, he would turn and wonder if this time the truth would spill out for all to see. It would wake with him in the morning and drag sleep from his tired bones throughout the long dark nights; replicating image after image of that day. It was retribution of a kind, yet as such, did not exact a final moment; one a person could look to and call done. John knew that peace could not be won, or lost, or placed softly into another's soul, so you could stand back and point to it. He would do that for Jane if he could.

The story would be told again and again, of that he was certain. Long after he and Jane were settled in their graves, in times to come, people would remember. Old women at their kitchen tables would speak of it to their grandchildren, and they in turn would fix the story to fresh words, but it would always and forever follow the direction of their gaze out across the bay to Bates Island.

Chapter Twenty-Three
The Storm

Johnny cursed when his bare feet hit the floor. His grandfather's forecast the day before was confirmed, as the nor' easter slammed against the house rattling the windows in the open chamber. He hated to wake his brother sleeping soundly under his quilt, his breath frosting in the cold air, yet as the eldest, he knew his help would be needed. Thank god for longjohns, he thought, even if they did itch the daylights out of you. Fastening his overalls, he hurried to the stairs taking comfort in the fact that he could smell bacon frying below.

"Mornin'", he said, entering the kitchen, nodding to his grandmother standing at the stove. "Guess we're gettin 'it full. Where's grandpa?"

"Went down to the barn, wanted to check on the animals in this weather."

"I'll go down to help him then," he said, eyeing the bacon.

Jane smiled and pulled a plate from the open shelf. "Guess you could have a bite to eat first. Need to keep your strength up."

"That's so. Want me to wake Gus up?"

"No, let him sleep, there isn't much to be done, he can fill the wood box when he gets up. There's still plenty there," she answered, nodding in the direction of the box. "These are the sort of days make me think of how good we have it in the summer. It seems to me winter gets colder every year. When you finish up, perhaps you'd best go on down, he's been a while now."

Johnny shoved in a last bite, then reached for his coat as his grandfather rushed in stamping his feet on the kitchen rug. "Boys, that's one old gale out there, can't see for the blowin 'snow." I'll need you and Gus's help as soon as I warm up a little, that old dory's liftin 'right off the ground!"

Johnny hauled on his coat and headed out, calling over his shoulder to Gus. The hard driven snow stung his face and eyes as he struggled to gain balance against the wind, searching for a patch of orange in the whiteness of the morning. Wading through the drifts, he cupped his hands to his face, hoping to see through the impenetrable blasts of the snow storm. Judging that he was half way to the shore, he turned to see if Gus had followed, when he caught sight of the dory in midair, rolling like a piece of driftwood making for the island's crest. Backtracking, he reached Gus in time to take hold of the dory's painter as Gus struggled at the stern. Holding fast, the dory flipped again hauling the boys up through the field, skittering like feathers along the barren ridge. Unable to find their footing, they slid along, tumbling and standing at turns until Gus caught his line around an outcrop of ledge snagging her still. Taking a breath, Johnny looked at Gus down on his knees, blanketed in snow. "Hadn't counted on a Nantucket sleigh ride this morning!" he yelled, laughing at Gus still holding on. "Can you keep her taut' til I get some more rope? I think she'll likely go again if we don't lash her down!"

Gus nodded once." Think so, but be quick about it," he yelled.

Leaving his brother with the dory, Johnny headed for the barn, sighting his grandfather plowing his way through the drifts toward Gus. Once inside, he searched for any rope he could find strong enough to hold the dory until the nor'easter passed. Seizing an old mooring line and seine anchor he hurried to the door stopping to coil the length and throw it over his shoulder. Outside, the dory's bright orange patch again marked his way as he plunged through the knee deep drifts reaching them as another gust shook her hull. Circling the dory until he found her midsection, he looped the line around once, ran it out on either side and caught one end to the nearest scrub tree, repeating the process with the other end. Taking up the slack to ensure the fix, his grandfather sat back into the snow. The men waited to see if she would hold to as the gale raged across the field and the snow battered their faces. Johnny finally gave the nod.

"Boys mother, I tell 'ya, we'd of lost her for sure if it hadn't been for those boys fast thinkin'," John announced brushing snow to the floor.

"Gram, did you see us out there? She was takin 'us for some old ride along that ridge!" Gus said. "Only wish I'd thought to enjoy it more!"

Jane laughed and ordered them out of their wet clothes, pushing the kettle over to heat. "I saw you! Looked to me like you might blow right off the other side of the island! Don't recall ever seein' that before."

"No," John said, "And I don't think I want to ever again."

Jane poured the tea, thinking she might take pity on Gus and get the wood herself. "How's my chances on gettin' that woodshed door open in this gale?" she asked. "I think you boys have earned a stay in."

"I'll get it directly," John answered. "You stay right where you are. Just need a few minutes to get warmed up."

"Let one of the boys, John...John? What's wrong?" she asked, walking around the table to stand at his side.

"I'm fine, just had a twinge, is all," he said, reaching for his coat. "Be back in a jiffy."

Jane turned momentarily and smiled at Gus, but the face staring back at her blanched as he watched his grandfather's body slump back into his chair and his head pitch forward. Hurrying to his aid, Johnny and Gus, each took an arm as Jane gently lifted his head from the table. In that instant, the instant she had turned away, Jane thought, John had simply given over to a pain he would not, or could not, admit to feeling. Standing back, the boys, sought an answer in her shocked expression.

Looking about the room, as if checking to see if everything was in its place, she pulled at her apron front, straightened her shoulders, uttering simply, "He's gone." Her face held a final look, as if trying to reorder the balance in the room; the look that measured a life from one day to another and never asked to go beyond. The boys knew her strength, but needed comfort, needed her to tell them what they should do.

Gus held her gaze, seeing her through his tears and confusion, not sure if he should move to her side or stay with Johnny and his grandpa, hoping that his brother would say something to put it right, but Johnny held to the stillness as if part of a plan Gus had not fully worked out. The fire cracked and popped in the silent kitchen, becoming a foreign world, binding them together, one they could not yet take in as to the shape, or the scope of its boundaries. Grappling with the silence, Jane gradually regained an understanding of her role, a sense of what seemed most natural to the moment, thinking not of the boys, but of the man she had loved, drawing him into her arms. The boys withdrew to stand beside her, waiting for her to speak. For as long as they had known their grandmother, neither boy had ever heard her utter a word without a purpose. And so they waited, waited as the light dimmed, and listened into the quiet. Perhaps it was an awareness of the seeping cold, or the screeching wind, or the simple clearing of a throat that prompted her to move, they'd all lost the chance to say for sure, yet eventually they moved and Jane took hold of their needs.

"We'll see to him tonight, then. If there's a chance tomorrow we'll get word over to Mose. Think you can do that, Johnny?"

"Yes, mam," Johnny choked through his tears, "I think I can do that for you."

Part Four
1889-1890

Ira

Chapter Twenty-Four
Belt Buckle

Each morning the conversation in her head began with picking up the belt buckle. She tried to recall the day Margaret so proudly displayed her first purchases with her wages from the Sunnyside. She could see her plainly now as she admired her new shawl and skirt, and hear her asking if Jane thought it was too fancy for a working girl. She just couldn't remember the belt as clearly, try as she would. They'd laughed together at Margaret's stories about the women who walked the clam shell promenade, twirling their parasols, dressed in their finery. It had been such a sweet moment, a moment when life tossed you pure happiness.

Sitting now at the table, she could hear the boys stirring overhead. She placed the buckle to one side and rose to start the morning, catching a glimpse of Mose from the kitchen window making his way up the path.

"Mornin'", he said, pushing through the door. "See I'm just in time for a mug-up."

"Mornin 'yourself, sit down then, the boys are just getting up."

"What's this then?" Mose asked, holding up the buckle." Looks a bit worse for wear, doesn't it?"

"It didn't at one time, Mose," she replied, holding out her hand to him.

"Doesn't look too special, was it yorn?" he asked, flipping it over in his hand.

"Not mine, Mose, belonged to Margaret."

"Where's it been? Looks like it's been in the ground to me."

"Found it by the barn, near the foundation," she said.

Mose stared at Jane, then at the buckle, before handing it to her. She watched his face closely, wondering if its significance would register and was not surprised to see the shadow cross over his eyes. She had waited too long for him to visit the boys and now felt she had her answer. She would not wait any longer to hear him tell the truth.

"That's an odd one," he finally said. "She must have taken it off down there or somethin'."

"Is that what you believe, Mose?" she asked.

"Well, how am I supposed to know? Don't want to speak ill, but you and I both know she was a flighty one. I 'magine she used it some way, maybe to put 'round a cow's neck, then dropped it. You know how she was. Never thought ahead that girl."

"Might of been," Jane said, sitting beside him now and placing the buckle on the table before them. "But, I'd wager, there's more to it."

"I'm not sure I follow," he said.

"I think you do, Mose. I think you know just how it came to be there and there's no use not talkin ''bout it. I'd appreciate you tellin ' me the truth. You owe me and John that much."

"Nothin 'to tell. Here, what are you sayin'? You think Ira was here that day?"

"I do. Always thought it was funny the way you hedged away from bein 'certain when you was asked direct."

"I told what I remembered and that's an end to it. God, Jane, It's been neigh on to thirteen years now. You can't expect me to think back now better than I did then, can you?"

"I can and I do, Mose. Say you do try and remember. Could be you had it mixed up with another day he visited with you at the fish house. Could be you thought more about your friendship with Ira than you did about the truth. You might as well tell me, Mose. Sooner or later it's goin' to eat you up and you'll not be a man your boys might want to know."

Mose turned away from her accusations and rose from the table. "I'll not have you call me a liar. I'm no liar and you know it. You know me, kind of man I am."

"I think I always have, Mose. You have a chance now to make it right, not just for you, but for Margaret's sake. He brought you here, where you met my Rosy, where your boys call home. I want this settled once and for all. That buckle," she said, pointing to the table, " tells the story I 'magine happened that day. As soon as I picked it up I saw how it could of been between them. He's a strong man."

"That don't mean he brought her harm. I can't believe what your sayin', you've just got it wrong. Let it drop, it will do no good to go back over it. It's said and done with."

"It may be for you, it may be, but I am not through with it. If you are not willin 'to tell me, I can't force you, but I will be honest with you. I plan to see this through."

"Even if what you think is true, what can be done 'bout it now? No one will listen or care, I wager. Look, I understand she meant somethin' to you and John, but she was just a girl with no family, and now she's gone, way I see it."

Jane turned away hiding the disgust she knew was showing on her face. She had believed in the end that Mose wouldn't try to argue, that he'd be a better man. "That's that then. I know how you are 'bout it now. I'll not bring it up again," she said, flatly turning away. "I'll just hurry the boys along. More than likely they'll be surprised to see you."

Chapter Twenty-Five
The Wager

Ira stood apart from the group of men gathering outside Sinnett's Store wondering if he still had the strength, or will, to join in the game. While waiting for the afternoon mail boat, Will Staples had begun to brag that his grandfather was strongest man who ever lived, then braced himself for the argument sure to follow. It wasn't long before his cousin, Harry, jumped in to agree. His comment caused old Mr. Sinnett to remark that he'd heard the stories, but felt pretty certain that he'd need some proof.

"Now, how in the hell am I goin 'to give you proof?" Will asked, incredulously.

"Yah," Harry defended, "what's he supposed to do, you old coot!"

Old Sinnett smiled and leaned back against the porch railing. Pulling out his pipe he filled it to the brim, tamped it down with his thumb, then nodded to Ira. "Seems to me that fella over there's 'bout same size as old George. I reckon if he can latch on to that barrel, carry it up those steps, and set it down in my store, then I'll have my proof."

"Not the same thing at all," Harry said. 'Sides, Ira couldn't lift a feather, let 'lone that barrel full of molasses."

"Oh, you think so, do you, sonny," Ira bristled at Harry. "You better run on home to mommy, or stand to, 'cause there isn't a man here can do what he says."

"Grandad could of," Harry quipped. "And we all know you're just about as old as Methuselah anyway."

"Older than you, that's for sure, but lookin 'at you I'd say a fair wind would blow you under the keel."

Thinking back on it later, Will would tell you that he had known the direction it was taking, and also took the blame for having started it, but he'd done what men do when challenged. "Not havin 'you talk that way 'bout my family, Ira. And, I'm sayin', there's not a chance in hell you can give that a go. But, if you was a mind to prove me wrong, I'd take a wager on it."

Ira ran his hand across his chin stubble and walked over to Will. He hadn't had a drop to drink in weeks and he saw his chance to make a little change. Hands on hips he stood back sizing up the barrel's heft, then grasping the edge to judge a hand hold, he turned to Will and reached out his hand.

"I'll put a dollar on it, Will," he said.

"Right then, a dollar it is," Will agreed, shaking the proffered hand.

Ira nodded once, threw his cigar into the road, and strode back to the barrel, inspiring Harry's sudden leap to the steps calling for the crowd inside to come quick. It was a busy mail day and the store's popularity on such occasions often found many islanders milling about. Women and children, old men, and young girls, all came stumbling through the door just as Ira leaned over and hove to.

Scooching down, he reached his arms firmly around the barrel, his fingertips almost touching on the other side. Giving a loud grunt he attempted the lift. Those assembled watched as his face grew beet red and his legs trembled under the effort. As Ira strained against its bulk, the barrel budged an inch or two, then settled back into the dirt. Determined to take one more stab, Ira stepped forward, positioned his left hand on the upper rim and reaching down pulled up with his right. Off balance, the barrel rolled up onto its bottom rim causing it's contents to slop around inside. Everyone present that day to witness the event guessed that Ira probably hadn't heard the slopping, or he would have righted the barrel. But Ira, intent on winning the bet, continued to lift. The more he struggled, the more the molasses sloshed. Inevitably, Ira lost command of the situation as the barrel fell over to its side popping its cover, spilling its sticky brown sweetness into the road.

Old Sinnett took a final draw on his pipe, stuffed it into his vest pocket and ascended the stairs disappearing into his store as the crowed roared at Ira, sprawled out face down in sludge. Will sauntered over and offered a hand up, thinking how much his granddad would have enjoyed the show Ira had just given them today.

"Come on then," Will said, stifling laughter. "Let's get you cleaned up."

"Ain't no need," Ira said, getting up and walking over to the barrel. "I'll just carry this inside the store first."

Will had to admit that he'd not said anything about the condition of the barrel in their wager and so dug in his pocket to pay up. "You know Ira, not sure I'd of thought of that. Got to hand it to ya, it takes a mighty strong man to be laughed at like that and still see it through."

"It wasn't my idea at first, Will, but it seemed to me the only way I was gonna part you of that money."

"Take it then, you earned it," he said, glancing over to old Sinnett standing behind the counter chatting. "Isn't that Mose, Ira?" he asked. "Bet he'll be sorry to have missed the fun."

"Probably so. Sure the old man's givin 'him an earful. Better go take my medicine," he said.

"Ira! Heard you've been entertaining this afternoon," Mose said, slapping him on the shoulder. "Boys I'd like to of seen that, I'll tell ya."

"Got it inside, just not quite like I planned."

"Planned, you damned fool," old Sinnett piped up." I've half a mind to charge ya for that molasses. I'll just take it out of your next catch, what I'll do."

"Now listen, it was your idea, in case you forget," Ira challenged.

"All right, all right, just next time you come 'round, I spect a nice halibut for my troubles."

Leaving him to stew, Ira walked with Mose down to his dory, holding on to his back complaining. "Tell ya one thing, Mose, I could sure do with a drink. Don't have any hidden up for'ard do ya?"

Mose shook his head, knowing there'd be nothing for it but to give Ira what he needed. After a rummage in his forward cubby, Mose handed Ira the whiskey bottle, then sat down in the stern to wait his turn. Passing the bottle back and forth, they shared a laugh about Ira's mishap, then Mose, thinking of the dwindling light, announced that he'd be heading home.

"Where you off to then?" Ira asked. "You still settled in over to Bates with that old biddy mother-in-law of yourn?

"Not tonight, I'll set for Chebeague. Where you hang your hat now? Haven't seen you 'round much?"

"Here and there," Ira laughed. "Mostly there," he said, enjoying his joke. "Don't suppose you'd put me up for the night?"

A quick look at Ira told Mose what he had guessed when he'd first set eyes on him at Sinnett's. Ira's hand to mouth living was conspicuous. Even if he took into account the day's accident and the molasses stains, he judged he'd been wearing the same clothes for weeks, if not longer. He had lost his paunch and his once muscled arms hung as if unattached, even his grin drooped in a one-sided effort to maintain its usual smirking self. If he was sure of anything, Ira had most likely been working on the docks mending nets for enough to buy his liquor and sleeping it off in the sheds. Since that morning with Jane, he hadn't been able to shake the looks she'd given him, now he was face to face with the man she'd accused of murder.

"I don't know Ira, I'm still bunking in at my folks when I'm not on the schooner. I just don't think they'd like it much," he said. "Haven't you got somebody here to put you up?"

"After today? I'd be lucky to sleep with old man Sinnett's dog tonight. Look, don't want to be a trouble to you, Mose. God knows you've helped me out plenty with that mess a few years back, and I appreciated you standin 'up for me. Boys, they was out for blood that crowd."

Mose looked at Ira and saw the man Jane had seen, a man capable of doing a wicked deed and then telling himself he didn't. Seeing him now made that realization all the more truthful.

"Ira, I've got to tell you plain," he began. "I just can't see my way clear to have you 'round the family, it's just that there's still hard feelin 'that way."

Sitting comfortably in the bow, Ira pitched forward and glared at Mose. "What in hell are you on 'bout, man? I thought we was friends. It's that old bag over there isn't it? I tell ya, never liked that woman, she was always on me for somethin', never once give a fella a chance." Ira's voice boomed, echoing across the water, his hand lurching and sloshing whiskey in emphasis. "Never liked her," he said, repeating himself. "I know you got to deal with her, but that should not matter between us, should it?"

Mose struggled with his growing dislike for the man and his need to be truthful, eventually deciding that Ira should be aware of Jane's suspicions. "Ira, I think you know that when I spoke for you that day in Portland, you know, before the coroner, I might have given them to think we were together that day. Might have gotten the days mixed up, 'cause you came by many a time, but now there's somethin 'come up."

Ira put the bottle to his lips, hauling the burning liquid deeply down his throat, lost in its sensation, then balanced the bottle on his knee. Adjusting his seat, he looked at Mose sitting in the stern, then focusing on the bottle again, he took another long pull.

"I can't tell you how much I appreciate this, Mose. It sure does make things go smooth. You've always been a good man, and I'm that obliged to you."

"That's good of you to say, but it doesn't change things. I talked with Jane and she's not sure but you didn't have somethin 'to do with Margaret, after all's said and done."

"What are you on 'bout now? That's over and done with. You told 'em. That's the end of it as far as I can tell. Said 'n done."

"Might 'of been, but Jane's found a belt buckle belonged to her."

About to drink, Ira settled the bottle back to his knee and fixed a stare. "What belt buckle?" he asked. "You tellin 'me she rummaged 'round and found a belt belonged to her and now wants to, what, to do what?"

"It wasn't in the house, Ira."

"Where then? She didn't have no belt on."

"Maybe, maybe not," Mose said, thinking he'd pushed Ira too far. "I'm not the one doin 'the accusin 'here. I wanted you to know. She's that riled up about it. Oh, she won't go on with anything now, been too long. Might be you ought to think about gettin' onto a vessel before the winter."

"Ha," Ira laughed, waving him off, "I'm not worried 'bout all that mess, you said it yourself, it's said 'n done, said 'n done. If she was here right now I'd tell her, don't you think I wouldn't. Had nothin 'to do with that girl and that's a fact. That old bitty just sittin 'out there on that god forsaken rock thinkin 'up all manner of shit. She's that bitter 'bout things she is," Ira said, lifting himself shakily from the foreword seat. "Guess you're right 'bout tonight, I'll go find me a bunk here."

"All right," Mose said, setting his oars, as Ira stumbled his way onto the dock. "Just keep in mind what I said. I mean it. It's up to you what you do, but if I was you I'd be gettin 'me a berth."

Ira stared down at Mose, tipped his hat, smirked, then walked off down the dock.

Chapter Twenty-Six
Esther

Jane watched the gulls sailing overhead, following the high currents off the strong northeast wind. Clouds hovered ominously over the islands, forecasting a day of rain. She had hoped to go out to her traps, left too long to set over, but white caps lifting off the water changed her plans. Having made her decision, she turned back toward the house, resigned to a day of inside work. There was still plenty to do, but she preferred being out on the water to a day cooped up with thoughts of Margaret's death, gathering like the storm overhead.

She made her tea and sat down at the table, reaching as she often had these past months, to hold the buckle, turning it over and over in her hand as she thought about the best way forward. Caroline's letter the week before confirmed what she had thought all along; the belt had not belonged to Rosy. As for Mary, she awaited a letter. If, as she thought, it belonged to Margaret, then she resolved to talk with Mose again. Although she understood his reluctance to change his testimony, she still felt he might tell her the truth. It was all she had.

Listening to the gale outside, she thought of other days like this when she and John had preferred to take a day together and sit before the fire to talk. His days as an English sailor had given her a chance to see the world she could only try to imagine. Stories of sailing to the West Indies, even the docks of London, with his descriptions of strange people and how they dressed in foreign places had fascinated her. It often made her wish she'd been born into a world where women could do the things that men did. Even though she'd lived a life unlike most women, doing the work alongside the men, she still understood the lure of far-off places and how a person might learn and change from those experiences.

The rain let up in the afternoon and patches of sun settled on her kitchen wall, turning her gloomy thoughts to the outside. Taking

John's old coat from the hook, she heard a knock at her door. She did not recognize the young girl standing on her porch, but welcomed a visitor and a chance to talk with another human being. Mose had started taking the boys with him on fish trips and she'd begun to realize how much she missed them. Throwing the door open wide, Jane stepped onto the porch noticing a young man standing by his dory at the shore.

"Hi, Mrs. Brown? I'm Esther, Margaret's friend from the Sunnyside?"

"Well, so you are," Jane said smiling, beckoning for her to come in. "What can I do for you?" she asked.

Reaching under her cloak, Esther withdrew a parcel wrapped in brown paper secured with twine. "I've been holding on to this for years and got to thinking it wasn't right for me to keep it. It was Mag's. See, I'm getting married soon and I was lookin 'through my trunk for some of my things from when I worked there, and this was at the bottom," she said, holding the parcel out to Jane. "Didn't seem right for me to keep it, and I'm sorry I did for so long, but here."

As she unwrapped the twine binding the parcel, Jane sensed the value of the gift she'd been handed. She held it tenderly in her hands feeling a mingling of joy and sadness. Lifting the embossed cover of Margaret's diary she glanced at the tiny script, recognizing Margaret's hand, then gently closed it shut.

Sensing her discomfort, Esther spoke softly to the older woman, understanding in that instant why Margaret had always longed to be home.

"I'm so sorry," she said, kindly, "I didn't mean to make you sad."

"No, that's all right. You did the right thing."

"Well, I'm glad of that. Will, he's my intended, said I shouldn't, but he agreed to bring me out just the same. And, you need to know, I haven't once read a word of it. None of my business to have even taken it in the first place, but with Mr. Jenks movin', I couldn't just leave it behind for someone to read. I mean, someone who didn't even know her like I did."

"Did you come all the way out here to bring me this?" Jane asked.

Judging she'd not been mistaken about her trip, Esther warmed to the old woman, feeling in her presence the connection she'd felt with Margaret.

"If you don't mind my sayin 'so, I never knew a girl so fond of anyone as she was of you and your husband. Talked about you the whole time, she did. Always lookin 'for a chance to get back here. 'Course it's a little out of the way for me. Will and I are plannin 'on movin 'up to the city. He's goin 'to work at the big hotel right there on Congress Street. Me too."

"Appreciate what you said about her," Jane said. "She's never our own, you know, but it felt like it."

"I'm very sure of that, Mrs. Brown. Never any doubt about it. I just wish things had worked out different. I hope that's all right to say."

"There's no harm." Jane said, absently reaching for the buckle.

"Say!" Esther said, pointing to the buckle, "that's Margaret's!"

Jane looked at her and back at the buckle in her hands. She'd grown so used to taking it up, she hadn't realized that she had, until the significance of Esther's remark cleared her mind.

"Are you certain?"

"Sure am! Remember the day she bought it, 'cause she was that nervous about tryin 'it on in the store. 'Fraid someone would think she was tryin 'to steal it she said. But I told her it was fine and she decided right there to have it. It was the first time we took the steamboat into the city and that was bad enough, she was nervous as an old hen. Boys, I tell ya, I surely do miss that girl. She was the best friend I ever had. I've never met anyone like her since."

After tea, Jane walked with Esther down to the shore to see her off. Her young man sat on the bow dangling his feet in the water, keeping the dory from grounding out. He greeted them smiling into the sun, reminding Jane of Jim. She wondered if he was some relation to the Johnson's. Watching them sail off past the point, Jane wandered over the beach and up to the woods, following their progress. She wished it was Margaret in that dory, happy to be starting her new life in the city with a young man so sure of their future.

***

Jane spent the weeks that followed Esther's visit mulling over her comments about Margaret. Sometimes she imagined her contentedly living her own life, eventually returning to her own sorrow for the

167

losses she'd known. Passing her days alone, she held to routine, dreading the feel of September's chill just months away. She found that in her solitude, memories poured out of every moment she breathed in and out. In the evenings now when she lit the kerosene lamp she saw her mother's hands lighting the flame and replacing the chimney, or John laughing at Rosy struggling with her books. More and more she walked the island picking up stones and driftwood, wasting afternoons, sitting idly by, while leaving her chores undone. She began to understand that she did not know how to be alone. There had always been someone to do for; a chore to complete, a dinner to make, a dress to sew. It was all so new and strange. She wondered why her freedom did not bring her happiness, some sense of release, yet in her liberation, she longed for the chains that had defined her. Without them to tell her what to do, she lingered more often in the past, unable to imagine the shape or dimensions of the time to come.

***

In late August, while strolling the back shore, she spied Mose's fishing schooner just sailing past the Cow. She waved, knowing they could not see her, yet she reached both arms high and flapped them about like an old coot drying its wings, making her smile at herself. If she'd been lost for awhile, she thought, so be it. Whatever she'd been going through she straightaway expected would change, she'd see to the rest of her days the best she could, because here at least she was home.

Arriving at the shore to wait, she realized that she was actually hungry and thought of what she had on hand that would do to feed them all, finally settling on the cod she'd salted drying on racks behind the shed. She'd boil potatoes and the cod, fry pork scraps and scrounge for greens left over in her garden.

Looking across her table at the boys and Mose, devouring their meal, she felt a contentment she'd not known since they left. It was good to have them home safe; hearing her mother's voice telling her to count her blessings.

"What's so funny, Gram?" Gus asked.

"Oh nothing, just thinking of what my mother used to say about counting my blessings. Made me smile to think how I used to get mad at her about it. It was silly, now that I think of it."

"If that's all it takes to get you laughin'," Mose said, "then I'll have to remember it."

"Go on with you. I laugh when there's somethin 'funny to laugh at."

"No, you don't, not really, Gram. Sometimes you get right sad, I reckon'," Johnny remarked.

"Well, I'm not now, so there's an end to it. How long will you be home this time?"

Mose stretched out his legs and reached for his pipe, wondering if he should mention what was on his mind, then looked to Johnny and Gus." I wonder boys if you might go on down to the barn and see to things for your grandmother, since she cooked you up such a good meal?"

"Come on Gus, he wants us out from underfoot so's to talk somethin 'over."

Mose looked closely at Jane, knowing that how she held her mouth was either a sign to proceed with his talk, or hold off for a better day. Judging that her mood had lasted, he began.

"I've been thinkin ''bout that will we talked 'bout. I've worried some that I couldn't pay the taxes, but since doin 'so well lately with the boys helpin 'out, I guess, well perhaps it'd be a good idea, that is, if you still want to."

Jane stopped clearing the table and pulled out her chair to sit. "I do want to. And if I can't keep on here with you and the boys gone for long stretches, I'll go live with Mary and Jacob."

"I think it could work out for the boys. They'd get Rosy's share and Mary could have the money. You trust me to don't you?" he asked, hoping she'd say she did.

"I made up my mind 'bout it long time ago, just waitin 'on you, Mose."

"Good, good, it's settled then. What do I need to do?"

"I'll sail the dory over to Joshua's and take the steamboat up. Make it legal. It will be in city hall if you need it. In the meantime, you might want to take on some things around here before too much longer."

"Tomorrow soon enough?" he laughed.

"That'd be just fine, Mose, plenty soon enough. No matter what's 'round the corner, we'll just have to face it when it comes."

***

As soon as Mose settled the schooner into a berth, he saw him. Unable to pretend that he hadn't, he walked over to him where he sat on a trawl tub smoking a cigar. Ira hadn't changed much since he last saw him at Sinnett's store covered in molasses and drunk on his whiskey.

"Mose, you old dog, you. How's it goin'?"

"Oh, can't complain, Ira. Ya'self?"

"Just fine 'n dandy, fine 'n dandy. Been workin 'steady now for months. Got nets in need of mendin'? 'Cause I'm your man."

"I think that could be arranged. You got time?"

"Nothin 'but," Ira said, picking up his needle and walking over to the nets he'd left hanging to dry. "Them's Doughty's rig," he said, nodding toward the schooner next to Mose's.

"Good to keep busy, Ira," Mose replied, heading off. "We'll start on those nets tomorrow, if that's agreeable, got some business in town."

Ira's head shot up hearing Mose mention business, wondering what scheme he might wrangle to his benefit out of Mose's business. "Wait up a minute," he yelled, "since you're goin 'that way, mind pickin 'me up some hooch? Just the cheap stuff, I'm not a rich man like you fishermen, ya know."

"Sure, Ira," he said, holding out his hand. "But, If I remember rightly 'nough, you already drank one off belonged to me, so I'll be expectin 'some coins for my trouble."

"That's the way it is, is it? Look, I'm a bit short at the moment, but maybe I can work it off on the nets. You know, kinda barter?"

"Figured you'd say that," Mose laughed, sizing him up." Ira, there's one thing 'bout you a man can always count on."

"Yah, and what might that be?"

"You never change," Mose said, laughing again, walking off down the wharf.

At dusk, Ira stowed his mending needle and twine under a tarp and sat down to wait for Mose, his thirst growing by the seconds. He was about to leave when Mose popped around the corner carrying a brown paper bag.

"Now, there's a sight for sore eyes!" Ira called. "I was beginnin' to think you'd scarpered out on me."

Sitting down beside him, Mose pulled the whiskey bottle from the bag and yanked the cork out with his teeth, taking a long pull for himself before handing it to Ira.

"What kept you so damn long?" Ira asked, gulping down whiskey.

"Just some paperwork, nothin 'to concern you 'bout," Mose said. "Think you might want to take it easy there, Ira. That's not water your haulin' down your gullet, you know."

"Don't be worryin 'ya'self none, I know what I can handle, sonny."

"So long as you do then. I'll just be puttin 'out for the island and see you in the mornin 'if you're still willin', or able."

"I'll be here, don't you worry. "Say, why don't I come 'long with ya, so's you won't worry so much 'bout me?"

"I don't think that'd be such a good idea. I'm livin 'on Bates now with the boys, and if my memory is right, you aren't the most popular fella out there."

"Is that old gal still kickin?" he asked, taking another drag." Once was a time I'd given my eyeteeth to live out there. Even asked old man Brown for that place out on the point, but he wouldn't go up against that old witch for nothin'. Kicked me right off," he said, shaking his head.

"You weren't very nice to her. She was just lookin 'out for her own. Lot a good it did her."

"What'd 'ya mean by that?" Ira asked.

"I mean, you damned fool, that she thinks you killed Margaret. What else do you think I mean?"

Ira lit his stogy and gazed up at Mose, tipping his head struggling to focus. "You still on 'bout that? I told ya', she didn't have no belt on that day, if that's what's botherin 'ya."

Mose stood gazing down at Ira, trying to figure out if he was drunk already, or if he was just plain ignorant, then stepped closer to face him.

"Looked at her that close, did ya?" he asked.

"On same boat weren't we. Long time ago. That was a damn shame, she was one pretty lass and I don't mind sayin 'so. Fella could of been happy as a clam livin 'with a girl like her. That pretty."

"Fancied her then? I wondered 'bout that," Mose said, encouragingly. "Jane always said you had eyes on her, but I never thought so. She was too young for ya. Well, it's all over now. You made sure of that, didn't ya? Don't matter now, Ira, it's said and done with, like you said."

Ira rested his bottle on his knee, then looked up at Mose. "I never meant to harm her, Mose. I don't get a minute's rest from it."

Mose stood for a moment searching for the right words to say to a man so broken down. He'd never thought that Ira amounted to much, but he never wanted to believe he'd killed her. Looking at him now he knew there wasn't much to say to him. Ira lived rough, he concluded, and others only came into his life if he could find a way to use them. Turning away, he walked across the wharf and stepped onto his schooner, leaving Ira to his drink and sorrow.

***

That evening, after the boys had turned in for the night, Mose told Jane the truth. He watched as her face changed, turning toward darkness as her anger grew. Uncertain that he'd made the right decision, he worried what she might do or say, but held his ground as she struggled with the reality of his candor.

"Did he tell you how?" she finally asked, searching his face for facts she knew she really did not want to hear, or live through again.

"I didn't think it was a good idea to ask," he simply stated.

"I want to know, Mose. I want him to pay for what he did."

"He's payin'. Pitiful to see him now, sittin' up in those docks, drunk everyday, nowhere to sleep. He's payin, plenty."

"That may be, Mose, but we know the truth now and what he's payin' isn't plenty. There's enough now to bring it to those who can take care of it."

"What are you sayin'? What can be done after they looked into it already? It's been too long a time for them to open it up. And what good would it do? Just stir things up, way I see it."

"The good, Mose, is just that. We can't go on livin' with this lie. Neither can he." Jane stared at Mose, unable to believe he could not see the anguish Margaret's death had caused her. Finally, she stood and quietly pushed in her chair, vacantly studying the things she touched everyday as if they might yield up an answer to Ira's meanness, as if she might turn suddenly and she'd see what was to be done. She wanted to count on Mose, but needed to find a way to help him see the right path, she felt she needed to as well.

Chapter Twenty-Seven
A Visit to Hope

Spring did not visit the island early this year. The morning's snow clung to the spruce trees' branches, occasionally drifting down in clumps past the kitchen window. Stamping his feet, carrying another armload of wood, Jim dumped the lot into the wood box, then lifted the stove lid poking in a few pieces of birch. His guest sprawled in the rocker, snoring in the warm kitchen, as Jim's wife cast sporadic baleful glances in his direction. She had not been at all pleased last night when Jim came walking through the door with Ira in tow. Her disapproval had begun to show in the little ways and Jim had learned over the years of their marriage not to treat it lightly. His only choice now was to wait until Ira left. In the meantime, he'd have to take his medicine as she tended to parcel out the bitterness in bits and pieces. Now and again, a cupboard door would bang shut, china would collide, or she'd simply walk past him, pulling her face into an exaggerated scowl. Oh, the storm was brewing. Jim promised himself that this would be the last time Ira would talk him into bringing him home.

As dinnertime approached, Sarah reluctantly set the table for three, flinging the dishes onto the table, while Jim did his best to stay out of her way. Finding there was little to be done, he managed to be just getting out of her way at every turn. As afternoons go, Jim thought, there couldn't be any way to make it worse, that is, until her heard voices coming from the path and saw Mose and his boys plodding through the snow. Whatever had brought them out today in the cold and snow would either lighten the mood, or make his life hell for longer than he'd anticipated.

"Hello the house!" Mose called, pushing in.

"Come right in," Jim said, glancing over his shoulder at Sarah. "Welcome strangers. To what do we owe this pleasure?"

Mose grinned widely, as the boys stomped in behind him, noticing Ira snoozing in the corner. "Sleepin 'it off?" he whispered to Jim.

"That's the sum of it, I'm afraid."

"Bum a ride?" Mose asked, nodding in Ira's direction.

Jim shook his head and frowned. "I felt so damn sorry for him, couldn't just leave him on the wharf."

"I know, Jim, I know, but you can't start bringin' him home either. He'll make a nuisance."

Jim lowered his voice, then glanced at Sarah. "Don't I know it. Sarah's fit to be tied," he said, smiling brightly at Sarah.

Returning a tight-lipped smile to Jim, then swiftly changing it to sweetness, she walked over to join them. "Hi boys, Mose," she said. "My, but this an awful day to be out, hopefully there's nothin ' wrong."

"No, no, nothins 'wrong, but the weather, and need for company besides ourselves. Thought you might be feelin 'the same," Mose replied.

Jim cast a weary eye toward Sarah, hunched his shoulders as if to say, it's not my fault this time, and asked them to stay for dinner. Although he meant well, he had of course, not given thought as to how they were to feed six with a meal prepared for three, as that thought was just now taking shape in Sarah's mind.

"Jim," she said, genially, taking his arm and guiding him to one side, "might I have a quick word?"

Mose chuckled as they left the room, knowing that showing up at dinner time was not exactly the best of plans, yet he'd needed to get off the island and this was his best idea. When they returned, Jim made his excuses, then disappeared down the cellar stairs returning with a canning jar of dandelion greens, left over from last spring, and another of canned mackerel. "This will have to do for extra sustenance," he said, twisting the lids free. "Think it will be all right?" he asked, turning to Sarah.

"Have to be," she said, "but it's goin 'to be one sorry excuse for a meal. Never served mackerel and ham together before."

The men settled at the table, as Sarah continued her campaign of abuse, taking out on the pots and pans the treatment she was planning for Jim. Between words with Mose, Jim wondered how it was possible she did not recognize her childish behavior.

During her rampage, Ira roused in the chair, opening his eyes to a world he apparently didn't recognize. Blinking, he rubbed his ruddy face, ran his hands through his greasy hair and stood to the amazement of those watching him closely.

"What?" he said. "What ya all lookin 'at? Never seen a man sleep before?" Grouchy from sleep and a powerful hangover, he scraped a chair back from the table and sat down, resting both arms on the tabletop.

Jim quickly glanced over to Sarah, but she was mercifully standing with her back to Ira's ungainly performance. Turning to Ira he leaned over and spoke quietly. "Think you might want to wash up 'fore dinner, Ira?"

"That's all right, Jim, don't matter," Ira said, eying the dinner Sarah set before them. "Sarah, my girl, you've got no idea how good that smells. Can't recall when anything looked that good to me," he said, turning to smirk at the boys, "unless you consider that pretty lass I was seein 'in town last night."

Jim dished out a portion of ham onto his plate, then handed it to Gus who had been unusually quiet, as had Johnny. They knew better than to bring up their grandmother's name in Sarah's presence, but Jim was their grandfather, and they never understood what exactly to say when confined to the house.

"Say," Ira said, suddenly casting a glance about the table, "it just dawned on me that Jim's your granddaddy. How 'bout that? Never thought much 'bout it 'til now. Don't that beat all," he concluded, shaking his head.

Jim looked over to the boys and smiled. "Don't pay him no mind. Crazy as a coot."

Jumping in, Mose complimented Sarah on her cooking, then suggested the boys could help with the washing up as the three men moved into the parlor for their smoke. Walking to the mantle Jim struck a match on the fireplace stones and lit his pipe, speaking around the cloud of smoke as he drew in. "You know, Mose, I don't quite buy your story," he said slyly.

"Oh?" Mose said, looking up." And what story might that be?"

"You know, the one 'bout you bein 'tired of your own company."

"Tell the truth, Jim, I have been botherin ''bout things some, but I think I'm comin ''round to it."

"Do you want to talk about it? I don't mean to pry into your business, just say if you don't want to."

"No, no, that's all right. You ought to probably know anyway as the boys are involved in it." Jim propped his elbow on the mantle and looked quizzically at Mose.

Hesitantly, Mose began. "Seems, Jane's gone and signed the place over to me in her will. I didn't ask for it. The idea's hers alone. I've been worried 'bout the money end of things, is all."

Jim stood mulling over Mose's news, then realized how intently Ira had been listening to the conversation. He judged that Mose would not have spoken the news, if he hadn't wanted Ira to know, yet he felt uneasy talking about family in front of him. "Listen, Ira, seems to me you could pay for your suppah. How 'bout goin 'out to the woodshed for a load, that is, if you're feelin' up to it."

Ira stared at Jim for a moment, peeved that he'd devised a way to get him out of the room. "'Course, no problem, could use some fresh air," he said, getting to his feet.

Hearing the door close shut, Sarah walked into the room. Making her apologies said she was tired and would be off to bed early and that the boys were content playing caroms at the kitchen table. Once alone, Mose leaned forward in his chair and confided his real concerns.

"Jim, I know there's not a thing you can do about it, but I need to talk it over with someone," he said quietly. "Jane's got it into her head to bring back up this business 'bout Margaret all over again and I'm that worried 'bout her."

Jim sat down next to Mose and stared in disbelief. "Has she lost her mind then?" he asked.

"Not that I can tell. She was so cut up 'bout it, it gutted her when she died. And, that fella stayin 'under your roof, 'cordin' to Jane, got a lot to answer to."

Jim's quiet nod encouraged him to continue. "She's got hold of a belt buckle belonged to her, to Margaret. Found it by the barn where the ladder was leanin 'that day. You'll remember her John always maintained there was no drag marks which made him think it was someone capable of lifting, instead of draggin', like a woman might."

"But, Mose, this came out in the inquest. I was there and heard him. The buckle could of been from any time she was 'round there, couldn't it?"

"That's what I said, but she's now got hold of a diary of hers and in it Margaret tells 'bout him," Mose said, gesturing over his shoulder with quick nod at the door. "She tells 'bout him pesterin' and followin' her 'round all the time."

"Still, that don't seem 'nough to me, Mose. Is there anything to it?" Jim asked.

Mose stood and walked over to peek into the kitchen. Satisfied that Ira had not returned yet, he said softly, "He told me he did it."

"Who? Ira?" Jim asked, raising his voice in disbelief.

Mose nodded. "I'll be settin 'off early, Jim. Jane's got it into her head to turn him in. Said she was goin 'tomorrow. Thought you might have an idea what to do."

"Whose goin 'where tomorrow?" Ira asked, coming into the room. I knew you two'd be chawin 'on some good stuff whiles I was gone."

"Nothin 'Ira, we was just talkin ''bout somethin 'happened long time ago.

"Somethin 'happen with me in it, is what I think."

Ignoring Ira, Mose stood and walked out into the kitchen with the boys.

Jim wondered how he could have have been so sure it wasn't Ira. They'd fished together, and if he was honest, he thought Jane had jumped to conclusions out of dislike for him. Now, he knew the truth and it unnerved him to think Ira would be sleeping under the same roof tonight. As soon as the sun was up, he'd be sailing Ira back to town. Of that he was certain. Thinking back to the night before, he realized he had viewed Ira with sympathy and he guessed he still did in some ways, yet for Ira to have been so careless and unaware as to admit to killing that girl, that was going too far. He wondered if he should go with Mose and talk with Jane. She'd not have luck with it, he was sure. The truth was he couldn't bear to see her come to harm. He'd see what Mose thought about it in the morning. Feeling helpless and tired he rose from his chair and stoked the fire, then went to the kitchen to brew strong coffee; there'd be no sleeping tonight. Shaking his head he chuckled inwardly thinking how foolish he'd been to think that Sarah was all he had to worry about.

Chapter Twenty-Eight
The Plan

Jane wrapped the belt buckle in a dish towel along with a few pieces of jewelry belonging to her mother. Sandwiched between the pages of Margaret's diary, Mose's signed statement swearing that Ira had confessed to the crime, secured in her mind all that needed to be said. Pulling on her long skirt, she thought of John's prized twenty-dollar gold piece she'd kept hidden nestled inside the bedsprings. Taking extra care, she pinned it inside her waistband and hurried herself along.

Approaching her dory, she waded in, unmindful of the cold, or the discomfort her wet boots might bring later. Determined to set things right for Margaret, she would hound those men at city hall until one of them saw fit to listen.

Her plan had been to sail to Chebeague and catch the morning steamer leaving Jenks 'Landing, thinking it safer than trying to sail off on her own. She'd hoped Mose might offer, but he'd shied away from taking part, telling her that he wanted to protect the boys, then he'd followed through on his own plans, taking them to Hope for the night. Thinking about his reasoning, she'd half agreed with him, knowing in the end that this was hers to do alone.

Once aboard, she stepped the mast and unfurled the sheet, expertly pulling her into the wind. It had picked up since early morning and she chided herself for taking so long to leave. Making her way to the stern, she sat down and hauled in the main as the dory swung to attention and keeled to port, just clearing the ledge outside the cove. In her haste to set off, she'd almost missed sighting Mose's dory clipping past the bar, perhaps he'd decided to help her after all, she thought, inwardly pleased at his change of heart.

Seeing that he was heading into the cove, she cut the tiller over and let out the main, reaching up to wave and call out as her dory slid in to shore next to his. He stood at the bow throwing half hitches, lashing the sail to the mast, then tossed the anchor onto the beach. In the brief seconds it took for him to turn, Jane's mind raced to clear her confusion, as Ira strode to her dory's bow, red-faced with anger.

"Heard you was planin 'a little trip to the city," he said, holding the dory's painter firmly in his grasp. "Thought you might enjoy some company."

"Let go of my boat," she shrieked. "What I do is my business."

"That's not the way I hear it. Now, step on out of there and we'll go up to the house and sort this out, 'fore someone regrets somethin ' they can't take back."

"I'll not be regrettin 'anythin', Ira, but you might. Now, I'll say again, let go of my painter and take Mose's dory back."

Ira wiped his hand across his face and grinned." Looks to me like we're at what you might call a standstill. I've got hold of your boat and you've got a bag full of nonsense, accordin' to what Mose was tellin 'Jim. Come on, get on out so's we can talk 'bout it."

"Nothin 'to say to you," she said, searching the horizon for signs of a boat, putting it together that he'd been with them and that he knew the purpose of her trip. She also thought there might be some reason to hope she'd see them coming if she could keep Ira thinking she might change her mind.

"Look, I'll just anchor the dory, give me a hand and we'll go on up to the house," she said, watching him closely.

"Now, ain't that nice. Thought you might listen to reason," he said, securing her dory. "This is more like it. Just hand me that satchel, so's you don't lose it overboard."

Jane gripped the bag firmly in her grasp, then realizing its heft and her advantage, hauled her arm back bringing its full weight against Ira's face, knocking him off balance. Floundering in the shallow water, he struggled with the wave surge pushing him in to shore. Watching her chance, Jane reached for the bait knife and scrambled to the bow, cutting the painter free of the anchor. Ira lurched forward, grabbing the gunnels with both hands, throwing his full weight against the dory, toppling Jane over the side. Still clutching her knife, she hurled forward, lashing out wildly, slicing at his face and neck.

"You bitch!" he yelled, reaching for his face."You goddamned bitch!" he yelled again, grabbing her by the arm. "You'll regret doin ' that, I swear! Stop strugglin 'and get over on the beach," he ordered, fuming, still fighting to keep his balance. Wrenching free, Jane waded toward the dory, attempting to swing her leg over, conscious of the deep red slash across Ira's jaw as he advanced. Holding tight to the gunnel, she fought against the sea, hauling her body out, then driving her back against the dory. Regaining her grip, Jane saw the white trashing water, the bulk of the man raising his arm back, bringing the anchor down hard across her knuckles. Slipping under, she opened her mouth to scream. She felt the saltwater filling her throat, then the full strength of his hands at her neck.

Ira struggled with the oars, pulling hard against the tide and wind catching the dory broadside. Once beyond the bar point he judged he'd gone far enough. He knew he'd have to act fast as the wind propelled the dory closer to the ledges. Still enraged, he pitched forward, stumbling to the bow where her body lay. Certain that he had heard her neck crack, he reached down and hauled her by the arms to the dory's rail, rolling her body onto the edge as the waves crashed against the hull. With a last surge of strength, Ira held her at the gunnel, then cast her over the side, watching as she slipped beneath the surface.

***

Jim stood on the shore waiting for Mose and the boys, wondering where Mose had anchored last night. Deciding that he must have beached her, he started walking toward Alex's cove when Mose hailed him from the path.

"What in God's name did you do with your boat?" Jim called.

"What did I do with it? I've been all the way down to the east end lookin'. I thought maybe you was pullin 'a prank."

"I had more on my mind last night than rowin 'boats 'round in the dark. Think maybe she's adrift?"

"Might be," Mose answered." Left Gus and Johnny to tie her up."

"What'd 'ya do with 'em, anyway?"

"Left 'em up to the house with strict instructions to keep an eye on Ira when he rolled out. 'Magine you'll be takin 'him back to the docks, won't ya?"

"That was the plan, but I think we'd better locate your dory first," Jim said, smiling. "Just can't see those two slippin 'up like that.

181

"Though, it was dark as pitch last night. Maybe tied her to a piece of driftwood?"

"Hardly likely," Mose said, looking at Jim to see if he was joking or serious, catching the twinkle in his eye. "Check down the other end, will ya? She's probably fetched up in the cove. I'm goin 'up to see what the boys have to say," Mose said, starting toward the house when he heard Johnny yell from the top of the path.

Mose and Jim looked at each other puzzled, then turned for the house, meeting Johnny just pulling on his coat. "Dad, he's gone!" he said, hurriedly.

"Whose gone?" Mose asked, concerned he meant Gus. "Where's Gus?"

"He's havin 'his breakfast with Sarah. Listen, when we went to turn Ira out, he was long gone and it don't look like he slept there neither," Johnny explained.

"Good God, Jim, that bastard took my boat!"

"Damn right he did," Jim said, then turned to Johnny. "Go on back, tell Sarah we've gone lookin 'for Mose's dory."

Johnny nodded, started off, then turned back. "Just wait for me, I won't be a tic."

Jim reached out and caught his arm. "Listen, son, I was wonderin ' if you'd mind stayin 'with Gus and Sarah? You know, 'case he comes back. I don't want her alone with that animal and Gus might need support of an older brother."

"Sure, sure, glad to," he said. "You can count on me."

Mose looked at his son realizing how much he'd grown, and at the moment, he was glad he had. "Johnny, keep a close eye on things," he cautioned. "Ira's well… Ira's fond of drink, and women, you understand?"

Johnny nodded, taking the bank in five strides, his hip boots tripping him up just once.

Mose looked out over the cove, judging the wind had picked up considerably while he waited for Jim to haul in his dory. "Should we take the sloop?" he asked. "Gettin 'pretty dusky out there. Might be faster."

"Not to mention dryer," Jim laughed. "Look, 'wouldn't be too worried, he can't have gotten too far in this chop. Which way do ya think he headed?"

"Could have gone to Chebeague, but he's such a crazy bastard, I'd say Portland."

As Jim rowed, Mose sat in the stern and pulled his cap lower over his ears. "Damn if it isn't cold for April. I'll be some glad to see summer. Ya know Jim, this isn't the first damn time he's made free with my dory. Wait 'til I get ahold of him."

Jim threw his leg over the sloop's side and waited for Mose. Once underway, facing a headwind and running tide, Jim tacked out into the gut, hoping to make Deer Point on a second tack. Looking back along the island's shoreline, Mose spied a dory making for Jenks' Landing and called to Jim.

"Better come 'bout, Jim. Looks to me like someone's out for a sail," he said, pointing. Jim nodded and hauled her about letting her sail before the wind. Closing in on her, Mose squinted for better focus, knowing without a close inspection that it was his. "Damn him, damn him all to hell, will ya look at that! She's adrift!" he said, as they pulled along side and Mose reached out to grab the painter. "If I ever set sights on him again, Jim, he's gonna get a piece of my mind. Let the sail go all loose and everything," he said, half-hitching in a longer piece for the tow. I'm that fed up with his ways, he'll not have any more work from my boat, if I can help it. He's got no regard for anyone's belongings.

"Looks like you'll have to wait 'fore you get your hands on him," Jim laughed. "Guess he's scarpered."

Mose shook his head and had to laugh at himself for getting so angry. "Least he's gone," he said. "And, unless I miss my guess, he's got a whole hell of a lot more to worry 'bout than me, if Jane gets her wish."

Jim held the wheel steady bringing her around to the starboard, keeling her over in the strong southwest wind. Thinking of Jane's tenacity, he laughed lightly and shook his head. "You know Mose, I don't doubt but you're right at that."

Mose and the boys spent another night with Jim and Sarah, as the wind continued to howl and sailing for Bates in the dory seemed more trouble than it was worth. Sarah had almost forgiven Jim for his lack of backbone and decided for the sake of the boys, who could do no wrong in her book, to make their stay worthwhile.

Sitting around the table together, Sarah and the boys laughed about Ira's theft, saying no harm was done, returning to pity and his sad condition. Jim and Mose remained quiet on the subject, preferring to enjoy Sarah's lobster stew and biscuits. As the evening wore on, Mose listened to the wind and wished he'd headed home instead. He knew Jane could fend for herself, understood she wanted it that way, but he also knew he should have sailed the boys home.

"You're quiet tonight, Mose," Sarah said, dipping her head forward to see past Gus. "You must be worried about Jane."

Mose looked back, surprised to hear her mention Jane in front of the boys. In all the years he'd know them, he'd never once heard her speak her name, let alone suggest worry for her. "No, she's all right," he answered. "She's used to it. In fact, truth be known, she probably likes it. Can't see it myself."

Jim moved to the rocker and lit his pipe, considering Mose's words and the life he might have had with Jane and the girls. He'd changed, had grown to see that his father had been right in many ways about her, but he'd made his bed and was content enough with it. A lull in the conversation brought an eery quiet over the room.

"Somebody just walked over my grave," Sarah said, laughing. "Well for heaven's sake, somebody say something!"

"How 'bout," Gus started, "you never use that expression again?"

"Fair enough," she replied, reaching over to give his hand a gentle pat.

Chapter Twenty-Nine
Asa

It was too damn cold for April, he thought, stepping out onto his front porch to survey the day. The woods, sky and water framed one solid gray, dark opinion, in his view, yet he needed wood and knew it would not be any warmer at night fall. After two days of ceaseless wind, Asa judged his best bet would be to scout the back shore and so set off down through the field with his wheelbarrow. Stumbling down the shale ledges to the shore he scuffed along at the high tide mark. His long mac trailed almost to his feet as he searched for the driest pieces of driftwood, stacking neat piles as he walked.

Not another soul knew, or cared, that he lived in the old house, abandoned for years, their mining adventures having failed. Asa could have told them it would amount to nothing and waited them out for his chance. He'd tossed around aimlessly for too long, taking odd jobs on the vessels out of Portland, mending nets, trying his hand at fishing from his dory. This seemed as good a spot as any to live out what might be left of his life. He was just too old now to think beyond keeping warm and digging up the ground to grow a few vegetables. Occasionally he'd wander the back shore to shoot a sea duck for his dinner. Mostly, he was content to live alone.

Stopping to rest and stretch his back, Asa scanned the shoreline ahead, keeping an eye out for the coming tide. Disappointed in the scarce pickings, he thought he might still find a lobster left by the tide in the Punch Bowl for his troubles.

Almost thirty feet across, the bowl never completely drained out. The outer ledges, nearest low tide, formed a perfect wall keeping whatever the sea washed in captive until the next tide. The sun warmed salt water was a perfect spot for summer bathing, although thinking of it now sent a chill through his bones.

At the moment, the bowl was rapidly filling with the rushing tide prompting him hurry. Looking down into the pool, Asa was

185

momentarily startled at his own reflection; distorted and mingling with the clouds 'reflection scaling across its surface. Kneeling down he reached in to peel back a layer of seaweed. It was then that he noticed the body floating on the pool's surface, thinking at first sight it must be a dead seal. He didn't favor the idea of going closer and stood arguing with himself as the tide pushed over the ledges and the pool began to fill. If he'd just stayed home, he said cursing his luck, he'd never been the wiser. Now, standing at the edge, he reached down and rolled up his hip boots and waded in. Coming closer, he realized that he was looking at a woman's body. She floated on her back, her long hair fanned out about her head and her long black skirt clung to her thighs. Bracing a wide stance, he slipped his hands under her arms and lifted her torso out of the water. Edging backward, one cautious step at a time, he dragged her to the beach head. Sitting down heavily, exhausted from the exertion, he rolled down his boots and took out his pipe wondering what he should do next.

Asa guessed he'd have to tell someone, but on that subject he was stuck. She had to belong to someone he surmised, but who? Looking at her more closely he supposed she'd not been in the water for more than a day. She might just be sleeping on the beach, he thought, then noticing how she was dressed, it occurred to him that she could have been a passenger on the steamer and somehow fallen overboard. All the same, she'd ended up in his pool and he wasn't about to take her any further than he had.

Taking another long pull on his pipe, the unsettling thought suddenly materialized that someone might think he'd had something to do with it, but he couldn't see how he could avoid it. Eventually, he stood and surveyed the horizon, pondering his bad luck, when he recalled seeing Jim's sloop tacking back and forth off the Cow the day before. He could have been fishing, but Asa thought it was unlikely given the wind. He'd just have to get himself over to Hope in the morning, he finally decided, then started out across the beach. Halfway to the cliff path, he stopped and retraced his steps. Shrugging out of his mac, he placed it gingerly over her body, cursing into the wind how he'd be needin 'it a damn sight more than she would, then walked off down the beach.

Chapter Thirty
The Search

At daybreak Jim and Mose sailed into the cove, hoping to find Jane in her kitchen frying bacon and full of news about her day in the city, but soon exchanged worried glances as they stepped onto the beach. Her dory was nowhere in sight. It meant she'd either gone adrift, or Jane was not back yet. Neither man wanted to voice an opinion, but each read the other's thoughts.

Mose stepped out and walked to the house, leaving Jim to wait with the dory. Straddling the bow, keeping her from grounding out in the falling tide, Jim looked across the bar toward Ministerial. Thinking it possible she'd walked over to visit, he thought he should mention his idea to Mose when he saw him striding down the path.

"She's not there," he said, "and hasn't been judging by the house. Fire's not been lit, cold as hell in there."

"What 'ya make of it then? She'd not have stayed in Portland?" he asked.

"Not very likely. Maybe over to Chebeague with Caroline and Barn."

"Could be," Jim said, without much enthusiasm, knowing how much Jane disliked staying with her sister. "Anyone over there?" he asked nodding across the bar.

"Cleared out."

They stood together silent for a few moments, then Mose started off across the beach in the direction of the barn, calling back over his shoulder, "Just goin 'to check on the critters, be back in a tic."

Jim stood at the dory's bow thinking about setting off across the beach in search of Jane's dory. It seemed reasonable that she could have beached out on Ministerial's front beach and a quick walk across the bar would set his mind at ease. Rolling up his boots, he waded in a short distance, then stood for a moment judging the tide's retreat. Once at the bow, he tied on the anchor, gave it a toss and shoved the dory off. Satisfied she'd stay put, he set out for the bar, searching the shore, growing more concerned with each forward step. Images of the dory abandoned, or in pieces, hurried him along until he rounded the shoreline, relieved to see an empty beach. A little more at ease, Jim still felt something had to be amiss. There was no sensible explanation for Jane's absence. She was too able in a boat, even in bad weather. Discouraged, he started across the flats, and had he not been mindful he might slip, he may have missed seeing the flattened satchel. Even covered in mud, Jim instantly recalled how often he'd seen it hanging by door. Reluctantly, he reached down and pried it free. They'd have to piece together the story, he thought, watching as Mose drew closer, but he supposed they'd be thinking in a different direction now.

Unfastening the satchel, Mose reached in gingerly lifting out the waterlogged diary. Completely soaked through, the pages clung together; Margaret's secrets now bleeding into one another, seeming to form an unfamiliar language.

"It's hers."

"I know," Jim replied, sadly. "What does it mean?"

"It means," Mose replied, "that Jane's gotten herself into a mess. She's either gone overboard in that blow or...there's been more foul play. This is Margaret's. Jane was takin 'it to Portland."

Looking at Mose, it began to dawn on him what Margaret's diary might mean about finding Jane, and what had happened to her. "Where should we start then?" he asked.

"I guess we ought to get a party together and go out lookin'. We'll go over to Chebeague and roust out as many boats as we can. But I'll tell ya Jim, I think we're lookin 'for a body, not anybody breathin'."

"Let's not get ahead of ourselves here, she might be right as rain. This could of fallen overboard and she gave up on the whole thing."

"Maybe," Mose replied, doubtfully. "Still 'n all, we've got to look."

Chapter Thirty-One
After Judgement

They picked their way clumsily up the shore path in the dark, both men tired and hungry after searching the inner bay for a sighting of Jane's dory. They knew that finding it would not bring them any closer to answers, but might give them a better idea where to look. Jim still held on to the hope that she'd stayed over in the city and suggested they sail up in the morning. Mose had agreed, but he kept seeing Jane holding the diary and his dory adrift that first day, wishing then that they'd had the foresight to worry.

The warm light from the kerosene lamp cast a welcome glow through the kitchen window as the two men approached the house. Sarah sat at the table quietly talking with John and Gus, rising abruptly the instant they opened the door.

"Jim, Mose," she said softly, "we've had a visitor this afternoon and I think you need to hear what he had to say."

Mose looked at the boys, and then to Sarah. "They found her then?" he asked.

"'Fraid so. That old man lives over to Jewels found her washed up in the Punch Bowl," she said, speaking frankly, not knowing how to break the news another way.

"Albert and Frank went over and brought her back. We didn't know what else to do."

"Where is she?" Mose asked.

John stood and walked over to his father. "We carried her up to the shed, Pa, wrapped her in a sheet. Best we could think of."

Mose understood that John was being strong for Gus and that he should say something comforting, but the manner of her death still bothered him. "I'll just go on out then," he said, turning a crooked, half smile to John.

"You want me to come?" Jim asked, kindly.

"No, you're all right," he said, closing the door behind him.

"What do you make of it, Jim? Did she fall overboard then?" Sarah asked.

Jim shook his head, then casting a worried glance at the boys, thought they might be better off thinking it had been an accident. "I don't know, Sarah. It was blowin 'awful hard that day. She told Mose she was plannin 'a trip to town, that's all I really do know."

Sarah caught the look in Jim's eye and reached over to touch his arm as she passed by, pretending to accept his answer. "Well, we'll know soon enough, I guess. Mose will have a better idea 'bout what she was up to than you would, I should think."

Starting on dinner, she left them and walked to the kitchen window. Mose sat outside the shed, elbows resting on his knees, holding his head in both hands. She wondered if she should say something to Jim, or the boys, but turned away, allowing him a moment to his grief without them watching on. He'd been fond of her after all, she thought sadly, knowing that no one could crawl inside another person's skin and feel what they felt. Perhaps he's thinking of the boys 'mother, Rosy, and the life they might have had together.

Jim retreated to his rocker, pulling it closer to the wood stove, leaving the boys to sort out their own feelings about the day. Mose would know what to do, he thought. He would help out where he could.

***

The dory was sighted at daybreak. Charles Horr had found it, half submerged at the head of Kennedy's cove on Cliff Island. Word had come by way of Albert, who had gone out early to his traps and hauled it back to Hope.

The men stood at the shore around the dory, awkwardly offering to help in any way they could. Seeing no use for Jane's dory, they hauled it above the high tide onto the bank and turned her over. Taking a place at the bow, Jim glanced down, then stepped around to call over to Mose. "What 'ya make of that?" he asked, pointing to the bow.

Mose studied the bow, aware of what Jim had seen. He could see where Albert had lashed a new piece in and where the old piece had

190

been cut. "Looks like it's been hacked off," he said. "Now why would she of done that?"

"Not rightly sure. Al, did you cut off the old bow piece?" Jim asked.

"Wasn't one, nothin 'but that little piece left, I was wonderin ' 'bout it, then forgot in all the excitement. Looks like she cut it off. Bit odd isn't it?"

"She must of had a reason," Jim added.

"Kinda looks like she was maybe caught down or somethin', had to cut it quick," Albert posed.

"Could be," Mose said, "but, on what?"

"Maybe she couldn't get the anchor up and was in a hurry?"

Mose shook his head, then walked to the stern, reaching inside, feeling along the ribs. "Bait knife's gone too," he said.

Jim looked at Mose, silently asking his question, not sure if he wanted to continue speculating, then turned to Albert. "We might never know, I guess, but might be how she come to fall over."

"I don't know, Jim. She was able as any man I know in that dory. More like someone else did the cuttin'," Albert said. "Far as that goes, the main was all hauled down in the bow, never was lashed down. Took it down and stowed it up forward."

Jim stepped to the bow, reached under the gunnel and untied the forward hatch, then unfurled the small mainsheet across the beach stones. A slight breeze rippled beneath the cloth and the morning's sun flicked across the surface of the small white triangle as Jim walked its edges. Al would not have noticed what Jim and the others could now see clearly in daylight. He would not have been thinking about the sail's condition in the urgency to get it stowed, but now he stood as a witness to the wide slash of red stain running the length of the main's foot.

"Think she cut herself?" Al asked.

Mose shook his head. "She wasn't hurt that I could see, not in that way."

"The anchor's gone, knife, sail's all blood…only one way to look at it," Jim said. " I haven't been able to put that coin you found in your dory out of my mind either."

"If it was Jane's, someone will know," Mose said. "But it don't make sense to me, Jim. What was she doin' aboard my dory?"

Jim stared at the sail, taking in Mose's question, reluctant to acknowledge the truth it carried. He imagined he could see on its surface one brutal moment at a time, falling into place, until he knew, as sure as he was standing there on the shore, that Jane's death could not have been an accident. Wanting to blot out the vision, he reached for a corner of the sail, gathering in the images, pulling the horror into its darkness, until it was a small patch of canvas cloth he could hold in his hand.

"There ain't but one way to see this, Mose. We've been blind to Ira and what he's done."

"I just can't see it, Jim. Ira's a bad actor, no one's denying that, but I just can't see it."

Jim heard Mose's protest, and in some ways he understood how he felt, yet he knew as well, that it fell to them to make things right. "You can't look the other way now, Mose. I'll see it through myself if you can't bring yourself to it. There's just too much here to go on thinking she did this to herself. That day we found your dory adrift and that coin sittin' there in the wash, you didn't wonder how it got there? You knew Ira took it and set her adrift. You knew that coin couldn't of been his. How else do you think it got there?"

"Look, Jim, what you're suggestin' seems a bit far fetched, is all I'm sayin'."

"It may be, Mose, but I intend to find out."

"Now, how in hell do you imagine you're goin' to do that? You just goin' to sail on up to the docks and call him out?"

Jim's firm gaze moved Mose's question out to the men, still standing about the Jane's dory, each one putting together for himself the pieces of the story now unfolding before them. Understanding their reluctance to go looking for trouble, coupled with a need to put things right, he waited through their silence, watching a path of morning sun settle along the dory's wet hull. Absently, Jim looked down at his hands, still grasping the sail, seeming shroud-like, as if a piece of Jane's life quietly spoke out into the day. Touched by its sadness, Jim stepped forward and set the canvas patch gently on the stern seat, making his answer clear.

***

Late that afternoon, Jim's sloop sailed into Portland Harbor finding a berth at Dyer's Wharf. Al had taken the news of their discovery to Elizabeth, mentioning that it would be best to keep the reason for their trip under wraps as Jim did not want to worry the family unnecessarily. Fueled by a growing anger, Jim carried inside, he saw little reason to try and convince Mose further. He had consented to travel with them, but Jim doubted he would actually confront Ira if they found him. Jim knew that Ira would deny, still he wanted to see his face when he did.

It was decided that they would search the wharf, thinking that after two days, Ira would feel it safe to show himself around the docks. They agreed that Al would stay with the sloop, while Jim and Mose scouted Ira's haunts. With a plan in place, Jim stepped up onto the wharf and walked toward Dyer's bait shed, knowing that Ira often slept rough inside. The shed encompassed the entire breadth of the wharf, and a person wanting to walk along its length, needed to pass through its covered alley. This narrow passageway skirted the wharf's edge and led directly out to Commercial Street. Along the shed's shingled front, two windows were placed askew either side of the only entrance. Approaching the lower window, Jim cupped his hands to his face, blinder style, hoping to see inside. Years of grime, mingled with coal smoke and dust, blocked most of his view, yet he was fairly certain he could just make out a cot against the further wall and what he hoped was Ira sleeping one off. Jim knew he needn't worry about waking him, still he took care lifting the latch, wanting time to survey the room. Seconds before stepping over the threshold, the thought occurred to him that perhaps he should have retrieved Al for backup, yet as he approached the sleeping man, he quickened his stride and gave voice to the outrage he'd been feeling since morning. "Ira!" he yelled. "Wake up!"

"What? Go away and let a man sleep, for God's sake."

"Ira, it's Jim. I need a word with you, now."

"Jim? Oh, Jim, is it? Need a hand with your nets? I'll just be with you, if you can give me a bit to get myself movin'."

"Guess you know well enough I'm not here 'bout nets, now roll out so's we can talk."

"I got nothin' to talk with you 'bout, Jim. I'm done with that island and all of ya. And good riddance."

"Well then, that's good to hear, but just to make sure you're done with us, I'd still like that talk, outside, where I can see you face to face."

Ira sat up and ran his hands through his hair, grumbling as he staggered to his feet and walked to the door. "Alright, hold your horses. But I got plans, so you better make it quick, Jim. I got me a berth on a schooner and soon's I'm out of here the better."

Jim answered Ira by grabbing his arm and leading him straight through the door and out onto the wharf, calling out to Al as he moved him along, finally standing him against the shed wall. Even in its shadow, Jim saw the long deep gash running along Ira's stubbled jaw.

"Jesus, Jim. What's got you so damn mad?"

"You know, Ira, if I didn't know better, I'd say you are pretty darn cocky for a fella that did what you did. Come to think on it, I do know better."

"What are you sayin', Jim? What are you damn people accusing me of now? I left your house and didn't come back. Now get on down into that lousy sloop of yours and sail on outta here. I know my rights! You can't be accostin' a man in his own bed," he complained, knowing the shaky ground he stood on by the look in Jim's eyes, and the sudden appearance of Al stalking over the wharf. "What in hell is this, anyway?"

"This is me, askin' you direct why you took Mose's dory when you left my house and what you did with it," Jim said, slowly forcing each word through anger.

Ira grinned. "Is that it then? All this over a damn borrowed dory?"

"No, Ira, that's the least of it. Tell me what happened to Jane. And I want the truth, not some story you think you can get away with, starting with that gash on your face?"

Ira unconsciously reached up to hide the knife slash, running his hand along his jaw, feeling again the rage he felt on the beach that day. "I don't have no idea what your talkin' 'bout, Jim. Now we fished together for a long time, shared a few laughs, and I can't see why you'd come roust me outta bed accusin' me of things I never done. Just like before with that girl down there. Now, I don't know a single, solitary, thing about Jane missing and that's the truth of it."

"Missing! Jesus, Ira! I never said a word about Jane being missing," Jim yelled, shoving Ira back against the wall. "You need to tell me what happened to her, you son of a bitch. You know, and I want some damn answers."

"Simmer down, Jim, there ain't no cause to fly off the handle so. I musta' heard it in town. You got everything wrong side to, way I see it. Now, if you'll just step aside," Ira said, brushing Jim away, "I've got better things to do than stand here jawin' with you two island boys 'bout some crazy idea you got hold of." As he spoke, Ira edged his way along the shed wall toward the alley's passageway, mindful that Jim would follow, yet he thought he could get through the alley and out to a busy street, where he hoped to give them the slip. Hurrying along, he entered the sudden darkness, feeling his boots slide along the mossy planks and his balance give way. Skidding to the edge, he reached out to grab the railing; disoriented, he stared down at the grassy pilings imbedded in the muck below, only slightly aware of his weight leaning against the decaying barrier.

Intent on finishing with Ira's excuses, Jim strode into the alley with Al at his side, glad to see Mose approaching from the opposite end. "Where in God's name have you been?" Jim called.

"Where we should of gone to begin with," Mose called back. "Is that him, then? What's he doin' just standin' there?"

Hearing Mose's voice, Ira turned to face him. Expecting he might have a better chance of talking his way out, he began slowly walking toward Mose, who seemed to wholeheartedly welcome the idea. Thinking that Mose was about to let Ira off the hook, Jim took a step forward, then stopped as Mose lifted his hand to warn him off. They all moved more deeply into the alley, Mose leading the way, with Ira blindly following along after him. Pausing to listen for the sound of following boots against the planks, Ira slowed his pace, then satisfied, moved on toward the dim light, relieved to see two men walking toward him. Caught as he was between Jim and freedom, he felt somewhat encouraged they might be fishermen, yet one man stood head and shoulders above the other. He knew for sure that one of them was Mose. The other called his name.

"Ira, Ira Gould," the voice echoed down the passage. "This man here wants a word with you."

It took Ira a few seconds to work out that the man with Mose was not another fisherman, but the police; a man Ira recognized as the one who patrolled the waterfront and had often warned him off the docks. He stood immobilized, watching as the men approached; their shadows growing as they paced into the gloomy alley, the light beyond outlining each man's frame. A slight tremble began pushing at his core as the tunnel seemed to deepen and hollowed voices bounced erratically, calling his name. Gradually, Ira realized that he had misplaced his faith in Mose's intentions; Jim and Al had blocked the route back, and Mose was after judgment.

"Ira, we've got good reason to believe that you had something to do with Jane's death. This man here wants to take you in and ask you about it. You fooled me once and I'm not havin' it again. So, you can come under your own power, or the four of us can see that you go along."

Ira held fast to the railing, gazing down at the water, his back to the men. Ultimately, he turned, drawing his hands across his face, covering the open wound marking his guilt.

"There's no cause to worry yourself, Mose. I'll go without you makin' a fuss, but you will find out the truth of it," he said, "and when it all comes out right, you'll be sorry, just like the last time you all came botherin' me. I don't know a damn thing about what happened out there. I wish to God I'd never laid eyes on the lot of ya."

"That may be so, Ira, but we want it done proper this time," Mose said. "God knows if we had, Jane would still be alive today, and that is the truth I know."

***

Mose knew he would have to arrange for the burial and planned to sail for Chebeague, taking the boys with him. He dreaded telling Caroline, knowing she'd insist on a proper funeral at the church; allowing himself a smile thinking what Jane might have to say about it. But, he'd promised to take care of her, and he reckoned she'd be pleased to rest beside her daughter.

Jim and Johnny had worked together all morning building the coffin, judging that it would be the most dignified manner in which to move her. Grateful, Mose thanked the men as they carried it down the shore path and placed it in the dory.

Last week's storm had blown itself out to sea, leaving them a windless day. Watching from the shore, Jim turned and placed his arm around Sarah's shoulders, thankful that she had made her way down to see them off. The boys sat in the stern, as Mose set his oars and pushed forward, rowing off through the calm water. He followed the morning light, setting to a direct path between the islands, listening to a tuneless squeal from his oars rolling against the thole pins. Further out, in the deeper water, Mose felt a slight breeze nudging at the bow, prompting him to turn in his seat and check his heading. Just ahead lay their destination, not more than a mile off. He could see the men in the cove readying to haul, and his mother's clothesline on the hill; home, he thought, then quickly dipped his oar in deep, pulling them about. He saw the boys' confusion, returning their question with a simple nod toward Bates.

"We were headed in the wrong direction, boys!"

Johnny retuned the nod. "Wondered 'bout that," he said. "Last night when you said we was goin' home, that's what I thought you meant. Isn't that what you thought, Gus?"

"It was, and that's a fact," Gus answered, reaching into his pocket, searching for the gold coin his father had placed in his palm the night before.

Character Chart

Edsel Bates purchased Newharbour Island (Bates) in 1791

<u>Edsel Bates m. Mary Wormwell (1802)</u>

|

<u>Caroline Bates m. Barnwell Johnson / Jane Bates (children with
James Johnson) m. John Brown (1856)</u>

↓

<u>Mary m. Jacob Frost /Sarah (died young) /Rose m. Moses Dyer</u>

|

Johnny
Gus
Margaret Douglas (orphan living with Jane and John)

Hope Island Family

<u>Alexander Johnson m. Rebecca</u>

↓

<u>James m. Sarah / Elizabeth m. Albert Coffin</u>

|

Albert (Frank)
William

Little Chebeague Family and Sunnyside Employees

<u>Joshua Jenks m. Nettie Perkins</u>

|

Harry
Edward

Mrs. Barker (cook)
Esther / Nellie / Margaret (house maids)
Ira Gould -Fisherman and hired hand

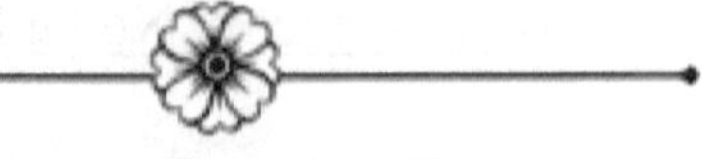

About the Author

Sharon lives on a small island off the coast of Maine, at home in the company of her family, lifelong friends and ancestors. At the age of sixteen she visited an elderly island resident who launched into a story bringing to light an unsolved mystery for over a century. The story sparked a desire to learn as much as possible about the fate of the woman whose history may have been lost in time.

A graduate of the University of New Hampshire, Sharon was accepted as a fellow with the 1999 Maine National Writing Project, and is recently retired from a career in teaching. Her writing focuses on Maine island life, the character of her people and history. She is presently working on a second island novel.